THE T

In a rickety hut on the borders of the Forest of Munza-Mulgar there lived three monkeys: Thumb, Thimble and Nod. They were no ordinary forest creatures for their father, Seelem, who had come to this land from the beautiful far-off valleys of Tishnar, was own brother to Prince Assasimmon, and he instructed them in many things that Mulla-Mulgars (or royal monkeys) should know. Above all, he taught them to walk upright, never to taste blood, and never, unless in danger or despair, to climb or to grow a tail.

After thirteen years away from the palace of Assasimmon, Seelem had a longing to see his home again, so one day he set off, promising to return and bring his family to Tishnar with him. But time passed and Seelem was not seen again, and without him his wife Mutta-matutta slowly pined away. On her death bed, calling her three sons around her, she told them Seelem's last words to her: that if he did not return they were to make the same perilous journey alone as best they could. She gave Thumb and Thimble each a red jacket with metal hooks, and to little Nod a coat of Sheep's wool with nine ivory buttons. And to Nod, because he had magic in him, she entrusted the milk-white Wonderstone of Tishnar.

So the brothers started on their long journey across forest, swamp, river and the Mountains of Arakkaboa. Many adventures lay before them, and many creatures were to help or hinder them, such as Mishcha the witch hare, the flesh-eating Minimuls, a stranded sailor and a lonely Water Midden. Often Nod would lose the precious Wonder-stone, but as often, luck or his quick wits would restore it; sometimes their lives would be in dreadful danger, but magic or cunning came to their aid. And so, gradually, they drew nearer to the fabled groves and fields of Tishnar.

The African jungle that this classic story so vividly portrays is half a real place that we might travel to, half an inner imaginative world that we can see only through the brilliant eyes of its famous author. Mysterious and fascinating, t his is one of those tales that can be enjoyed by young and old alike, and no bookshelf is complete without it.

Walter de la Mare

The Three
Royal Monkeys

Illustrated by Mildred E. Eldridge

Puffin Books
in association with Faber & Faber

Puffin Books, Penguin Books Ltd, Harmondsworth, Middlesex, England
Penguin Books, 625 Madison Avenue, New York, New York 10022, U.S.A.
Penguin Books Australia Ltd, Ringwood, Victoria, Australia
Penguin Books Canada Ltd, 2801 John Street, Markham, Ontario, Canada L3R 1B4
Penguin Books (N.Z.) Ltd, 182–190 Wairau Road, Auckland 10, New Zealand

First published by Faber & Faber Ltd
under the title *The Three Mulla-Mulgars* 1910
Published in Puffin Books 1979
All rights reserved

Made and printed in Great Britain by
Richard Clay (The Chaucer Press) Ltd.,
Bungay, Suffolk
Set in Linotype Times

To
F. and D.
&
L. and C.

CHAPTER ONE

The Wonderstone

On the borders of the Forest of Munza-Mulgar lived once an old grey Fruit Monkey of the name of Mutta-matutta. She had three sons, the eldest Thumma, the next Thimbulla, and the youngest, who was a Nizza-neela, Ummanodda. And they called each other for short, Thumb, Thimble, and Nod. The rickety, tumble-down old wooden hut in which they lived had been built 319 Munza years before by a traveller, a Portugall or Portingal, lost in the forest 22,997 leagues from home. After he was dead, there came scrambling along on his fours one peaceful evening a Mulgar (or, as we say in English, a *monkey*) named Zebbah. At first sight of the hut he held his head on one side awhile, and stood quite still, listening, his broad-nosed face lit up in the blaze of the setting sun. He then hobbled a little nearer, and peeped into the hut. Whereupon he hobbled away a little, but soon came back and peeped again. At last he ventured near, and, pushing back the tangle of creepers and matted grasses, groped through the door and went in. And there, in a dark corner, lay the Portingal's little heap of bones.

The hut was dry as tinder. It had in it a broken fire-stone, a kind of chest or cupboard, a table, and a stool, both rough and insect-bitten, but still strong. Zebbah sniffed and grunted, and pushed and peered about. And he found all manner of strange and precious stuff half-buried in the hut – pots for Subbub; pestles and basins for Manaka-cake, etc.; three bags of great beads, clear, blue, and emerald; an old rusty musket; nine ephelantoes' tusks; a bag of Margarita stones; and many other things, besides cloth and spider-silk and dried-up fruits and fishes. He made his dwelling there, and died there. This Mulgar, Zebbah, was Mutta-matutta's great-great-great-grandfather. Dead and gone were all.

Now, one day when Mutta-matutta was young, and her father had gone into the forest for Sudd-fruit, there came limping along a most singular Mulgar towards the house. He was bent and shrunken, shivering and coughing, but he walked as men walk, his nut-shaped head bending up out of a big red jacket. His shoulder and the top of his head were worn bare by the rubbing of the bundle he carried. And behind him came stumbling along another Mulgar, his servant, with a few rags tied round his body, who could not at first speak, his tongue was so much swollen from his having bitten in the dark a poison-spider in his nuts. The name of his master was Seelem; his own name was Glint. This Seelem fell very sick. Mutta-matutta nursed him night and day, with the sourest monkey-physic. He was pulled crooked with pain and the shivers, or rain-fever. The tips of the hairs on his head had in his wanderings turned snow-white. But he bore his pain and his sickness (and his physic) without one groan of complaint.

And Glint, who fetched water and gathered sticks and nuts, and helped Mutta-matutta, told her that his master, Seelem, was a Mulla-Mulgar – that is, a Mulgar of the

Blood Royal – and own brother to Assasimmon, Prince of the Valleys of Tishnar.

He told her, also, that his master had wearied of Assasimmon's valley-palace, his fine food and dishes, his music of shells and strings, his count-less Mulgar-slaves, beasts, and groves and gardens; and that, having chosen three servants,

Jacca, Glutt, and himself, he had left his brother's valleys, to discover what lay beyond the Arakkaboa Mountains. But Jacca had perished of frost-bite on the southern slopes of the Peak of Tishnar, and Glutt had been eaten by the Minimuls, or Earth Monkeys.

He was very silent and gloomy, this Mulla-Mulgar, See-lem, but glad to rest his bruised and weary bones in the hut. And when Mutta-matutta's father died from sleeping in the moon-mist towards the end of the season when ripens the Monkey-fruit called Sudd, Seelem untied his travelling bundle and made his home in the hut. Mutta-matutta was a lonely and rather sad Mulgar, so at this she rejoiced, for she had grown from fearing him to love the royal old wanderer. And she helped him to put away all that was in his bundles into the Portingal's chest – three shirts of cotton; two red jackets, like his own, with metal hooks; a sheep's-coat, with ivory buttons and pocket-flaps; three skin shoes (for one had been lost out of his bundle in the forest); a cap of Mamasul skin (very precious); besides knives, fire-strikers, a hollow cup of ivory, magic physic-powder, two combs of Impaleena-horn, a green serpent-skin for sweeten-ing water, etc., and, beyond and above all, the milk-white Wonderstone of Tishnar.

Here they lived, Seelem and Mutta (as he called her), in the Portingal's old hut, for thirteen years. And Mutta was happy with Seelem and her three sons, Thumb, Thimble, and Nod. They had a water-spring, honey-boxes or baskets for the bees in the Ollaconda-trees, a shed or huddle of green branches for Glint, and a big patch of Ummuz-cane. Nod slept in a kind of cubby or burrow in the roof, with a tiny peeping-hole, from which he used to scare the birds from his father's Ummuz, or sugar-cane.

Mutta wished only that Seelem was not quite so grim and broody; that the Munza-Mulgars, or Forest-Monkeys, would not come stealing her Subbub-syrup and honey; and

9

that the Portingal's hut stood quite out of the silvery moon-mist that rose from the swamp; for she suffered (as do most Fruit-Monkeys) from the bones-ache. Seelem was gentle and easy in his own moody way with Mutta and his three sons, but, most of all, he cheered his heart with tiny Nod, the Nizza-neela.

Sometimes all day long this old travel-worn Mulla-Mulgar never uttered a sound, save at evening, when he sang or droned his evening hymn to Tishnar. He kept a thick stick, which he called his Guzza, to punish his three sons when they were idle and sullen, or gluttonous, or with Munza tricks pestered their mother. And he never favoured Nod beyond the others more than all good fathers favour the youngest, the littlest, and the gaysomest of their children.

One of the first things that Nod remembered was Glint's tumbling from the great Ukka-tree, which he had climbed at ripening-time, bough up to bough from the bottom, cracking shells and eating all the way, until, forgetting how heavy he had become, he swung his fat body on to a slender and withered branch, and fell all a-topple from top to bottom on to the back of his thick skull. Beneath this same dark-leaved tree Seelem buried his servant, together with a pot of Subbub, seven loaves or cakes, and a long stick of Ummuz-cane. But Mutta-matutta after his death would never touch an Ukka-nut again.

Seelem taught his sons how to make fire, what nuts and roots and fruits and grasses were wholesome for eating; what herbs and bark and pith for physic; what reeds and barks for cloth. He taught them how to take honey without being stung; how to count; how to find their way by the chief and brightest among the stars; to cut cudgels, to build leaf-huts and huddles against heat or rain. He taught them, too, the common tongue of the Forest-Monkeys – that is the language of nearly all the Mulgars that live in the forests of Munza – Jacquet-Mulgars, Mullabruks, purple-faced and saffron-headed Mulgars, Skeetoes, tuft-waving Manquabees, Fly-catchers and Squirrel-tails, and many more than I can mention.

Seelem taught them also a little of the languages of the dreaded Gunga-Mulgars, of the Collobs, and the Babbaboo-mas. But the Minimul-Mulgars' and the Oomgars' or Man-Monkeys' languages (white, black, or yellow) he could not teach, because he did not know them. When, however, they were alone together they spoke the secret language of the Mulla-Mulgars dwelling north of the Arakkaboas – that is, Mulgar-Royal.

This language in some ways resembles that of the Portu-galls, in some that of the Oggewibbies, and, here and there – but in very little – Garniereze. Seelem, of course, taught his sons, and especially Thumb, many other things besides – more, certainly, than would contain itself in a little book like this. But, above all, he taught them to walk upright, never to taste blood, and never, unless in danger or despair, to climb trees or to grow a tail.

But now, after all these thirteen years of absence from Assasimmon's palace in the beautiful Valleys of Tishnar, Seelem began to desire more and more to see again his home and his brother, with whom as a child he had walked in scarlet and Mamasul, and drunk his syrup from an ivory cup. He grew more gloomy and morose than ever, squatted alone, his eyes fixed mournfully in the air. And Mutta would whisper to Nod: *'Sst, zun nizzaneela, tusweeta zan nuome!'*

The more cunning of the Forest-Mulgars at first had come in troops to Seelem, laden with gifts of nuts and fruits because they were afraid of him. But he would sit in his red jacket and merely stare at them as if they were no better than flies. And at last they began in revenge to do him as much mischief as their wits could contrive, until he grew utterly weary of their scuffling and quarrelling, their thumbs and colours, fleas and tails. At last he could bear himself no longer, and one morning, in the first haze of sunrise over the sleeping forest, he called Mutta and his three sons to where he sat in the shadow of Glint's great budding Ukka-tree. And he told them he was going on a long journey – 'beyond and beyond, forest and river, forest swamp and river, the mountains of Arakkaboa, leagues, leagues away' – to seek again the Valleys of Tishnar.

'And I will come back,' he said, leaning his hand upon the ground and blinking at Nod, 'with slaves and scarlet and food-baskets and Zevveras, and bring you all there with me. But first I must go alone and find the way through dangers thick as flies, O Mulla-Mulgars. Wait here and guard your old mother, Mutta-matutta, my sons, her Ummuz and Ukkas. And grow strong, O tailless ones, till I return. *Zu zoubé seese muglareen, een suang no nouano zupbf!'* And that was all he said.

But Mutta-matutta, though she could not hide her grief at his going, helped him in every way she could to be quickly gone. He seemed beside himself, this white, old, crooked Mulla-Mulgar. His eyes blazed; he went muttering; he would throw up his hands and snuff and snuff, as if the very wind bore Tishnar on its wings. And even at night he would rise up in the darkness and open the door and listen as if out of the immeasurable and solitudinous forests he heard voices calling him from far away.

At length, in his last shirt (which had been carefully kept these thirteen years with a dead kingfisher and a bag of civet, to keep off the cockroaches); in his finest red jacket and his cap of Mamasul-skin; with a great bundle of Manaka-cake and Ummuz-cane, knife and fire-striker and physic, and the old Portingal's rusty musket on his shoulder, he was ready to be off. In the early morning he came stooping under the little hut-door. He looked at his hut and his water-spring, at his bees and canes; he looked at his three sons, and at old Mutta-matutta, with a great frown, and trembled. And Mutta could not bear to say good-bye; she lifted her crooked hands above her old head, the tears running down her cheeks, and she went and hid herself in the hut till he was gone. But his three sons went a little way with him.

Thumb and Thimble hopped along with his heavy bundle on a stick between them to the branching of the Mulgar-track, which here runs nearly two paces wide into the gloom of Munza-Mulgar; while Nod sat on Seelem's shoulder, sucking a stick of Ummuz-cane, and clutching the long cold, rusty barrel of his musket.

The trees of the forest lifted their branches in a trembling haze of heat, hung with grey thorny ropes, and vines and trailing creepers of Cullum and Samarak, vivid with leaves, and with large cuplike waxen flowers, moon-white,

13

amber, mauve, and scarlet. Butterflies like blots and splashes of flame, wee Tominiscoes, ruby and emerald and amethyst, shimmered and spangled and sipped and hovered. And a thin, twangling, immeasurable murmur like the strings of Noomanossi's harp rose from the tiny millions that made their nests and mounds and burrows in the forest.

Seelem took his sons one by one by the shoulders, and looked into their eyes, and touched noses. And they lifted their hands in salutation, and watched him till he was gone from sight. But though his grey face was all wizened up with trouble and wet with tears, he never so much as once looked behind him, lest his sons should cry after him, or he turn back. So, presently, after they all three lifted their hands once more, as if his Meermut* might still haunt near; and then they went home to their mother.

But the rains came; he did not return. The long days strode softly by – the chatter and screams of Munza at dawn, the long-drawn, moaning shout of Mullabruk to Mullabruk as darkness deepened. Nod would sometimes venture a little way into the forest, hoping to hear the gongs that his father had told him the close-shorn slaves of Assasimmon tie with leopard-thongs about their Zevveras' necks. He would sit in the gigantic shadows of evening, watching the fireflies, and saying to himself: 'Sst, Nod, see what they say – to-morrow!' But the morrow never came that brought him back his father.

Mutta-matutta cared and cooked for them. She made a great store of Manaka-cake, packed for coolness all neatly in plantain-leaves; she made them Nano-cheese, and two or three big pots of Subbub. She kept them clean and combed; plastered and physicked them; taught them to cook, and many things else, until, as one by one they grew up, they

---

* 'Meermut' means shadow, phantom, spectre, or even the pictured remembrance of anything in the mind.

knew all that she *could* teach them, except the wisdom to use what they had learnt. She would often, too, in the first hush of night, tell them stories of their father, and of her own father, back even to Zebbah and the Portingal dangling with his bunch of wild-cats' tails in the corner. But as the years wasted away, she grew thin and mournful, and fell ill of pining and grief and age, and even had at last to keep to her bed of moss and cotton in the hut.

Her sons worked hard for her, pushing into the forest and across the narrow swamp in search of fruits to tempt her appetite. Nod heaped up fresh leaves for her bed, and sang in his shrill, quavering voice every evening Tishnar's hymn to his poor old mother. He baked her sweet potatoes and Nanoes wrapped in leaves, and would dance round, 'wriggle and stamp – wriggle and stamp', as Seelem had told him dance the Oomgar-Nuggas, or Black Men, to try to make her cheerful.

But by and by she began to languish, her teeth chattering, her eyes burning, unable to eat . . . And one still afternoon, when only Nod was near (his brothers, tired of the heat and buzzing in the green hut, having gone to gather nuts and sticks in the forest), as Mutta-matutta sat dozing and mut-tering in her corner, came the voice of Tishnar, calling in the hush of evening: and she knew that she must die.

Nod crept close to her, thinking at first the strange voice singing was the sound of Seelem's Zevveras' distant gongs, and he held the hard thin hand between his. When Thumb

and Thimble returned with their bags and faggots of smoulder-wood, she called them all three, and told them she too must go away now, perhaps even, if only in Meermut, to find their father. And she besought them to be always true and faithful one to another, and to be brave.

'Five fingers serve one hand, my brave ones,' she said. 'And oh, remember this always: that you are all three Mulla-Mulgars, sons of Seelem, whose home is far from here – Mulla-Mulgars who never do walk flambo – that is, on all fours – never taste blood, and never, unless in danger and despair, climb trees or grow a tail.'

It was hot and gloomy in the tangled little hut, lit only by the violet of the dying afterglow. And when she had rested a little while to recover her breath, she told them that Seelem, the night before he left them, had said that, should he perish on his journey and not return, in seven Munza years they were, as best as they could, bravely to follow after him. In time they would perhaps reach the Valleys of Tishnar, and their uncle, Prince Assasimmon, would welcome them.

'His country lies beyond and beyond,' she said, 'forest and river, forest, swamp and river, the mountains of Arak-kaboa – leagues, leagues away.' And, as she paused, a feeble wind sighed through the open window, stirring the dangling bones of the Portingal, so that, with their faint clicking, they too, seemed to echo, 'leagues, leagues away'.

'It will be a long and dreary journey, my sons. But the Prince Assasimmon, Mulla-mulla of the Mulgars, is great and powerful, and has for hut a palace of ivory and Azma-mogreel, with scarlet and Mamasul, slaves and peacocks, and beasts uncountable; and leagues of Ukka and Barbary-nuts; and boundless fields of Ummuz, and orchards of fruit, and bowers of flowers and pleasure. And his, too, is the Rose of all the Mulgars.' And as he listened Thimble shuffled from foot to foot, his heart uneasy, to hear her cry so hollowly of the strangeness of that rose. And at her bidding, out of the cupboard they took the civeted bundles of all the stuff and little Mulgar treasures she had been hoarding up for them all these years against this last day.

She gave Thumb and Thimble each a red Oomgar's or White Man's jacket with curved metal hooks, and to Nod the little coat of mountain-sheep's wool, with its nine ivory buttons. She divided and shared everything between them – their father's knives and cudgels, the beads blue and emerald, the Margarita stones. The Portingal's rusty hatchet, burned with a cross on its stock, she gave to Thumb; a litle fat black greasy book of sorcery, made of Exxzwixxia leaves, to Thimble; and to Nod, last of all, picking it out of the stitched serpent-skin lining of her great wool cap, she gave the Wonderstone.

'I give this to Nod,' she said to his brothers, 'because he is a Nizza-neela, and has magic in him. Come close, my sons, Thumb and Thimble, and see. His winking eye* has green within the hazel; his thumbs grow lean and long; he still keeps two milk-teeth; and bears the Nizza-neela tuft betwixt his ears.' With her hot skinny fingers she stroked softly back his hair, and showed his brothers the little velvety patch, or tuft, or badge, or crest, on the top of his head, above the parting. 'O Mulla-Mulgars, how I begged your father to take this Wonderstone with him on his journey! but he would not. He said, "Keep it, and let my sons, if need be, carry it after me to the kingdom of my brother. He will know by this one thing that they are indeed my sons – Mulla-Mulgars, Princes of Tishnar. *Sibbetha eena manga Môh!*" '

'Never, little Nod,' said his old dying mother – 'never lose, nor give away, nor sport with, nor even lend this

* The winking eye is the left eye. On the right or cudgel side, the Mulgars say, sits Bravery; on the winking, woman, or left side, sits Craft.

Wonderstone; and if in your long journey you are in danger of the Third Sleep,* or lost, or in great fear, spit with your spittle on the stone, and rub softly three times with your left thumb, Samaweeza: Tishnar will hear you; help will come.'

Then, with her small, clumsy fingers, she tied up the sleeping milk-white Wonderstone in the hem of his woolly sheep's coat, and lay back in her bed, too feeble to speak again. Thumb, Thimble, and Nod sat all three, each with his little heap of house-stuff before him, which it seemed hateful now to have, staring through the doorway. In the purple gloom the fireflies were mazily flickering. The night was still, like a simmering pot, with heat. And out of the swamp they heard the Ooboë calling to its mate, singing marvellously sweet and clear in the darkness above its woven nest; while over their heads the tiny Nikka-nakkas, or mouse-owls, sat purring in the thatch. And Nod said: 'Listen, Mutta, listen; the Ooboë's telling secrets!' And she smiled with tight-shut lids, wagging her wizened head.

And in the deepest dead of night, when Thimble sat sleeping, his long arms thrown out over the Portingal's rough table, and Thumb crouching at the door, Nod heard in the silence a very faint sigh. He crept to his mother's bed. She softly raised her hand to him, and her eyes closed.

So her three sons dug her a deep grave beside Glint's, under the Ukka-tree, as she had bidden them. And many of the Forest-Mulgars, especially those of her own kind and kindred, came down solemnly out of the forest towards evening of that day, and keened or droned for Mutta-matutta, squatting together at some little distance from the Portingal's hut. Beyond their counting (though that is not

* First Sleep is night-sleep; Second Sleep is swoon-sleep; Third Sleep is death, or Noomanossi. So, too, the Mulgars say, the first is 'Little-go', the second is 'Great-go', and the third is 'Come-no-more'; as if their bodies were a lodging, and sleep a kind of out-of-doors.

a hard matter) was the number of the years she and her father and her father's father, back even to Zebbah, had lived in the hut. But they did not come near, because they feared the Portingal's yellow bones hung up in the corner.

CHAPTER TWO

Fire and Snow

At first the three brothers lived so forlorn and solitary together that they could scarcely eat. Everything they saw or handled told them only over and over again that their mother was dead. But there was work to be done, and brave hearts must take courage, else sorrow and trouble would be nothing but evil. This, too, was no time for sitting idle and doleful. For a little before the gathering of the rains there began to seem a strangeness in the air. After the great heat, there had flown up a tempest of wind and lightning of such a brightness that Nod, peering out of his little tangled window-hole, could see beneath the gleaming rods of rain and the huge, bowed, groaning trees no less than three leopards crouching for shelter under the Portingal's sturdy little hut. He could hear them, too, in the pauses of the tempest, mewling, spitting, and swearing, and the lash of their angry tails against the wall of the hut.

After the tempest, it fell cold and very still, with sometimes a moaning in the air. Strange weather was in the sky at rise and set of sun. And the three brothers, looking out, and seeing the numberless flights of birds winging their way all in one direction, and hearing this moaning, hardly knew what to be doing. They went out every day to gather great bundles of wood and as many nuts and fruits and roots as they could carry. And they found everywhere wise creatures doing the same – I mean, of course, collecting food – for none beside the Minimuls, the Gungas, and the Mulla-Mulgars have fire-sticks, and most of them fear even the sight and smell of flames.

And Nod, having his mother's quick hand, made a great store of Manaka-cake and Sudd-bread. He dried some fruits, pulped others. And some he poured with honey or Ummuz-juice into the Portingal's little earthen pots, many of which were still unbroken, while he who had first used them was but a bony shadow-trap in the corner. And Nod and Thumb made two great gourds of Subbub, very sweet and potent, so that, because of the sweet smell of it, the four-clawed Weddervols came barking about their hut all night. But the Manga-cheese their mother had made melted in the heat of the great fires they burned, and most of it ran down out of the cupboard. They filled the wood-hole with fire-wood, and stacked it outside, above Nod's shoulder, all against the hut.

And it was about the nineteenth week after Mutta's death that Thumb, as he came stooping to the door one night, saw fires of Tishnar on the ground. Over the swamp stood a shaving of moon, clear as a bow of silver. And all about, on every twig, on every thorn, and leaf, and pebble; all along the nine-foot grasses, on every cushion and touch of bark, even on the walls of their hut, lay this spangling fiery meal of Tishnar – frost. He called his brothers. Their breath stood round them like smoke. They stared and snuffed, they coughed in the cold air. Never, since birds

wore feathers – never had hoar-frost glittered on Munza-Mulgar before.

These Mullas danced; they crouched down in the dreadful cold, thinking to warm their hands at these uncountable fires. And, lo and behold! in a little while, looking at one another, each was a Mulgar, white and sparkling too. Their very hairs, down-arm and up-arm, every tuft stood stiff and white with frost. Like millers they stood, all blazing in the night.

And that was the beginning of *Witzaweelwulla* (the White Winter). For it was only three days after Tishnar's fires were kindled that Nod first saw snow. Now one, two, three, a scatter of flakes, just a few. 'Feathers,' thought Nod.

But faster, faster; twirling, rustling, hovering. 'Butterflies,' thought Nod.

And then it seemed the sky, the air, was all aflock. He ran out snuffing and frightened. He clapped his hands; he leapt

and frisked and shouted. And there, coming up out of the swamp, were his brothers, laden with rushes, and as woolly with snow as sheep. Because it looked so white and crisp and beautiful, Nod even brought out a pot and filled it with snow to cook for their supper. But there, when he lifted the lid, was only a little steaming water.

By and by they began to wonder and to fear no more. How glad they were of all the wood they had brought in, and of their great cupboardful of victuals! They made themselves long poles, and would go leaping about to keep themselves warm. They built such roaring fires on the hearth they squatted round that the sparks flew up like fireflies under the black, starry sky. Snug in their hut, the brothers would sit of an evening on their three stools, with their smoking bowls between their legs. And they would open their great mouths and drone and sing the songs their father had taught them, beating to the notes with their flat feet on the earth floor.

Nevertheless, they pined for the cold and the snow to be over and gone, so that they might start on their journey. Every morning broke bleak and sparkling. Often of a night new snow came, till they walked between low white walls on their little path to the forest. But in spite of the cold which made them ache and shiver, and their toes and fingers burn and itch, they went out searching for frozen nuts and fruits every morning, and still fetched in faggots.

Often while they squatted, toasting themselves round their fire, Nod would look up, blinking his eyes, to see the faces of the Forest-Mulgars peeping in at the window, envying the Mullas their warmth, though afraid of their fire, and calling softly one to another: 'Ho, ho! look at the Mulla-Sluggas [lazy princes] sitting round their fire!' And Thumb and Thimble would grin and softly scratch their hairy knees. Thumb, indeed, made up a Mulgar drone, which he used to buzz to himself when the Munza-Mulgars came miching and mocking and peeping. (But it was a bad and dull drone, and I will not make it worse by turning it into my poor English from Mulgar-Royal.)

Nod often sat watching the Forest-Mulgars frisking in the forest, though every morning the light shone through on many perched frozen in the boughs. The Mullabruks and Manquabees made huddles in the snow. But the tiny Squirrel-tails, with their dark, grave, beautiful eyes and silken amber coats, still roosted high where the frost-wind stirred in the dark. Sometimes on a crusted branch of snow Nod would see five – seven – nine of these tiny, frost-powdered Mulgars cuddling together in a row – poor little

23

frozen and empty boxes, their gay lives fled away. And when his brothers were gathering sticks in the forest, he would smuggle out for the rest two or three handfuls of nuts and pieces of cake and Sudd-bread. All the crusts and husks and morsels he kept in a shallow grass-basket, which his mother had plaited, to feed these pillowy Squirrel-tails, the lean Skeetoes, and the spindle-legged Fly-catchers.

Birds of all colours and many other odd little beasts came in the snow to Nod to be fed. He summoned them with the clapping of two sticks of ivory together, till his brothers began to wonder how it was their victuals were dwindling so fast. But once, when Thumb and Thimble were away in the forest with their jumping-poles, and he had ventured out on this errand with his basket full of scraps, he forgot to put up the door behind him. When he returned, skipping as fast as his fours would carry him, wild pigs and long-snouted Brackanolls, Weddervols, and hungry birds had come in and eaten more than half their store. The last of their mother's treasured cheese was gone, and all their Ummuz-cane. That night Thumb and Thimble went very sulky to bed. And for the next few days all three brothers sallied out together, with their poles, searching and grubbing after every scrap of victuals they could find with which to fill their larder again.

Some time after this, so hard and sharp grew the cold that Thumb and Thimble were minded to put on their red metal-hooked jackets when they went out stick-gathering. They took their knives and nut-sacks over their shoulders, and muffled and bunched themselves up close, with cotton-leaves wound round their stomachs, and their skin caps pulled low over their round frost-enticing ears. And they told Nod to cook them a smoking hot supper against the dark, for now the snow was so deep it was a hard matter to find and carry sticks, and they meant to look for more before matters worsened yet. So Nod at once set to his cookery.

He made up a great fire on the hearthstone. But in spite of its flames, so louring with gathering snow-clouds was the day that he had to keep the door down to give him clearer light; and, though he kept scuttling about, driving out the thieving Brackanolls and Peekodillies that came nosing into the hut, and scaring away the famished birds that kept hopping in through the window-hole, even then he could not keep himself warm.

So at last he went to the lower cupboard, under the dangling Portingal, and took out his sheepskin coat. He put away the dried kingfisher which his mother had wrapped in the fleece to keep it sweet, and buttoned the ivory buttons, and skipped about nimbly over his cooking in that. Then he heaped more wood on – logs and brush and smoulder-wood – higher and higher, till the flames leapt red, gold, and lichen-green out of the chimney-hole. Then he said to himself, flinging yet another armful on: 'Now Nod will go down and get some ice to melt for water to make Sudd-bread.' So he went down to the water-spring.

And he stood watching the Mulgars frisking at the edge of the forest, vain that they should see him with his pole and basket, standing in his sheep's jacket. He broke up some ice and put it into his basket. Then he plodded over to his mother's grave and cleared away the hardened snow that had fallen during the night on her little heap of stones. '*Kara, kara* Mutta, Mutta-matutta,' he whispered, laying his bony cheek on the stones – 'dearest Mutta!'

And while he stood there thinking of his mother, and of how he would go and bring down a pot of honeycomb for her death-shadow; and then of his father; and then of the strange journey they were all going to set out on when Tishnar returned to her mountains; and then of his Wonder-stone; and then of Assasimmon, Prince of the Valleys, his peacocks and Ummuz-cane, and Ummuz-cane, and Ummuz-cane – while he was thus softly thinking of all these happy things, he suddenly saw the gigantic Ukka-tree above him, lit up marvellously red, and glowing as if with the setting of the sun. He shut his eyes with dread, for he saw all the Forest Monkeys lit up too, stock-still, staring, staring; and he heard a curious crackle and whs-s-s-ss.

Nod turned his little head and looked back over his shoulder. And against the snowy gloom of the forest he saw not only sparks, but flames, wagging up out of the chimney hole. The door of the hut was like the frame of a furnace. And a trembling fear came over him, so that for a moment he could neither breathe nor move. Then, throwing down his basket of ice, and calling softly, 'Mutta, O Mutta!' he scrambled over the snow as fast as he could and rushed into the hut. But he was too late; before he

could jump, spluttering and choking, out of the door again, with just an armful of anything he could see, its walls were ablaze. Dry and tangled, its roof burnt like straw – a huge red fire pouring out smoke and flame, hissing, gushing, crackling, bubbling, roaring. And presently after, while Nod ran snapping his fingers, dancing with horror in the snow, and calling shriller and shriller,

> Thumb, Thimble; Thimble, Thumb,
> Leave your sticks and hurry home:
> Thicker and thicker the smoke do come!
> Thumb, Thimble; Thimble, Thumb!

he heard above the flames a multitudinous howling and squealing, and he looked over his shoulder, and saw hundreds upon hundreds of faces in the forest staring out between the branches at the fire.

By the time that Thimble and Thumb in their red jackets came scampering on all fours, helter-skelter, downhill out of the forest, a numberless horde of the Forest-Mulgars were frisking and howling round the blaze, and the flames were floating half as high as Glint's great Ukka-tree. They squealed, *'Walla, walla!'* grinning and gibbering one to another as they came tumbling along; but they might just as well have called 'Moonshine!' for every drop of *walla*, or water, was frozen. Nor would twenty flowing springs and all Assasimmon's slaves have quenched that fire now.

When the Forest-Mulgars saw that the Mulla-Mulgars had given up hope of putting the fire out, they pelted it with snowballs, and scampered about, gathering up every stick and straw and shred they could find, and did their utmost to keep it in. For at last, in their joy that the little Portingal's bones were in the burning, and in their envy of the Mulla-Mulgars, their fear of fire was gone.

And so Night came down, and there they all were, hand-in-hand in a huge monkey-ring, dancing and prancing

round the little Portingal's burning hut, and squealing at
the top of their voices; while countless beasts of Munza-
Mulgar, too frightened of fire to draw near, prowled, with
flame-emblazoned eyes, staring out of the forest. And this
was the Forest-Mulgars' Dancing Song:

Bhoor juggub duppa singlee – duppa singlee – duppa singlee;
    Bhoor juggub duppa singlee;
        Sal rosen ghar Bhoosh!

They sing at first in a kind of droning zap-zap, and
through their noses, these Munza-Mulgars, their yelps
gradually gathering in speed and volume, till they lift their
spell-bound faces in the air and howl aloud. And with
such a resounding shout and clamour on the *Bhoosh* you
would think they were in pain.

    For the best part of that night the fire flared and smoul-
dered, while the stars wheeled in the black sky above the
forest; and still round and round the Mulgars jigged and
danced in the glistening snow. For the frost was so hard
and still, not even this great fire could melt it fifteen paces
distant from its flames. And Thimble and Thumb in their
red jackets, and Nod in his cotton breeches and sheepskin
coat, shivered and shook, because they were not hardened,

like the Forest-Mulgars, to the icy night-wind that stole fitfully abroad.

When morning broke, the fire had burned down to a smother, and most of the dancing Mulgars had trooped back, tired out and sleepy, to their tree-houses and huddles and caverns and hanging ropes in the forest. But no sleep stole over those Mulla-Sluggas, Thumb, Thimble, and Nod, sitting on their stones in the snow, watching their home-smoke drooping down and down. Nod stared and stared at the embers, his teeth chattering, ashamed and nearly heart-broken.

But his brothers looked now at the smoke, and now at him, and whenever they looked at Nod they muttered, *'Foh! Mulla-ugguba, foh!'* – that is to say, 'Foh! Royal-Flaming-Shining One!' or 'Your Highness Firebright!' or 'What think you now, Prince of Bonfires?' But they were too sullen and angry, and Nod was too downcast, even to get up to drive away the little mole-skinned Brackanolls and the Peekodillies which came nosing and grunting and scratching in the ashes, in search of the scorched oil-nuts and the charred Sudd and Manaka-cake.

The three Mulla-Mulgars sat there until the sun began to be bright on their faces and to make a splendour of the snow; then they did not feel quite so cold and miserable. And when they had nibbled a few nuts and berries which a friendly old Manquabee brought down to them, they began to think and talk over what they had best be doing now – at least, Nod listened, while Thumb and Thimble talked. And at length they decided that, their hut being burnt, and they without refuge from the cold, or any hoard of food, they would wait no longer, but must set off at once into the forest on the same long journey as their father Seelem had gone, to seek out their Uncle Assasimmon, Prince of the Valleys of Tishnar.

This once said, Thumb lifted his fat body stiffly from his

30

stone, and took his jumping-pole, and frisked high, leap-ing to and fro to make himself warm again. Soon he began to tingle, and laughed out to cheer the others when he tumbled head over heels into a snowdrift. And they combed themselves, and stood up to their trouble, and thought stubbornly, as far as their monkey-wits would let them, only of the future (which is easier to manage than the past).

Then they searched close in the cooling ashes and embers of the hut, and found a few beads undimmed by the heat, and all the Margarita stones, which, like the Salamander, no flame can change; also, one or two unbroken pots and jars and an old stone kettle or Ghôb. Nod, indeed, found also a piece of gold that had lain hid in the Portingal's rags. But all the little Traveller's bones except his left thumb knuckle-bone were fallen to ashes. Nod gave Thumb the noddle of gold, and himself kept the knuckle-bone. '*Sootli*,'* he whispered, touched his nose with it, and put it secretly into his pocket. And glad were they to think that only that morning they had fetched out their red jackets and Nod his wool coat.

When the Forest-Mulgars heard that the three brothers were setting out on their long journey, they came trooping down from their leafy villages, carrying presents – two skin water-bags (for the longed-for time when the ice should bestir itself), a rough stone knife, a wild-bee honeycomb, a plaited bag of dried Nanoes and nuts, and so on. But of these Mulgar tribes few, like ants, or bees, or squirrels, make any store, and none uses fire, nor, save one or two solitaries here and there, can any walk upright or carry a cudgel. They munch and frisk and chatter, and scratch and quarrel and mock, having their own ways and wisdom and

* That is, Magic, or Strangeness. When the Mulgars of Munza see anything strange or unknown, they will whimper to one another, as they stand with eyes fixed, '*Sootli, Sootli, Sootli*', or some such sound.

their own musts and mustn'ts. There are few, too, that
cherish not some kindness, if not for all, at least for one
another – the leopard for her cubs, the Coccodrillo for her
eggs. But back to our Mulla-Mulgars.

The forest of Munza-Mulgar saw a feast upon its borders
that day. The Forest-Mulgars sat in a great ring, and ate and
drank, and when the sun had ascended into the middle of
the sky and the snow-piled branches shone white as Tishnar's lambs, Thumb, Thimble, and Nod rose up and sang,
'Gar Mulgar Dusangee' – the Mulgars' Farewell. While
they sang, all the Forest-Mulgars, in their companies and
tribes, sat solemnly around them, furred and coloured and
pouched and tailed. Shave their chops and put them in
breeches, they might well be little men. And they waved
slowly palm-branches and greenery to the time of the tune;
some even moaned and grunted, too.

> Far away in Nanga-noon,
> Lived an old and grey Baboon,*
>   Ah-mi, Sulani!
> Once a Prince among his kind,
> Now forsaken, left behind,
> Feeble, lonely, all but blind:
>   Sulani, ghar magleer.
>
> Peaceful Tishnar came by night,
> In the moonbeams cold and white;
>   Ah-mi, Sulani!
> 'Far away from Nanga-moon,
> Thou old and grey Baboon;
> Is a journey for thee soon!'
>   Sulani, ghar magleer.

* So I have translated 'Babbabooma'.

'Be not frightened, shut thine eye;
Comfort take, nor weep, nor sigh;
Solitary Tishnar's nigh!'
　　Sulani, ghar magleer.

Old Baboon, he gravely did
All that peaceful Tishnar bid;
　　Ah-mi, Sulani!
In the darkness cold and grim
Drew his blanket over him;
Closed his old eyes, sad and dim:
　　Sulani, ghar magleer.

And here the Mulgars all lay flat, with their faces in the
snow, and put the palms of their hands on their heads;
while the three Mulla-Mulgars paced slowly round, singing
the last verse, which after the doggerel I have made of the
others, I despair of putting into English:

Talaheeti sul magloon
Olgar, ulgar Nanga-noon;
　　Ah-mi, Sulani!
Tishnar sootli maltmahee,
Ganganareez soongalee,
Manni Mulgar sang suwhee:
　　Sulani, ghar magleer.

Then the Mulla-Mulgars cut down stout boughs to make
cudgels, and, having tied up their few possessions into three
bundles, and filled their pockets with old nuts, they took
palm-leaves and honeycomb and withered scarlet and green
berries, with which they canopied as best they could their
mother's grave, nor forgot poor gluttonous Glint's. They
stood there in the snow, and raised their hands in lamentable salutation. And each took up a stone and jerked it (for
they cannot throw as men do) as far as he could towards the

forest, as if to say, 'Go with us!' Then, with one last sorrowful look at the befrosted ashes of their hut, they took up their bundles and started on their journey.

At first, as I have said, the Mulgar-track is wide, and even in this continually falling snow was beaten clear by hundreds of hand and foot prints. But after a while the lofty branches began to knit themselves above, and to hang thickly over the travellers, and to shut out the light. And the path grew faint and narrow.

One by one their friends waved good-bye and left them, until only Noll and Nunga (Mutta-matutta's only sister's only children) accompanied them. Just before sunset, when the forest seemed like a cage of music with the voices of the birds that now sang – many of them desperately from cold and hunger rather than for delight – Noll, too, and Nunga raised their hands, touched noses, and said good-bye. And the three brothers stood watching them till they had waved their branches for the last time. Then they went on.

CHAPTER THREE

The Three Princes set out on their Journey

It was now, what with the snow and what with natural evening, growing quickly dark. The birds had ceased to sing; only the Munza nightjar rattled. Now near, now far away, the Mulla-Mulgars heard the beasts of the forest beginning to range and roar in the gloom. Nod buttoned up his sheep's-jacket, for there was a frost-mist beneath the trees. He was cold, and began to be tired and very homesick. But Thumb was broad and fat and prodigiously strong, Thimble lean and sinewy. And when Thumb saw that Nod went stumbling under his bundle, he said: 'Give it to me, Mulla-Jugguba!' And Thimble laughed.

But Nod refused to give up his bundle, and trudged on behind his brothers, until night came down in earnest. Then, when it was quite dark, after listening and muttering together, they thought that if they spent the night down here they would certainly sleep 'in danger'. So Thumb clambered into a great Ollaconda-tree, and let down a rope or twist of the thick creeper called Cullum, and drew up all three bundles. Then Thimble pushed and Thumb pulled, and up went Nod, too stiff and cold to climb up by himself, after the bundles, sheep's-jacket and all. Then Thimble climbed up too. They made their supper of Mulgar-bread and frost-cockled Mambel-berries, which are sour and quench the thirst, and they drank or sucked splinters of ice, plenty of which hung glassy in the great, still, winter-troubled tree. And for fear of leopards (or 'Roses', as their Munza name

signifies), they agreed to keep watch in turn, Thumb first, then Thimble, then Nod. They tied their bundles to the boughs, chose smooth forks to squat in, and soon Thimble was fast asleep.

But when Nod found himself alone in the midst of the great icy tree in the black forest, he could not sleep for thinking of it. He stroked his face with his brown hand over and over to keep his eyes shut. He nuzzled down into his sheep's-jacket. He counted his fingers again and again. He repeated the lingo of the Seventy-seven Travellers from beginning to end. It was in vain. Far and near he heard the cries and wanderings of the forest beasts; the Ollaconda-tree was full of the nests of the weaver-birds; and, worse still, soon Thimble began to snore so loud and so sorrowfully that poor Nod trembled where he sat. He could bear himself no longer. He stooped forward and called softly: 'Thumb, my brother, are you awake, Thumb?'

'Sleep on, little Ummanodda,' said Thumb; 'if I watch, I watch.'

'But I cannot sleep,' said Nod; 'these weavers chatter so.'

Thumb laughed. 'Thimble sings in his dreams,' he said. 'Why shouldn't the little tailors sing too?'

'Do you think any leopards will come?' said Nod.

'Think good things, my brother, not bad,' Thumb answered. 'But this we will do – wait a little while awake, and I will sleep, and as soon as sleep begins to come, call me and wake me; then, little brother, you shall sleep in peace till morning.'

He put his head under his arm without waiting for an answer; and soon, even louder and more dismal than Thimble's, rose Thumb's snoring into the Ollaconda-tree.

Nod sat cold and stiff, his eyes stretched open, his ears twitching. And a thin moonlight began to tremble between the leaves. The light cheered his spirits, and he thought, 'Nod will soon feel sleepy now,' when suddenly out of the gloom of the forest burst a sounder or drove of wild pig, scuffling and chuggling beneath the tree. Peeping down, Nod could just see them in the faint moonshine, with their long, black, hairy ears and tufted tails.

And presently, while they were grubbing in the snow, one lifted up its snout and cried in a loud voice: 'Co-older – and colder!'

'Co-older – and colder,' cried another.

'Co-older – and colder,' cried a third. And all silently grubbed on as before.

'The Queen of the Mountains is in the Forest,' began the first again, 'with fingers of frost.'

'And shoulders of snow.'

'And feet of ice,' screamed the third.

'The Queen of the Mountains!' they grunted all together; and went on burrowing, and shouldering, and faintly squeaking.

'Hungrier and hungrier,' cried one in a shrill voice, suddenly lifting its head, so that Nod could see quite clearly its pale-green, greedy slits of eyes.

'Leaner and leaner,' answered another.

'All the Sudd hid, all the Ukkas gone, all the Boobab frozen!' squealed a third.

'The Queen of the Mountains is in the Forest!' they grunted all together. But the pig that had looked up into the tree was still staring – staring and wrinkling his narrow snout, till at last all the pigs stopped feeding. 'Pigs, my brothers; pigs, my brothers,' he muttered. 'Up in this tree are Mulgar three, which travellers be ... Ho, there!' But Nod thought it best to make no answer. And the pig turned round and beat with his hind-feet against the bole or trunk of the Ollaconda. 'Ho, there, little Mulgar in the sheep-skin coat!'

'If you beat like that, horny-foot, you'll wake my brothers,' said Nod.

'Brothers!' said the pig angrily. 'What's brothers to

Ukka-nuts? What's your names, and where are you going?'

'My brother's names,' said Nod, 'are Thumma and Thimbulla, and I am Nod. We are going to the palace of ivory and Azmamogreel that is our Uncle Assasimmon's, Prince of the Valleys of Tishnar.'

At that all the pigs began muttering together. 'Come down and tell us!' said a lean yellow pig; and as he snapped his jaws Nod saw in the moonbeam the frost-light blinking on his bristles.

'Tell you what?' said Nod.

'About this Prince of Tishnar. Oh, these false-tongued Mulgars!' Nod made no answer.

Then a fat old she-pig began speaking in a soft, pleasant voice. 'You must be very, very rich, Prince Nod, with those great bags of nuts; and, surely, it must be royal Sudd I smell! And Assasimmon his uncle! whose house is more than a thousand pigs'-tails long; and gardens so thick with trees of fruit and honey, one groans to have only one stomach. Come down a little way, Prince Nod, and tell us poor hungry pigs of the Royal Assasimmon and the dainty food he eats.'

So pleasant was her flattering voice Nod thought there could not possibly be any harm in scrambling down just one or two branches. And though his fingers were still stiff with cold, he began to edge down.

'Oh, but bring a bundle – bring a bundle, little Prince. It's cold for gentlefolk sitting in the snow.'

'Pigs – pigs must naked go; but not for gentlefolk the snow,' squealed the herd shrilly.

'Come gently, Prince Nod; do not stir your royal brothers, Prince Nod!' said the old crafty one.

Nod listened to her flattery, and, having untied his precious bundle, he slid down with it softly to the ground.

'A seat – a seat for Prince Nod,' cried the old sow. 'Oh, what a royal jacket – oh, what a handsome jacket!' So Nod sat down on his bundle in the moonlight of the snow, and all the wild pig, scenting his Sudd, pressed close – forty wild pig at least.

'Assasimmon, Assasimmon, Prince of Tishnar, Prince of Tishnar,' they kept grunting, and at every word they squeezed and edged closer and closer, their hungry snouts in air – closer and closer, till Nod had to hold tight to keep his seat; closer and closer, and again they began squealing: 'Pigs are hungry, brother Nod. Cakes of Sudd, cakes of *Sudd*!' And then, like a great scrambling wave of pigs, they rushed at him all together. Over went Nod into the snow. Scores of little sharp hoofs scuttled over him. And when at last he was able to get up and look about him, bruised and scratched and breathless, no trace of pigs was there, no trace of bundle; every nut and crust of Sudd and crumb of pulpy Mulgar-bread was gone.

Suddenly there sounded a loud, harsh voice out of the tree. 'Ho, ho, and ahôh! What's the trouble? What's the trouble?' Nod looked up, and saw Thumb and Thimble staring down between their out-stretched arms through the moon-silvery leaves. And he told them, trembling, of how he could not sleep, and about the pigs and the bundle.

'O most wise Nizza-neela!' said Thumb when he had finished. 'Last night Mulla-Jugguba; this night Noddanel-lipogo' (Prince of Bonfires, Noddle

of Pork). But Thimble was too sore to say anything, for his little Exxzw-ixxia-book of sorcery had been stuffed into Nod's bundle, and now it was lost for ever. And they left Nod to climb up again by himself. Once safely back on his fork, he was so tired and miserable that, with his hands over his face, he fell almost instantly fast asleep.

When he opened his small clear eyes again, sunrise was glinting here and there through the green twilight on the icicles and snow in the trees. He looked down, and saw Thumb and Thimble combing themselves. So down he went, too, and took off his jacket, and skipped and frisked till he grew warm. Then he, too, combed himself, and went and sat down beside his brothers at the foot of the Ollaconda-tree to eat his morning's share of musty nuts. At first his brothers sat angry and sullen, munching with their great dog-teeth, and seeming to begrudge him every Ukka-nut he cracked. But as the daybeams brightened, here where the trees grew not so dense, and the birds, some almost as small as acorns, flashed and zig-zagged, and Parrakeetoes squeaked and screamed in hundreds on the branches, watching the three hungry travellers, they began to forget Nod's supper with the pigs. And when they had eaten, into the gloom of Munza they set out once more.

As a dog smells out the footsteps of his master, so these Mulla-Mulgars seemed to smell out their way. No path was to be seen except where pig-droves had rambled by, or droves of Mullabruks and packs of Munza-dogs. And once Thumb, on a sudden, stood still, and pointed to the ground, opening his great grinning mouth, with its little wall of glistening teeth, and muttered, 'Roses!' They stood together looking down at the frozen footprints of a mother-leopard and her cubs in the fresh-laid snow. Nod fancied, even, he could smell her breath on the icy air. After this they went forward more warily, but carried their cudgels with a bravery, looking very fierce in their red jackets and great caps of furry skins.

And, after a while, the huge trees gathered in again, and soon arched loftily overhead as thick as thatch, so that it was all in a cold and sluggish gloom they walked, like the dusk of coming night. So thick was the leafy roof overhead, but little snow had floated into its twilight. Only a rare frost shimmered on the spiky husks of fruit thrown down by the Tree-Mulgars. Huge frozen ropes of Cullum and wild pepper dangled in knots and loops from bough to bough, and sometimes a troop of Squirrel-tails or spidery Skeetoes swung lightly down these hoar-frost ropes, chattering and scolding at the three strangers. But though Thumb called to them in their own tongue, *'Ullalulla-ubbajubba'*, or some such sounds as that, meaning, 'We are friends', they skipped off, hand, foot, and tail, into their leafy roofs and shadows, afraid of these cudgel-carrying travellers in their red jackets, who walked, like the dreaded Oomgar, heads in air.

Yet Nod was glad even of such company as this, so silent was the forest. In this darkness they sat and ate their handful of food, with scorpions and speckled tree-spiders watching them from their holes, not knowing where the sun was, nor daring to kindle a fire with their fire-sticks for fear of the tree-shadows. And at night they slept huddled close together for warmth and safety, while Thumb and Thimble kept watch in turn.

In this way many days passed almost without blink of sunlight. Once and again they would cross over some pig-track, or stand, with club in hand, to watch a leopard pass. And often troops of Mulgars kept pace with them awhile, swinging from branch to branch, and chattering threats at the travellers. But most of the forest creatures, parched and famished by such a cold as had never fallen on Munza-Mulgar before, had been driven out of the forest in search of food and warmth. And often the travellers were compelled to search the bark of the trees and in the crevices of rocks and under stones, as do the Babbaboomas, and eat whatever creeping things they could find.

Apart from the dangling Skeetoes, and now and then father, mother, and chidderkins of some old sour-faced mournful Mullabruk, they saw few things living, except the little ivory-gnawing M'boko, Peekodillies, and poison-spiders. But many of these, too, had died of cold and hunger. And now, instead of the pale green and amber lamps of firefly and glow-worms, burned only the fires of Tishnar's frost. Birds rarely ventured down into this snowy shadowland, except only the tiny, Telateuties, blood-red as lady-birds, that ran chittering up the trees. These birds haunt only where daylight rarely steals, and it is said they talk with the tree-spirits, or giant Noomas, that roam these shades.

At last, their feet sore with poison-needles, which some-times pierced clean through their thick skins, their eyes aching with the darkness, the three travellers, on the eighth day, broke out of the dense forest into broad daylight and shining snow again. Down and down they descended into a frozen swampy valley. And about noon, half-hidden in the fume and steam of their own breath, they saw a great herd or muster of Ephelantoes feeding. They stood in a line beyond Nod's counting – big, middling-sized, and little – tearing down the rime-laden branches of the trees, whose leaves and fruits they first warmed with their bellows-breath before stuffing them into their mouths. The swampy ground shook with their tramplings. Nod gazed in wonder as he and his brothers, marching abreast, paced softly but doggedly on. And very soon the watchful eyes—that glitter small in the great stone-coloured heads of these mountainous beasts – perceived the red jackets moving betwixt the grasses. And a silence came; the beasts stopped feeding.

'*Meelmutha glaren djhar!*' muttered Thumb.

So the Mulla-Mulgars pushed quietly and bravely on, without turning their heads or letting their eyes wander. For it is said that there is nothing frets and angers these monsters so much as a watchful eye. They leave their feeding and wallowing, even the big Shes their suckling. Their great bodies trembling, they stand in disquiet and unrest if but just one small clear eye beneath its lid be fixed too close or earnestly upon them. Oomgars, Mulgars, leopards, even down to the brooding Mullabruk, with its clay-coloured face – they abhor all scrutiny. But why this is so I cannot say.

It may be, then, that Nod, in his first wonder, dwelt too lingeringly with his eye on these Lords of Munza : for a behemothian bull-Ephelanto, with one of his tusks broken, lurched forward through the long grasses, his tail stock-stiff behind him, and stood in their path. And as the Mulgar travellers passed him by, he wound his long, two-fingered trunk round Nod's belly, shook him softly, and lifted him high above the sedge into the air.

At this many other of the Ephelantoes stamped across the swamp and stood in the mist around him. Nod's hand was in his pocket and pressed against his slim thigh-bone, and there, hard and round, he felt as in a dream his Wonder-stone. And he caught back his fears, and thus, up aloft twenty feet or more between earth and sky, he twisted his head and said softly: 'Deal with the Nizza-neela gently, Lord of the Forest; we are servants of Tishnar.' At the sound of the name of Tishnar all the Ephelantoes lifted up their trunks, and with a great blast trumpeted in unison. Whereupon the bull-Ephelanto that had, half in sport, tossed Nod up into the air set him gently on the earth again. And the three brothers, hastening their hobbling pace a little, journeyed on once more.

CHAPTER FOUR

Fleas

A little before evening Thumb suddenly stopped, and stood listening. They went on a little farther, and again he stood still, with lifted head, snuffing the air. And soon they all heard plainly the sound of a great river. In the last light of sunset the travellers broke out of the forest and looked down on the waters of the deep and swollen Obea-Munza. Along its banks grew giant sedge, stiff and grey with frost like meal. In this sedge little birds were disporting themselves, flitting and twittering, with long plumes of every colour that changes in the sunlight, brushing off with their tiny wings the gathered hoar-frost into the still sunset air. The Mulgars stood like painted wooden images, with their bundles and cudgels, staring down at the river, which flowed beneath them wide and turbulent, its gloomy hummocks of ice and frozen snow nodding down upon the pale green waters. They glanced at one another as if with the question on their faces, 'How now, O Mulla-Mulgars?'

'"His country lies beyond and beyond,"' muttered Thimble. '"Forest and river, forest, swamp, and river." Could, then, our father Seelem walk on water?'

Thumb coughed in his throat. 'What matters it? He went: we follow,' he grunted stubbornly. 'We must journey on till our wings grow, Mulla Thimble, or till your long legs can straddle bank to bank.' And they all three stared in silence again at the swirling icy water.

Now it was just beginning to be twilight, which is many times more brief than England's in Munza, and the frozen forest was utterly still in the fading rose and purple, the

beasts not yet having come down to drink. And while the travellers stood listening, there came, as it were from afar off, the beating of a drum – seven hollow beats, and then silence.

'What in Munza, Thumb, makes a noise like that?' Nod whispered. 'Listen, listen!'

They all three hearkened again, with heads bent and eyes fixed, and soon once more they heard the hollow drumming. Thumb shook his head uneasily.

'It is wary walking, my brothers,' he said; 'maybe there are Oomgar-Nuggas by the riverside; or maybe it is one of the great hairy Gunga-Mulgars whose country our father Seelem told me lies five days' journey towards the daybreak. Whicheversoever, Mulla-Mulgars, we will hobble on and discover.'

Thimble dropped lightly, and rested on all-fours a moment. His eyes squinted a little, for he greatly feared the drumming they had heard.

But Thumb, moving softly, edged watchfully on, and Thimble and Nod followed as he led along the reedy bank of the river. Ever and again they heard the drumming repeated, but it seemed no less distant, so they squatted

down to eat while there was light enough in the sky to find the way from fingers to mouth. They sat down under a twisted Boobab-tree, opened their bundles, and took out the frosted nuts and fruits which they had lately gathered for their supper. But it was so bitterly cold by the water-side Nod could scarcely crack his shells between his chattering teeth.

And now the waning moon was beginning to silver river and forest. From the farther bank rose the cries of Munza's beasts come down to drink, mournful, lean, and fierce from hunger and cold. Soon the long-billed river-birds began their night-talk across the water. And while the Mulgars were sitting silently munching, out of the shadow before their faces came on her sound-less pads a young she-leopard, and with cat-like face stood regarding them.

Thumb and Thimble dropped softly their hands, and very slowly stooped their stiff-haired heads. But the leopard after regarding them awhile, and seeing them to be three together and Mulgars-Royal, drew back her head, yawned, and leapt lightly back into the shadowy grasses from which she had stolen out. 'One Roses may bring many,' said Thumb sourly; 'let us hobble on, Mulla-Mulgars, until we find a quieter sleeping-place.'

But it was now so dark beside the river that the Mulgars had to stop and walk on the knuckles of their hands, as do all the Munza-Mulgars or Forest Monkeys. And while they walked heedfully forward, they heard the trump-billed river-birds calling their secret to one another:

I see Mulgars, one, two, three,
Creeping, crawling, one, two, three.

Once Thumb trod on a forest-pig that was lying half-dead with cold under a root of Samarak. But the pig was too weak to squeal. Nod stooped and gave him three Ukka-nuts and a pepper-pod. 'There, pig,' he said, 'tell your brothers who stole my bundle that Nod Nizza-neela gave you these when you were frozen.' And the pig, being a pig, opened its slits of eyes and feebly snapped at his fingers. Nod laughed and hastened after his brothers.

Over the half-moon a cloud of snow was drawing, and soon the whispering flakes began to float again between the branches. The wind that blew steadily down the river was sharp and icy. The travellers were afraid, if they slept in the trees again, they would be frozen. And if even one big toe of any one of them got frost-bitten, how distant would the Valley of Tishnar seem then! They heard, too, now and then the faint sounds of snapping twig and rustling reed, and a low whimpering growl would sometimes set the giant grasses trembling. Stiff and crusted with frost, and in constant danger of falling into the river, they crawled stubbornly on.

And suddenly straight before them burned out a light in the darkness that was neither of moon, star, nor frost-fire. On they rustled, very warily now, because they knew somewhere here must lurk the Oomgar-Nugga or the Gunga-Mulgar whose drumming they had heard. One by one they presently crept out of the sedge, and stood up a few paces from a kind of huddle or hut, standing crooked and smoking in the moonlight, and built of two or three rows of huge stakes, three times plaited, very fast and close, with Samarak and withies of all kinds. It stood about three Mulgars high, and its walls were more than four spans thick.

The light which the travellers had espied burning in the

distance streamed from a mis-shapen window-hole far above Thimble's head. The Mulgars stood staring at one another in the shadow of the black forest, and now and then they would hear a rumble or clatter from behind the thick walls, and presently a sneeze or cough, after which would suddenly roll out the loud and hollow drumming of the great creature within.

So Thumb bade Nod climb softly on to Thimble's shoulder, and very slowly lift his face up and look in. Up went Nod, and softly drew his sheep-skinned head into the light.

And the first thing he noticed was a wonderful steaming smell of broth cooking, and then, as he pushed his head farther through the window-hole, he looked down into the hut. And he saw, sitting there on a huge bench before his eating-board, a gigantic Gunga-Mulgar in a shift or shirt of fish-skin.

He was guzzling down broth out of a gourd, and fishing for titbits of fish-fat in it with a wooden prong or skewer. He knew his comfort, this ugly Gunga. He sat with crossed legs before a blazing fire. It shone on his fangs and teeth and flaming eyes. A huge axe, made out of a stone, hung on the wall. In one corner lay a heap of brushwood and fish-bones, and in a hole in the ground a pile of logs. There were skins, too, on the walls, of fishes and birds and little furry beasts, and two fat hog-fish shone silvery in the firelight. Besides these, there was an Oomgar-Nugga's, or Black Man's bow of wood, thrice strung with twisted string. But what pleased Nod most to see, as he peeped stealthily down

51

through the thorny wattle window, was an old grey Burb-hrie cat, which sat washing her face in front of the fire.

He was still peeping and peering into the hut, when Thumb pinched his leg to bid him come down. So he slid cautiously down Thimble's back into the cold moonlight again, and told his brothers all he had seen.

'Yes, Mulla-Mulgars,' he said, 'and beside his bow and his sharp-nosed darts, he has three big knubbly cudgels in the corner higher than is Nod. He sits there, muttering and chuffing and sticking a long wooden spit into his soup, and then he coughs, and says, "Ug!" and beats his black fists on his chest till the flames shake.'

Thumb's short thick scalp twitched to and fro as he sat on his heels, staring into the moonlight. 'Is he very big and strong? Is he as broad and thick as Thumb?' he said.

'He's sitting in a spangly shirt,' said Nod, 'and his arms are like Boobab-roots – like Boobab-roots – and his eyes, Mulla-Mulgars, they burn in bony houses, and his face is black as charcoal.'

Thumb lifted his face uneasily and yawned. 'We will push on; we will not meddle with the Gunga, my brothers,' he said. 'Better sleep cold than never wake.' He laughed, and patted Nod on the head with his stump-thumbed hand, just as Seelem used to do when Nod was a baby. So they crept softly past the huddle on their fours, turning their heads this way, that way, snuffing softly along on an icy path that led through the sword-grass to the river's edge. And there, tossing lightly on the water, they found a boat, or Bobberie, of Bemba-wood and skin pegged down with wooden pegs. It was moored fast with a rope of Samarak, and two broad paddles lay inside it. All this the travellers saw faintly in the moonlit dusk. Far away they heard the barking and weeping of Coccadrilloes as they stooped together over the Bobberie, rising and falling on the gloomy water.

'Let us not trouble the Gunga at his supper,' said Thimble, 'but get in first and ask leave after.'

And Thumb began softly hauling on the rope. But the smooth round stone on which they stood was coated green with ice, and as he pulled his foot slipped. He flung out his arms: down went Thumb; down went Nod. No sooner had their uproar died away than an angry and ogreish voice broke out from the hut. Thumb, with Thimble at his heels, had only just time enough to scramble off and hide himself in the giant sedge before down swung the gibbering Gunga on the crutches of his hairy arms to see what was amiss, and who was meddling with his boat.

There he found Nod, floating like a sheeny bubble in his puffed-out sheep's-jacket on the icy water. He stooped down and clawed him up with one enormous paw, and carried him off into his hut. Then, putting up the wooden door, he sat him down with a shout before his blazing fire.

'Ohé, ohé, ohé!' he bellowed. 'Zutha mu beluthli zakketi zanga xoot!'

Nod, cold and trembling, lifted his little grey face out of his streaming sheep's-coat and shook his head.

Then the Gunga, seeing this crackle-shell did not understand his language, bawled at him in Munza-Mulgar: 'Thief, thief! What were you after, fishing from great Gunga's boat?' Nod shook his head again, for he expected every moment that great hand to clutch him up and fling him into the fire.

'Thief, thief, and son of a thief!' squalled the Gunga again, opening his great mouth.

But at that Nod's wits grew suddenly clear and still. 'Not so fast – not so fast, Master Gunga,' he said. 'Mulla-Mulgars are neither thieves nor sons of thieves. Squeal that at the Munza-Mulgars, not at Ummanodda!'

The old Gunga stared with jutting teeth. 'Mulla-Mulgars,' he grunted mockingly. 'Off with that sheep-skin, Prince of Fleas! I'll skin ye 'fore I cook ye!'

Nod stared bravely into the glinting sooty face. '*Gunga duseepi sooklar!* by Noomanossi's harp!'

The old Gunga stooped closer on his fleshless legs and blinked. 'What knows a fly-catching Skeeto of Noomanossi's harp?' he said.

'What knows a fish-bait Gunga of the Princes of Tishnar?' Nod answered, and calmly sat down beside the old Burbhrie cat on a log in front of the fire. The savage old Puss stretched out her claws, spread back her tufted ash-coloured ears, and with grey-green eyes stared fiercely into his face. But Nod clutched tight his Wonderstone, and paid no heed; and soon she lazily turned again to the flames, and began to purr like a nestful of Nikka-nakkas.

The Gunga stared, too, snapped his great jaws, coughed, then beat with his warty fist on his great breast. '*Ohé, ohé!*' he said. 'I meant no evil to the Mulla-Mulgar. Princes of Tishnar journey not often past old Gunga's house. I hutch alone, far from my own country, Royal Stranger, with only my Black Man's Bobberie for friend.'

Nod, when he heard this, almost laughed out. 'Not now, "Prince of Bonfires", nor "Noddle of Pork",' he thought, 'but "Royal Stranger", and "Prince of Tishnar".'

'Why, then,' he said aloud to the Gunga, 'tongues chatter best when they have something good to say. I'll take a platter of soup with you, Friend of Fishes. And better still, I'll dry my magic coat.'

He slipped out of his dripping jacket, and spread it out in

front of the fire, and there he sat, slim and silky, in his little cotton-leaf breeches, scratching Puss's head and pretending himself at home. But the old Fish-catcher's bloodshot eyes were watching – watching all the time. He was thinking what snug and beautiful breeches that sheep's-coat would make him this icy weather. But he thought, too, it would be best to speak civilly and smoothly to his visitor – at least, for the present. Not even a Gunga-Mulgar cares to quarrel with peaceful Tishnar.*

'Make yourself easy, Traveller,' he said, nodding his peaked head with a hideous smile. 'The moon was at hide-and-seek when I found you in the water; I could not see your royal countenance. But Simmul, she knows best.' The old Burbhrie cat turned to her master at sound of her name, put up a tufted paw towards Nod, and mewed.

'Ohé, ohé!' said the Gunga mournfully. 'She's mewing "Magic". And what knows a feeble old Fish-catcher of Magic?' He poured out some soup into a bowl, put in a skewer, and handed it to Nod.

'I will hang the Royal Stranger's beautiful sheep's-coat on a hook,' he said slyly. 'There it will dry much quicker.'

But Nod guessed easily what he was after. Once hung up there, how was he ever going to reach his jacket down again? 'No, no,' says he; 'it's nearly dry already.'

He took the gourd of soup between his knees. It tasted strong of fish, and was green with a satiny river-weed; but it was hot and sweetish, and he supped it up greedily. And just as he was tilting the bowl for the last mouthful he looked up and saw Thumb's round, astonished face staring in at the little dark window. He put down his gourd and burst out laughing.

'What makes the stranger laugh?' said the old Gunga-Mulgar. 'It's very good broth.'

'I was laughing,' said Nod, 'laughing at that last fish I caught.'

* See page 261.

'Was it a big fish – a fat, heavy fish?' said the Gunga.

Nod stared, with one eye shut and his head a little awry, at the two hog-fish dangling on the wall. 'Five times as big as them,' he said.

'Five?' said the Gunga.

'Five or six,' said Nod.

'Or six!' said the Gunga.

'Truly,' said Nod softly, 'he fishes not for minnows who knows the magic fish-song of the Water Middens.'

The old Gunga turned his great black skull, and beneath the beetling porches of his eyes glowered greedily on Nod. 'And what,' he said cunningly – 'what song is that, O Royal Stranger?' And he stooped down suddenly and pushed Nod's jacket under the bench.

'Why do you push my sheep's-coat under the bench?' said Nod angrily.

'I smelt – I smelt,' said Gunga, throwing back his head, 'scorching. But softly, Mulla-Mulgar. What *is* this Water Middens' song that catches fishes five – six times as big as mine? And if you know all this wisdom, and are truly a Prince of Tishnar, why do you sit here, this freezing night, supping up a poor old Fish-catcher's broth?'

CHAPTER FIVE

Magic and Bobberie

By this time it was plain, Thimble and Thumb had found something to raise them to the window-hole, for Nod, as he glanced up, saw half of both their astonished faces (one eye of each) peering in at the window. He waved his lean little arms, and their faces vanished.

'Why do you wave your long thumbs in the air?' said the old Gunga uneasily.

'I wave to Tishnar,' said Nod, 'who watches over her wandering Princes, and will preserve them from thieves and cunning ones. And as for your filthy green-weed soup, how should a Mulla-Mulgar soil his thumbs with getting fish? And as for the Water Middens' song, *that* I cannot teach you, nor would I teach it you if I could, Master Fish-catcher. But I can catch fish with it.'

The old Gunga squatted close on his stool, and grinned as graciously as he could. 'I am poor and growing old,' he said, 'and I cannot catch fish as once I could. How is that done, O Royal Traveller?'

Nod stood up and put his fingers on his lips. 'Secrets, Puss!' says he to the purring Burbhrie, and stepped softly over and peeped out of the door. He came back. 'Listen,' he said. 'I go down to the water – at daybreak; oh yes, just at daybreak. Then I row out a little way in my little Bobberie, quite, quite alone – no-one must be near to spy or listen; then I cast my nets into the water and sing and sing.'

'What nets?' said the Gunga.

Nod dodged a crisscross with his finger in the air.

'*Sootli, Sootli,*' mewed Puss, with her eyes half-shut.

57

The old Gunga wriggled his head with his great lip sagging. 'What happens then?' said he.

'Then,' said Nod, 'from far and near my Magic draws the fishes – head, fin, and tail – hundreds and hundreds, all to hear my Water Middens' lovely song.'

'And what then?' said Gunga.

'Then,' said Nod, peeping with his eye, 'I look and I look till I see the biggest fish of all – seven, eight, nine times as big as that up there, and I draw him out gently, gently, just as I choose him, into my Bobberie.'

'And wouldn't *any* fish come to the little Prince unless he fished alone?' said the greedy Gunga.

'None,' said Nod. 'But there, why should we be gossiping of fishing? My boat is far away.'

'But,' said the Gunga cunningly, 'I have a boat.'

'*Ohé*, maybe,' said Nod easily. 'One cannot drown on dry land. But *I* did speak of a Bobberie of skin and Bembawood, made by the stamping Oomgar-Nuggas next the sea.'

'Ay,' said the Gunga triumphantly, 'but that's just what my Bobberie *is* made of, and I broke the backbone of the Oomgar-Nugga chief that made it with one cuff of my cudgel-hand.'

Nod yawned. 'Tishnar's Prince is tired,' he said, 'and cannot talk of fishes any more. A bowlful more broth, Master Fish-catcher, and then I'll just put on my jacket and go to sleep.' And he laughed, oh, so softly to himself to see that sooty, gluttonous face, and the red, gleaming eyes, and the thick, twitching thumbs.

'*Ootz nuggthli!*' coughed the Gunga sourly. He ladled out the broth, bobbing with broken pods, with a great nutshell, muttering angrily to himself as he stooped over the pot. And there, as soon as he had turned his back, came those two dark wondering faces at the window, grinning to see little Nod so snug and comfortable before the fire.

And when the Gunga had poured out the broth, he

brought his stool nearer to Nod, and, leaning his great hands on the floor, he said: 'See here, Prince of Tishnar, if I lend you my skin Bobberie tomorrow morning, will you catch *me* some fish with your magic song?'

Nod frowned and stared into the fire. 'The crafty Gunga would be peeping between the trees,' he said, 'and then –'

'What then?' said he.

'Then Tishnar's Meermuts would come with their silver thongs and drive you squalling into the water. And the Middens would pick your eyes out, Master Fish-catcher.'

'I promise, I promise,' said the old Gunga, and his enormous body trembled.

'Where is this talked-of Bobberie?' said Nod solemnly. 'Was it that old log Nod saw when whispering with the Water Middens?'

'Follow, follow,' said the other. 'I'll show the Prince this log.' But first Nod stooped under the bench, and pulled out his sheep's-coat and put it on. Then he followed the old Fish-catcher down his frosty path between its banks of snow, clear now in the silver shining of the moon.

The Fish-catcher showed him everything – how to untie

the knotted rope of Samarak, how to use the paddles, where the mooring-stone for deep water was. He held it up in his hand, a great round stone as big as a millstone. Nod listened and listened, half-hiding his face in his jacket lest the Gunga-Mulgar should see him laughing. Last of all, the Fish-catcher, lifting him lightly in his hand, pointed across the tumultuous water, and bade him have care not to drift out far in his fishing, for the stream ran very swiftly, the ice-floes or hummocks were sharp, and under the Shining-one, he said, snorting River-horses and the weeping Mumbo lurk.

'Never fear, Master Fish-catcher,' said Nod. 'Tishnar will watch over me. How many big fish, now, can the old Glutton eat in comfort?'

The Gunga lifted his black bony face, and glinted on the moon. 'Five would be good,' he said. 'Ten would be better. *Ohé*, do not count, Royal Traveller. It makes the head ache after ten.' And he thought within himself what a fine thing it was to have kept this Magic-Mulgar, this Prince of Tishnar, for his friend, when he might in his rage have flung him clean across Obea-Munza into that great Boobab-tree grey in the moon. 'He shall teach me the Middens' song, and then I'll fish for myself,' he thought, all his thick skin stirring on his bones with greed.

So he cozened and cringed and flattered, and used Nod as if he were his mother's son. He made him lie on his own bed; he put on him a great skin ear-cap; he filled a bowl with the hot fish-water to bathe his feet; and he fetched out from a lidded hole in the floor a necklet of scalloped Bamba-shells, and hung it round his slender neck.

But Nod, as soon as he lay down, began thinking of those poor Mulla-Mulgars, his brothers, hungry and shivering in the tree-tops. And he pondered how he could help them. Presently he began to chafe and toss in his bed, to sigh and groan.

Up started the old Gunga from his corner beside the fire. 'What ails the Prince? Why does he groan? Are you in pain, Mulla-Mulgar?'

'In pain!' cried Nod, as if in a great rage. 'How shall a Prince sleep with twice ten thousand Gunga fleas in his blanket?'

He got up, dragging after him the thick Munza ram's fleece off his bed, and, opening the door, flung it out into the snow. 'Try that, my hungry hopping ones,' he said, and pushed up the door again. 'Now I must have another one,' he said.

The old Fish-catcher excused himself for the fleas. 'It is cold to comb in the doorway,' he said, rubbing his flat nose. And he took another woolly skin out of his earth-cupboard and laid it over Nod.

'That's one for Thumb,' Nod said to himself, laughing. And presently once more he began fretting and tossing. 'Oh, oh, oh!' he cried out. 'What! More of ye! more of ye!' and with that away he went again, and flung the second ram's fleece after the first.

'Master Traveller, Master Traveller!' yelped the old Fish-catcher, starting up, 'if you throw all my blankets out, those thieves the smudge-faces will steal them.'

'Better no blankets than a million fleas,' said Nod; 'and yours, Master Fish-catcher, are as greedy as Ephelanto ticks. And now I think I will sleep by the fire, then the first peep of day will shine in my eyes from that little window-hole up there, and wake me to my fishing.'

'*Udzmutchakiss,*' growled the Gunga. But he was very angry underneath. 'Wait ye, wait ye, wait ye, my pretty Squirrel-tail,' he kept muttering to himself as he sat with crossed arms. 'For every blanket a Bobberie full of fish!'

But Nod had never felt so merry in his life. To think of his brothers wrapped warm in the Gunga-Mulgar's blankets! – He laughed aloud.

'What ails the Traveller? What is he mocking at now?' said the Fish-catcher, glowering out of his corner.

'Why,' said Nod, 'I laughed to hear the mice in this box hanging over my head.'

'Mice?' said the Gunga.

'Why, yes; a score or more,' said Nod. 'And one old husky Muttakin keeps saying, "Nibble all, nibble all; leave not one whole, my little pretty ones – not the crumb of a crumb for the ugly old glutton." I think, O generous Gunga, she means the bread of Sudd I smell.'

At that the Gunga flamed up in a fury. He rushed to his food-box, shouting. 'Will ye, oh, will ye, ye nibbling thieves!' And, opening the door, he flung it after the blankets – Sudd-loaves, Nanoes, river-weed, and all. And he stood a minute in the doorway, looking out on the cold moonlit snow.

'Shut to the door, shut to the door, Master Fish-catcher,' called Nod. 'I hear a distant harp-playing.'

The Gunga very quickly shut the door at that. But he came to the fire and stood leaning on his hands, looking into it, sullen and angry. 'Did I not say it, Prince of Tishnar?' he said. 'My blankets are gone already. Stolen!'

'Sleep softly, my friend,' said Nod, 'and weary me not with talking. There's better rams in the forest than ever were flayed. Your blankets will creep back, never fear. Even to a Mullabruk his own fleas! But, there! I'll make magic even this very moment, and to-morrow, when you go down to the river to fetch up the fish, there shall your blankets be, folded and civeted, on the stones by the water.'

Then he rose up in his littleness, and began to dance slowly from one foot to the other, waving his lean arms over the fire, and singing, in the secret language of the Mulla-Mulgars, as loud as ever he could:

> Thumb, Thimble, Mulgar meeze,
> In your blankets dream at ease,
> And never mind the frozen fleas;
> But don't forget the loaves and cheese!

'That is strange magic,' said the Fish-catcher.

'Nay,' said Nod; 'but they were very strange fleas.'

'And "Thumthimble" – what does that mean?'

'"Thumb" mean short and fat, and "Thimble" means long and lean, which is Mulgar-Royal for both kinds, Master Fish-catcher.'

'Ohé, the Prince knows best,' said the Old Gunga; 'but I never heard such magic. And I've watched the Dancing Oomgars leagues and leagues from here, and drummed them home to their Shes.'

Nod yawned.

As soon as it was daybreak the old Fish-catcher, who had scarcely slept a wink for thinking of the fishes he was to have for his breakfast, came and woke Nod up. And Nod said: 'Now I go, Master Fish-catcher; but be sure you do not venture one toe's breadth beyond the door till you hear me bringing back the fishes.'

'How can the Prince carry them, fishes big as that?' said the Gunga.

'One at a time, my friend, as Ephelantoes root up trees,' said Nod, staring at the Gunga's bristling arms and tusks of teeth.'*Ohé!*' he went on, 'when you hear my sweet-sounding Water Middens' song, you will not be able to keep yourself from peeping. You must be bound with Cullum, Master Fish-catcher. Oh, I should weep riverfuls of salt tears if the Water Middens picked your gentle eyes out.'

At first the cunning old Gunga would not consent to be bound up. But Nod refused to stir until he did. So at last he fetched a thick rope of Samarak (which in fact is stronger and tougher than Cullum) out of his old chest or coffer, and Nod wound it round and round him – legs, arms, and shoulders – and tied the ends to the great fish-scaly table.

'Sit easy, my friend,' said he; 'my magic begins wonderfully to burn in me.' And, without another word, he skipped out and pulled-to the door-flap behind him.

Words could not tell how rejoiced were his brothers to see him from their tree-tops come frisking across the snow. Away went the travellers in the first light, hastening like thieves in their jackets; Nod in his sheep's-coat leading the way. They left the blankets as Nod had promised the Gunga. Then, one, two, three, they pushed the Bobberie into deep water.

In jumped Nod, in jumped Thimble, in jumped Thumb. Out splashed the heavy paddles, and soon the Bobberie was floating like a cork among the ice-humps in the red glare of dawn. They shoved off, Thumb at one paddle, Thimble and Nod at the other. The farther they floated, the swifter swept the water. And soon, however hard they pushed at the heavy paddles, the Bobberie began twirling round and round zig-zagging faster and faster down with the stream.

But scarcely were they more than fifteen fathoms from the bank when a shrill and piercing '*Illa olla! illa olla!*' broke out behind them. No need to look back. There on the bank in his glistening fish-skins, gnashing his teeth and beating with his crusted hands on the drum of his great chest, stood the terrible Gunga-Mulgar, his Samarak ropes all burst asunder. He stooped and tore up huge stones and lumps of ice as big as a sheep, and flung them high into the air after the tossing Bobberie.

Splash, splash, splash, they fell, around the three poor sweating travellers, drenching them with water and melting snow. The faster they paddled the faster swirled the water, and the thicker came tumbling the Gunga's huge boulders of stone and ice. Let but one fall plump upon their Bobberie, down they would go to be Mumbo-meat for good and all. But ever farther the surging water was sweeping them on. Suddenly the hailstones ceased, and they spied their dreadful enemy swinging furiously back on his thick five-foot arms.

'Gone, gone!' cried Thimble in triumph, leaning breathless on his paddle.

'Crow when your egg's hatched, brother Thimble,' muttered Thumb. 'He's gone to fetch his bow.'

True it was. Down swung the gibbering Gunga, his Oomgar-Nugga's bow across his shoulder. Crouching by the water-side, he stretched its string with all his strength. And a thin, keen dart sang shrill as a parakeet over their heads. Again, again, and then it seemed to Nod a red-hot skewer had suddenly spitted him through the shoulder, and he knew the Fish-catcher had aimed true. He plucked the arrow out and waved it over his head, scrunching his teeth together, and saying nothing save 'Paddle, Thimble! Paddle, O Thumb!'

Mightily they leaned on their broad and unwieldy paddles. But now, not looking where the water was sweeping them, of a sudden the Bobberie butted full tilt into a great hummock of ice, and water began welling up through a hole in the bottom. Nod knelt down, and, while his brothers paddled, he flung out the water as fast as he could

with his big fish-skin cap. But fast though he baled, the water rilled in faster, and just as they floated under a long, snow-laden branch of an Ollaconda-tree, the Bobberie began to sink.

Then Thimble cried in a loud voice, *'Guzza-guzza-nahoo!'* and, with a great leap, sprang out of the boat and caught the drooping branch. Thumb clutched his legs and Nod Thumb's; and there they were, all three swinging over the water, while the branch creaked and trembled over their heads.

Down sank the staved-in Bobberie, and up – one, two, three, four, five – floated huge, sluggish Mumboes or Coccadrilloes, with dull grass-green eyes fixed gluttonously on the dangling Mulgars. And a thick muskiness filled the air around them.

Inch by inch Thimble edged along the bough, until, because of the jutting twigs and shoots, he could edge no farther. Then, slowly and steadily at first, but gradually faster, the three travellers began to swing, sweeping to and fro through the air, above the enraged and snapping Coccadrilloes. The wind rushed past Nod's ears; his jacket flapped about him. 'Go!' squealed Thumb; and away whisked Nod, like a flying squirrel across the water, and landed high and dry on the bank under the wide-spreading Ollaconda-tree. Thumb followed. Thimble, with only his own weight to lift, quickly scrambled up into the boughs above him. And soon all three Mulla-Mulgars were sitting in safety, munching what remained of the Gunga's Sudd-bread, and between their mouthfuls shouting mockery at the musky Coccadrilloes.

While they were thus eating happily together Thumb suddenly threw up his hands and cried: 'Blood, blood, O Ummanodda! – blood, red blood!' And then it seemed to Nod, trees, sky, and river swam mazily before his eyes. Darkness swept up. He rolled over against a jutting root of the Ollaconda, and knew no more.

CHAPTER SIX

The Mouse-Faces

When Nod opened his eyes again, he found himself blinking right into the middle of a blazing fire, over which hung sputtering a huddled carcass on a long black spit. Nod's head ached; his shoulder burned and throbbed. He touched it gently, and found that it was swathed and bound up with leaves that smelt sleepily sweet and cool.

He looked around him as best he could, but at first could see little, because of the brightness of the flames. Gradually he perceived small grey creatures, with big heads and white hands that reached almost to the ground, hastening to and fro. His smooth brown poll stood up stiff with terror at sight of them, for he knew he must be lying in the earthmounds of the flesh-eating Minimuls.

Memories one by one returned to him – the Bobberie, the river, the yapping Coccadrilloes, the burning dart. One thing he could not recall – how he came to be lying alone and helpless here in the root-houses of these cunning enemies of all Mulgars, great and small. He remembered the stories Mutta-matutta used to tell him of their snares and poisons and enticements; of their earth-galleries and their horrible flesh-feasts at the full moon. His one comfort was that he still lay in his sheep's-jacket, and felt his little Wonderstone pressed close against his side.

When one of the Minimuls that stood basting the spit saw that Nod was awake he summoned others who were standing near, and many stooped softly over, staring at him and whispering together. Nod put his finger to his tongue, and said, '*Walla!*' One of them instantly shuffled away and brought him a little gourd of a sweetish juice like Keeri, which greatly refreshed him.

Then he called out, 'Mulgars, Mulla-Mulgars?' This, too, they seemed at once to understand. For, indeed, Seelem had told Nod that these Minimuls are nothing but a kind of Munza-Mulgar, though their faces more closely resemble the twilight or moonshine Mulgars, and for craft and greed the dwarf Oomgar-Nuggas, that long ago had trooped away beyond Arakkaboa. Nod heard presently many faint voices, and then thick guttural cries of pain and anger. And by turning his head a little he could see a host of these mouse-faced manikins tugging at a rope. At the end of this rope, all bound up with Cullum, with sticky leaves plastered over their eyes, and hung with dangling festoons of greenery and flowers, like jacks-in-the-green, Thumb and Thimble hobbled slowly in from under an earthen arch. Nod was weak with pain. He cried out hollowly to see his brothers blind and helpless.

Thumb heard the sound, and answered him boldly in Mulgar-Royal. 'Is that the voice of my brother, the Mulla-Mulgar, Nizza-neela Ummanodda?'

'Oh Thumb!' Nod groaned, 'why am I here in comfort, while you and Thimble are dragged in, bound with Cullum, and hung all over with dreadful leaves and flowers?'

'Have no fear, Prince of Bonfires,' said Thumb with a laugh. 'The Minimuls caught us smelling at their Gelica-nuts, and sleeping in the warmth of their earth-mounds. We were too frozen and hungry to carry you any farther. They are fattening us for their Moon-feast. But it will be little more than a picking of bones, Ummanodda. And even if they do spit us over their fire, we will taste as sweet as Mulla-Mulgars can.' And he burst out into such a squeal of angry laughter the Minimuls began chattering again and waving their hands.

'Talk not of meat and bones to me, Thumb. If you die, I

die too. Tell me, only so that they do not understand, what Nod is to do.'

Then Thimble, who was standing in the shadow, hobbled a little nearer into the light of the fire, and lifting up his leaf-smeared face as if to see, said: 'Have no fear for yourself, Nod. They have caught us, but not for long. But you they dare not frizzle a hair of, little brother, because of Tishnar's Wonderstone sewn up in your sheep's-coat. They have smelt out its magic. Keep the stone safe, then, Ummanodda, and, when you are alone, rub it Sāmaweeza-wise as Mutta told you before she died. Tishnar, perhaps, will answer. See only that none of these miching Mouse-faces are near. Had we but been awake when they found us! ...'

But the Minimuls began to grow restless at all this palaver, for, though the Munza-Mulgar tongue is known to them, they cannot understand, except a word here and there, the secret language of Mulgar-Royal. So they laid hold of the Cullum-ropes again, and lugged Thumb and Thimble back under the sandy arch through which they had come. Thumb had only time enough to cry in a loud voice, 'Courage, Nizza-neela', before he was dragged again out of sight and hearing.

And Nod remembered that when the Gunga-Mulgar had led him down out of his huddle to show him the Bobberie, the moon was shining then at dwindling halves. So he knew that, unless many days had passed since then, it would be some while yet before these Minimuls made their cannibal Moon-feast. He lay still, with eyes half-shut, thinking as best he could, with an aching head and throbbing shoulder.

The firelight glanced on the earthy roof far above him. Here and there the contorted root of some enormous forest-tree jutted out into the air. There was a continuous faint rustle around him, as of bees in a hive or ants in a pine-wood. This was the shuffling of the Minimuls' shoes, which are flat, like sandals, are made of silver grass plaited together, that rustles on the sandy floor of their chambers and galleries. This plaited grass they tie, too, round their middles for a belt or pouch, beneath which, as they walk, their long lean tails descend. Their fur shines faintly shot in moon or firelight, and is either pebble-grey or sand-coloured. It never bristles into hair except about their polls and chops, where it stands in a smooth, even wall, about one and a half to two inches high, leaving the remnant of their faces light and bare. They stand for the most part about three spans high in their grass slippers. Their noses are even flatter than the noses of the Mullabruks. Their teeth stand out somewhat, giving their small faces a cunning mouse-look, which never changes. Their eyes are round and thin-lidded, and almost as colourless as glass. Yet behind their glassiness seems to be set a gleam, like a far and tiny taper shining, so that they are perfectly visible in the dark, or even dusk.

Thus may they be seen, a horde of them together in the evening gloom of the forest when they go Mulgar-hunting. When they are closely looked on, they can, as it were within their eyes, shut out this gleam – it vanishes; but still they continue to see, though dimly. By day their eyes are as empty as pure glass marbles. Their smell is faintly rank, through eating so much flesh. The she and young Minimuls feed in the deeper chambers of their mounds, and never venture out.

Nod was falling into a drowse from weariness and pain, when there came spindling along an old sallow-hued Earth-Mulgar, whose eyes were pink, rather than glass-grey like the others. He shook his head this way, that way, muttering his magic over Nod; then, with a mottled gourd beside him, he very gently and dexterously rolled back the strip or bandage of leaves on Nod's shoulder, and peered close into his poisoned wound. He probed it softly with his hairless fingers. Then out of the pouch hanging on his stomach

71

he took fresh leaves, smeared and stalked, a little clay pot of green healing-grease, and anointed the sore. This he rubbed ever so smoothly with his two middle fingers. After which he bound all up again so skilfully with leaves and grass that it seemed to Nod his wounded shoulder was the easiest and most comfortable part of his body. Out of his pinkish eyes he gazed greedily into Nod's face for a moment, and took his departure.

After he had gone, Nod smoothed his face, and with his own comb combed himself as far as he could reach without pain. Presently shuffled along two or three more of the Mouse-faces carrying roasted Nanoes and Mambel-berries, and a kind of citron, like a Keeri, very refreshing; also a little gourd of thin Subbub.

But, although he was too wretched and too much afraid to be hungry, and shuddered at sight of the Minimul food, Nod knew he must quickly grow strong if ever he and his brothers were to reach the Valleys of Tishnar. So he ate and drank, and was refreshed. Then he turned to a little sleek Minimul that tended him, and asked him in Munza-Mulgar: 'Is it day – sunshine? Is it day?'

The little creature shook his head and shut his eyes, as if to signify he did not understand the question.

Nod at that shut his eyes too, and laid his cheek on his lean little hand, as if to say, Sleep.

Thereupon eight thickish Minimuls came – four on either side – and hoisted up by its handles the grass mat on which he lay, while others went before, strewing dried leaves and a kind of forest-flower that smells like mint when crushed, and carrying lanterns of candle-worms, while others wad-dled with them, beating on little tambours of Skeetoskin – all this because Nod breathed magic, part his own, part his Wonderstone's.

They laid him down in a sandy chamber strewn with flowers. And, bowing many times, their heads betwixt their

bandy legs, they left him. When they were gone, Nod wriggled softly up and looked about him. The chamber was round and caved, and on the walls were still visible the marks of the Minimuls' hands and scoops which had hollowed it out. Through the roof a rugged root pierced, crossed over, and dipped into the earth again. The candleworms cast a gentle sheen on the golden sanded walls. Hung from the roof were strings of dried flowers, shedding so heavy and languid a smell in the narrow chamber that Nod's drowsy eyelids soon began to droop. His bright eyes glanced like fireflies, darting to and fro with his thoughts. But the odour of the flowers soon soothed them all to rest. Nod fell asleep.

The next day (that is, the next Minimul day, which is Munza night) crept slowly by. Nod was never left alone. Every hour the little soft-shuffling Mouse-faces tended and fed and watched him, and burnt magic incense sticks around him. When he was carried into the big fire-chamber, or kitchen, again, three dead Skeetoes, with fast-shut eyes, lay on the floor, shot by their poisoned darts in the dusk of the evening. They were soon skinned and trussed by the hungry Minimuls, and stretched along the spit. The smell of their roasting rose up in smoke.

At last came sleeping-time again. And then, when all was silent, Nod rose softly from his grass-mat, and stealing down the low, narrow earth-run, looked out into the kitchen where he had lain all day. The fire was dying in faintly glowing embers. All was utterly still. But which way should he go now, he wondered, to seek his brothers? And which of these dark arches led to the open forest, the snow, and the Valleys?

His quick eyes caught sight of the thin smoke winding silently up from the logs. Somewhere that must waft out into the air. But on high it was so dim he could scarcely see the roof, only the steep walls, ragged with snake-skins, and the huge pods of silky poison-seed. He crept stealthily under one of the arches hung at the entrance with the dried carcass of a little fierce-faced, snow-white Gunga cub, and presently came to where, all in their sandy beds, with their tails curled up, side by side in double rows, the mousy Earth-Mulgars slept. He returned to the kitchen, and called softly in the hollow cavern, 'Thumb, Thumb!'

Only his own voice echoed back to him. Yet a sound feeble even as this awoke the light-sleeping Minimuls. For their mounds echo more than mere hollowness would seem to make them. The lightest stir or footfall of beast walking above in Munza may be heard. Nod had only just time enough to scamper up his own narrow corridor and throw himself on his mat before a score of shuffling footfalls followed, and he felt many glassy eyes peering closely into his face.

All the rest of that night (and for the few nights that followed) Minimuls stood behind his bed beating faintly on their skin Zoots or tambours, while two others sat one on each side of him with fans of soporiferous Moka-wood. But though they might lull Nod's lids asleep, they couldn't still his busy brain. He dreamed and dreamed. Now, in his dreams he was come in safety to his Uncle Assasimmon's, and they were all rejoicing at a splendid feast, and he was dressed in beads from neck to heel, with a hat of stained ivory and a peacock's feather. Now he was alone in the forest in the dark, and that tiny bird of the darkness, the Telateuti, was lamenting in his ear, '*Noom*-anoss-i, Noom-anoss-i.' And now it seemed he sat beneath deep emerald waters in the silver courts of the Water Middens, amid the long gold of their streaming hair. But he would awake babbling with terror, only to smell the creeping odour of broiling Mulgar on the air.

One day came many Earth-Mulgars from distant mounds to see this Prince of Magic, whom their kinsmen had captured in the forest. They stared at him, sniffed, bowed, and burned smoulder-sticks, and then were led off to gloat on fat Thumb and fattening Thimble. And that same day the Minimuls dragged into their kitchen a long straight branch of iron-wood, which with much labour they turned by charring into a prodigious spit. And Nod knew that his hour was come, that there was no time to be lost.

When he had once more been carried on his mat into his own chamber or sleeping-place, he drove out the drumming and fan-waving Minimuls, making signs to them that their noise and odour banished sleep away instead of charming it to come. He waited on and on, tossing on his mat, springing up to listen, hearing now some forest beast tread hollowly overhead, and now a distant cry as if of fear or anguish.

But at last, when all was still, he very cautiously fumbled and fumbled, gnawed and gnawed with his sharp little dog-teeth, until in the dim light of his worm-lantern peeped out the strange pale glowing milk-white Wonderstone, carved all over with labyrinthine beast and bird and unintelligible characters. It lay there marvellously beautiful, as if in itself it were all Munza-Mulgar, its swamps and forests and mountains lying tinied in the pale brown palm of his hand, and as full of changing light as the bellies of dead fishes in the dark. He got up softly, clutching the stone tightly in his hand. He listened. He stole down his sandy gallery, and stood, small and hairy, in his sheep-skin, peering out into the great evil-smelling kitchen.

Then he spat with his spittle on the stone, and began to rub softly, softly, three times round with his left thumb Sāmaweeza-wise, dancing lightly and slowly the while, with eyes tight shut and ears twitching.

And it seemed of a sudden as if all his care and trouble had been swept away. A voice small and clear called softly within him: 'Follow, Ummanodda, follow! Have now no fear, Prince of Tishnar, Nizza-neela; but follow, only follow!'

He opened his eyes, and there, hovering in the air, he saw as it were a little flame, crystal clear below, but mounting to the colour of rose, and shaped like a little plu-plu fruit, or pear. As soon as he looked at it, it began softly to stir and to float away from him across the glowery kitchen. And again the mysterious voice he had heard called softly: 'Follow, Prince of Tishnar, follow!' With shining eyes he hobbled warily after the little flame that, burning tranquil in the air, about a span above his head, was floating quietly on.

It led him past the gaunt black spit and the dying fire. It

wafted across the great kitchen to the fifth of the gloomy arches, and stealthily as a shadow Nod stole after it. Under this arch and up the shelving gallery gently slid the guiding flame. And now Nod saw again the furry Earth-Mulgars, lying on their stomachs in their sandy beds, whimpering and snuffling in their sleep. On glided the flame; after it crept Nod, scarcely daring to breathe. 'Softly, now softly,' he kept muttering to himself. And now this gallery began to slope downward, and he heard water dripping. A thin pallid moss tufted the stony walls. It felt colder as he descended. But Nod kept his eyes fixed on the clear, unswerving flame. And in the silence he heard a muffled groan, and a harsh voice muttered drowsily, *'Oo mutchee, nanga,'* and he knew Thumb must be near.

The strange voice whispered in his mind: 'Hasten, Ummanodda Nizza-neela; full moon is rising!' Then Nod whimpering in his fear a little, like a cat, edged on once more through a gallery where was laid up on sandy shelves a great store of nuts and pods and skins and spits and sharp-edged flints. And at last he came to where, in a filthy hollow, cold and lightless, and oozing with dark-glistening water-drops, his brothers Thimble and Thumb were sleeping.

They were tied hand and foot with strands of Cullum to the thick root of a Boobab-tree, even their eyes bound up with sticky leaves. Nod hobbled over and knelt down beside Thumb, and put his mouth close to his ear. 'Thumb, Thumb,' says he, 'it is Nod! Wake, Mulla-Mulgar; it is Nod who calls!' And he shook him by the shoulder. Thumb stirred in his sleep and opened his mouth, so that Nod could see the hovering flame glistening on his teeth. *'Oohmah, oohmah,'* he grunted, *'na nasmi mutta kara theartchen!'* Which means in Mulgar-Royal: 'Sorry, oh sorry! Don't whip me, mother dear!' And Nod knew that he was dreaming of long ago.

He shook him again, and Thumb, with an inward groan, rolled over, trembling, and seemed to listen. 'Thumb, Thumb,' Nod whispered, 'it is only me. It is only Nod, with the Wonderstone!' And while he was stripping off the leaves and bandages which covered Thumb's eyes he told him everything. 'And don't cry out, Thumb, if Tishnar's flame burns your shins. They've tied your legs in knots so tight with this tough Cullum, my fingers can't undo them.' So Thumb stretched out his legs, and as though it were that of a little lamp in unseen fingers, the flame descended and burned through his fetters. He rubbed his singed shins where the flame had scorched them, and then he stood up. Soon his arms were unbound, and Thimble, too, was roused and unloosed: and they were all three ready to tread softly out.

'Lead on, my wondrous fruit of magic!' said Nod.

The light curtsied, as it were, in the air, and glided up through the doorway; and the three Mulla-Mulgars crept out after it, Thumb and Thimble on their fours, being too stiff to walk upright.

'Hasten, hasten, Mulla-Mulgars!' said Nod softly. 'The full moon is shining; night is come. The pot is ready for the feast.'

So one by one, with Nod's clear flame for guide, they trod noiselessly up the sandy earth-run. It led them without faltering past the huddled sleepers again; past, too, where the she-Minimuls lay cuddling their tiny ones, and up into the big empty kitchen. Under another arch they crept after it, along another gallery of rough steps, hollowed out of the sandy rock, beneath great tortuous roots, through such a maze as would have baffled a weasel.

And suddenly Thumb stopped and snuffed and snuffed again. 'Immamoosa, Immamoosa!' he grunted.

Almond and evening-blooming Immamoosa it was, indeed, which they could smell, shedding its fragrance abroad

79

at nightfall. And in a little while out at last into the starry darkness they came, the great forest-trees standing black and still around them, their huge boughs cloaked with snow.

CHAPTER SEVEN

Mishcha the Hare

It was bitterly cold, and as the three travellers stood there, ragged and sore and hungry, it seemed they would never weary of gazing at the starry sky and sniffing the keen night air between the trees. But which way should they go? No path ran here, for the Earth-Mulgars never let any path grow clear around their mounds. Thumb climbed a little way up a Gelica-tree that stood over them, and soon espied low down in the sky the Bear's bright Seven, which circle about the dim Pole Star. So he quickly slid down again to tell his brothers.

It so happened, however, that in this tree grows a small round, gingerish nut that takes two whole years to ripen, and hangs in thick clusters amid the branches. They have a taste like cinnamon, and with these the Earth-Mulgars flavour their meat. And as Thumb slid heavily down, being stiff and sore now, and very heavy, he shook one of these same clusters, and down it came rattling about Nod's head. They had but thin shells, these nuts, and are not heavy, but they tumbled so suddenly, and from such a height, that Nod fell flat, his hands thrown out along the snow. He clambered up, rubbing his head, and in the quietness, while they listened, they heard as it were a distant and continuous throbbing beneath them.

Thimble crouched down, with head askew. 'The Minimuls, the Zoots!' he grunted.

But even at the same moment Nod had cried out too. 'Thumb, Thumb, O Mulla-Mulgar, the Wonderstone! the Wonderstone! the snow, the snow'. No pale and tapering

81

light hovered clearly beaming now beneath these cold and starlit branches. The Mounds of the Minimuls were awake and astir. Soon the furious little Flesh-eaters would come pouring up in their hundreds, and to-morrow, their magic gone, all three brothers would be quickly frizzling, with these same Gelica-nuts for seasoning, on the spit.

Nod flung himself down; down, too, went Thumb and Thimble in the ice-bespangled snow. At last they found the stone, shining like a pale moon amid the twinkling starriness of the frost. But it was only just in time. Even now they could hear the far-away crying and clamour, and the surly Zoot-beating of the Earth-Mulgars drawing nearer and nearer.

Without pausing an instant, Nod slid the stone into his mouth for safety, and away went the three travellers, bundle and cudgel, rags and sheep's-coat, helter-skelter, between the silver breaks of the trees, scampering faster than any Mulgar, Mulla, or Munza had ever run before. The snow was crisp and hard; their worn and hardened feet made but the faintest flip-flap in the hush. And scarcely had they run their first short wind out, when lo and behold! there, in a leafy bower of snow in their path, three short-maned snorting little Horses of Tishnar, or Zevveras, stood, rearing and chafing, and yet it seemed tethered invisibly to their frosty stable by bridles from which they could not break away.

They whinnied in concert to see these scampering Mulgars come panting over the snow. And Nod remembered instantly the longed-for gongs and stripes of his childhood, and he called like a parakeet: 'Tishnar, O Tishnar!' He could say no more. The Wonderstone that had lain couched on his tongue, as he opened his mouth, slid softly back, paused for his cry, and the next instant had glided down his throat. But by this time Thumb had straddled the biggest of the little plunging beasts. And, like arrows from the

Gunga's bow, each with his hands clasped tight about his Zevvera's neck, away went Thumb, away went Thimble, away went Nod, the night wind whistling in their ears, their rags a-flutter, the clear stripes of the Zevveras winking in the rising moon.

But the Little Horse of Tishnar which carried Nod upon his back was by much the youngest and smallest of the three. And soon, partly because of his youth, and partly because he had started last, he began to fall farther and farther behind. And being by nature a wild and untamable beast, his spirit flamed up to see his brothers outstripping him so fast. He flung up his head with a shrill and piercing whinny and plunged foaming on. The trees winked by. Now up they went, now down, into deep and darkling glades, now cantering softly over open and moon-swamped snow. If only he could fling the clumsy, clinging Mulgar off his back he would soon catch up his comrades, who were fast disappearing between the trees. He jumped, he reared, he kicked, he plunged, he wriggled, he whinnied. Now he sped like the wind, then on a sudden stopped dead, with all four quivering legs planted firmly in the snow. But still Nod, although at every twist and turn he slipped up or down the sleek and slippery shoulders, managed to cling fast with arms and legs.

Then the cunning beast chose all the lowest and brushiest trees to run under, whose twigs and thorns, like thick besoms, lashed and scratched and scraped his rider. But Nod wriggled his head under his sheep's-coat, and still held on. At last, maddened with shame and rage, the Zevvera flung back his beautiful foam-flecked face, and with his teeth snapped at Nod's shoulder. The Mulgar's wound was not quite healed. The gleaming teeth just scraped his sore. Nod started back, with unclasped hands, and in an instant, head over heels he shot, plump into the snow, and before he could turn to scramble up, with a triumphant squeal of delight, the little Zevvera had vanished into the deep shadows of the moon-chequered forest.

At last Nod managed to get to his feet again. He brushed the snow out of his eyes, and spat it out of his mouth. The Zevvera's hoof-prints were plain in the snow. He would follow them, he thought, till he could follow no longer. His brothers had forsaken him. His Wonderstone was gone. He felt it even now burning like a tiny fire beneath his breast-bone. He limped slowly on. But at every step he stumbled. His shoulder throbbed. He could scarcely see, and in a little while down he fell again. He lay still now, rolled up in his jacket, wishing only to die and be at peace. Soon, he thought, the prowling Minimuls would find him, stiff and frozen. They would wrap him up in leaves, and carry him home between them on a pole to their mounds, and pick his small bones for the morrow's supper. Everything he had done was foolish – the fire, the wild pig, the Ephelantoes. He could not even ride the smallest of the Little Horses of Tishnar.

The languid warmth of his snow-bed began to lull his senses. The moon streamed through the trees, silvering the branches with her splendour. And in the beautiful glamour of the moonbeams it seemed to Nod the air was aflock with tiny wings. His heavy eyelids drooped. He was falling softly – falling, falling – when suddenly, close to his ear, a harsh, small, angry voice broke out.

'Hey, Mulgar! hey, Slugabones! how come you here? What are you doing here?'

He opened his eyes drowsily, and saw an old grey Quatta hare staring drearily into his face with large whitening eyes.

'Sleep,' he said, softly blinking into her face.

'Sleep!' snarled the old hare. 'You idle Mulgars spend all your days eating and sleeping!'

Nod shut his eyes again. 'Do not begrudge me this, old hare,' he said; ''tis Noomanossi's.'

'Where did you steal that sheep's-coat, Mulgar? And how came you and the ugly ones to be riding under my Dragon-tree on the Little Horses of Tishnar?'

'Why,' replied Nod, smiling faintly, 'I stole my sheep's-coat from my mother, who gave it me; and as for "riding on the Little Horses" – here I am!'

'Where have you come from? Where are you going to?' asked the old hare, staring.

'I've come from the Flesh-mounds of the Minimuls, and

I think I'm going to die,' said Nod – 'that is, if this old Quatta will let me.'

The old hare stiffened her long grey ears, and stamped her foot in the snow. 'You mustn't die here,' she said. 'No Mulgar has ever died here. This forest belongs to me.'

In spite of all his aches and pains, Nod grinned. 'Then soon you will have Nod's little bones to fence it in with,' he said.

The old hare eyed him angrily. 'If you weren't dying, impudent Mulgar, I'd teach you better manners.'

Nod wriggled closer into his jacket. 'Trouble not, Queen of Munza,' he said softly. 'I shouldn't have time to use them now.' He shut his eyes again, and all his pain seemed to be floating away in sleep.

The old hare sat up in the snow and listened. 'What's amiss in Munza-Mulgar?' she muttered to herself. 'First these galloping Horses of Tishnar, one, two, three; now the angry Zoots of the Minimuls, and all coming nearer?' But Nod was far away in sleep now, and numb with cold.

She tapped his little shrunken cheek with her foot. 'Even in your sleep, Mulgar, you mustn't dream,' she said. 'None may dream in my forest.' But Nod made no answer even to that. She sat stiff up again, twitching her lean, long, hairy ears, now this way, now that way. 'Foh, Earth-Mulgars!' she said to herself. She stamped in the snow, and stamped again. And in a minute another old Quatta came louping between the trees, and sat down beside her.

'Here's an old sheep's-jacket I've found,' said the old Queen Quatta, 'with a little Mulgar inside it. Let us carry it home, Sister, or the Minimuls will steal him for their feast.'

The other old Quatta raised her lip over her long curved teeth. 'Pull out the Mulgar first,' she said.

But Mishcha said: 'No, it is a strange Mulgar, a Mulla-Mulgar, a Nizza-neela, and he smells of magic. Take his

86

legs, Sister, and I will carry his head. There's no time to be lost.' So these two old Quatta hares wrapped Nod round tight in his sheep-skin coat, and carried him off between them to their form or house in an enormous hollow Dragon-tree unimaginably old, and very snug and warm inside, with cotton-leaf, feathers, and dry tree-moss. There they laid him down, and pillowed him round. And Mishcha hopped out again to watch and wait for the Minimuls.

Sheer overhead the pygmy moon stood, when with drums beating and waving cudgels in their silvery girdles, leopard-skin hats, and grass shoes, thirty or forty of the furry Mini-muls appeared, hobbling bandily along, following the hoof-prints of the galloping Zevveras in the snow. But little clouds in passing had scattered their snow, and the track had begun to grow faint. The old hare watched these Earth-Mulgars draw near without stirring. Like all the other creatures of Munza-Mulgar, she hated these groping, glut-tonous, cannibal gnomes. When they reached the place where Nod had fallen, the Minimuls stood still and peered and pointed. In a little while they came scuttling on again, and there sat old Mishcha under a great thorn-bush, gaunt in the snow.

They stood round her, waving their darts, and squeaking questions. She watched them without stirring. Their round eyes glittered beneath their spotted leopard-skin hats as they stood in their shimmering grasses in the snow.

'When so many squall together,' she said at last, 'I can-not hear one. What's your trouble this bright night?'

Then one among them, with a girdle of Mullabruk's teeth, bade the rest to be silent.

'See here, old hare,' he said, 'have any filthy Mulgars passed this way, one tall and bony, one fat and hairy, and one little and cunning?'

Mishcha stared. 'One and one's two, and one's three,' she said slowly. 'Yes, truly – three.'

87

'Three, three!' they cried all together – 'thieves, thieves!'

Mishcha's face wrinkled. 'All Mulgars are thieves,' she said; 'some even eat flesh. Ugh!'

At this the Minimul-Mulgars grew angry, their glassy eyes brightened. They raised their snouts in the air and waved their darts. But the old hare sat calmly under her roof of poisonous thorns.

'Answer us, answer us,' they squeaked, 'you dumb old Quatta!'

'H'm, h'm!' said Mishcha, staring solemnly. 'Mulgars? There are hundreds, and tens of hundreds of Mulgars in my forest, of more kinds and tribes than I have hairs on my scut. How should old Mishcha raise an eyelid at only three? *Olory mi*, my third-gone grandmother used to tell me many a story of you thieving, gluttonous Mulgars, all alike, all alike. It's sad when one's old to remember – but it's sadder to forget.'

Clouds had stolen again over the moon, and snow was falling fast. Let these evil-smelling Minimuls chatter but a little longer, she thought; not a hoof-print would be left.

'Listen, old hare,' said the chief of the Minimuls. 'Have you seen three Mulgars pass this way, two in red jackets, and one, a Nizza-neela, in a sheep's-coat, and all galloping, galloping, on three Little Horses of Tishnar?'

Mishcha gazed at him stonily, with hatred in her eyes. She was grey with age, and now a little peaked cap of snow crowned her head, so still she had sat beneath the drifting flakes. 'I am old – oh yes, old, and old again,' she said. 'I have ruled in Munza-Mulgar one hundred, two hundred, five hundred years, but I never yet saw a Mulgar riding on a Little Horse of Tishnar. Tell me, Wise One, which way did they sit – *with* the stripes, or criss-cross?'

'Answer us, grandam,' squealed one of the Minimuls in a fury, 'or I'll stick a poisoned dart down your throat.'

Mishcha smiled. 'Better a Minimul's dart than no supper at all,' she said. 'Swallow thy tongue, thou Mulgar!' she said; and suddenly her lips curled upward, her two long front teeth gleamed, her hair bristled. 'Hobble off home, you thieving, flesh-eating, sun-hating earth-worms! Hobble off home before ears and nose and thumbs and toes are bitten and frozen in Tishnar's snows! Away with you, moon-maggots, grubbers of sand!' She stamped with her foot, her old eyes greenly burning under the bush.

The Minimuls began angrily chattering again. At last the first who had spoken turned mousily and said: 'To-day you go unharmed, old Quatta, but to-morrow we will come with fire and burn your Dragon-tree about your ears.'

Mishcha stirred not one hair. 'It's sad to burn, but it's sadder still to freeze.' Her round eyes glared beneath her snow-cap. 'A long march home to you, Minnikin-Mulgar! A long march home! And if I should smell out the Sheep's-jacket on his Little Horse of Tishnar, I will tell him where to find you – burnt, bitten, brittle, baked hard in frozen snow!' She turned and began to hop off slowly between the shadow-casting trees.

At this, one of the Minimuls in his fury lifted a dart and flung it at the old hare. It stuck, quivering, in her shoulder. She turned slowly, and stared at him through the falling flakes; then, drawing the dart out with one of her forefeet, she spat on the point, and laid it softly down in the snow.

And so wildly she gazed at them out of her aged and whitening eyes that the Minimuls fell into a sudden terror of the old-witch-hare, and without another word turned back in silence and scuffled off in the thick falling snow by the way they had come.

Old Mishcha watched them till they were hidden from sight by the trees and the clouding snowflakes; then, muttering a little to herself, nodding her thin long ears, she, too, turned and hopped off quickly to her house under the old Dragon-tree.

CHAPTER EIGHT

Snared

Nod still lay huddled up in his jacket, his small, hairy face all drawn and grey, his eyes tight-shut and sorrowful beneath their thick black lashes. Mishcha squatted over him, and put her head down close to his little body. 'He breathes no more, sister, than a moth or an Immamoosa-bud.'

'Let us drag him out of his sheep-skin, and bury him in the snow,' said Môha.

But Mishcha listened more closely still. 'I hear his heart beating; I hear his drowsy blood just come and go. But what is it that, sweeter than a panther's breath, smells so of Magic? We must not harm the little Mulgar, Sister; he is cunning. A Meermut of Magic would soon return to plague us.' So she wrapped him up still closer in dry leaves and tree-moss, and opened his mouth to sprinkle a pinch of snow between his lips.

All that night and the next day Nod slept without stirring. But the evening after that, when the snow had ceased falling again, he opened his eyes and called *'Walla, walla!'* Mishcha hopped off and brought him snow in a plantain-leaf, and wrapped him up still warmer. But the little dry herbs and powdered root she put on his tongue he choked at, and could not swallow. His shoulder burned, he tossed to and fro with eyes blazing. Now he would start up and shout, 'Thumb, Thumb!' then presently his face would pucker up with fear, and he would scream, 'The fire, the fire!' and then soon after he would be whispering, *'Muzza, muzza, mutta; kara mutta, mutta!'* just as if he were at home again in the little dried-up Portingal's hut.

91

Mishcha did all she could to soothe and quiet him. And at last she managed to make him swallow a little hard bright blue seed called Candar, which drives away fever and quiets dreams. But old Môha eyed him angrily, and wanted to throw him out into the forest to die. 'Who'd sleep in a jacket that a gibbering Mulgar has died in?' she said.

When the next night was nearly gone, but before it was yet day, Nod awoke, cool and clear, and stared into the musty darkness of the Dragon-tree, wondering in vain where he was. Only one small spark of light could he see – the red star Antares, that was now burning through a little rift in the bark. He thought he heard a faint rustling of dry leaves.

'Hey, there!' he called out. 'Where is Nod?'

'Hold your tongue, thieving Mulgar,' cried an angry voice, 'and let honest folk sleep in peace.'

'If I could see,' Nod answered weakly, 'you wouldn't sleep much to-night, honest or no.'

'You can't see,' answered the voice softly, 'because, my man of bones, you are dead and buried under the snow.'

Nod grew cold. He pinched his legs; he opened and shut his mouth, and took long, deep breaths; then he laughed. 'It's none so bad, then, being dead, Voice-of-Kindness,' he said cheerfully, 'if it weren't for this sore shoulder of mine.'

But to this the morose voice made no answer. Not yet, even, could Nod remember all that had happened. 'Hey, there!' he called out again presently, 'who buried me, then?'

'Buried you? Why, Mishcha and Môha, the old witch-hares, who found you snuffling in the snow in your stolen sheep's coat – Mishcha and Môha, who wouldn't touch monkey-skin, not for a grove of green Candar-trees.'

'I remember Môha,' said Nod meekly, 'a gentle and sleek, a very, very handsome old Quatta. And is she dead, too?'

But again the sour voice made no reply.

'Once,' said Nod, in a little while, 'I had two brave brothers. I wonder where those Mulla-Mulgars are now?'

'He wonders,' said the voice slowly – '*he wonders*! Frizzling, frizzling, frizzling, my pretty Talk-by-Night, with seven smoking Gelica-nuts for company on the spit.'

At this Nod fell silent. He lay quaking in his warm rustling bed, with puckered forehead and restless eyes, wondering if the voice had told him the truth, while daybreak stole abroad in the forest.

When dusk began to stir within the Dragon-tree, Mishcha awoke and came and looked at him.

She hearkened at his ribs and mouth, and there seemed, Nod thought, a little kindness in her ways. So he put out his shrunken hand, and said: 'Tell me truly, witch-hare. A voice in the night was merry with me, and told me for pleasure that my brothers Thumb and Thimble were frizzling on the cannibal Minimuls' spit. That is not true?'

' "One long and lean," ' said Mishcha, ' "one fat and very hairy, and one sly and tiny, a Nizza-neela." Here's the Nizza-neela Mulla-Mulgar; I know nothing of the others.'

'Ah, then,' said Nod, starting up out of his bed, 'I must be off to look for them. Their Little Horses ran faster than mine. And mine, he was a coward, and nibbled my sore shoulder to make me loose hold. But he could not buck or scrape me off, witch-hare, tried he never so hard. I must be off to look for my brothers. If they are dead, then I die too.'

'Well, well,' said the old hare, 'it's sad to die, but it's sadder to live alone. But tell me first one thing,' she said. 'Where have these strange Mulgars come from in their rags and bravery?'

'*Ohé*,' said Nod, and told her who they were.

'And tell me just one thing more,' she said, when he had finished. 'Where, little Mulgar, is all this Magic I can smell?'

93

And at that question Nod thought he could never keep from laughing. But he looked very solemn, and said: 'There are three things, old hare, I always carry about with me – one is my sheep's-jacket, one is hunger, and the other is Magic; and the Magic just now is where my hunger is.'

The old hare eyed him narrowly. 'Well,' she said, 'wherever it is, if it hadn't been for the Magic, little Mulgar, the Jaccatrays would have been quarrelling over your bones. But there! remember old Mishcha sometimes in your travels, who hated every Mulgar except just one little one!' She bade him be very quiet, for her Sister, after the night's talk, still lay fast asleep, her eyes wide open, in the gloom.

And she put Ukka-nuts, and dried berries and fruits of many kinds, and seven pepper-pods into his pockets, and buttoned the flaps. And gave him also some powdered physic-nuts, three bright-blue Candar-seeds and a little bunch of faded saffron-flower for a protection against the teeth of the dreaded Coccadrillo. She tied up his shoulder with soft clean moss, and fetched him a stout stick for cudgel, out of the forest. And then she hobbled out with him to see him on his way. Dawn lay rosy and still upon the snow-laden branches.

'Where burns the Sulemnāgar, old hare?' said Nod, pretending utter bravery. And the wise old Quatta hare pointed

out to him where still the Sulemnāgar gleamed faint and
silver above the glistening trees.

So Nod thanked her, went forward a few paces, and
stepped back to thank her again; then set out truly and for
good.

He walked very cautiously, spying about him as he went.
The red sun glinted on his cudgel. Once he saw a last night's
leopard's track in the snow. So he roved his eyes aloft as
well as to left and right of him, lest she should be lying in
wait crouched in the branches. A troop of Skeetoes pelted
him with Ukka-nuts. But these, as fast as they threw them
down, he gathered up and put into his bulging pockets, and
waved his cap at them for thanks. They gibbered and
mocked at him, and flung more nuts. 'So long as it isn't
stones, my long-tailed friends,' he said to himself, 'I will
not throw back.'

After a while he came to where Cullum and Samarak
grew so dense amid the tree-trunks that he could scarcely
walk upright. But he determined, as his mother had bidden
him, to keep from stooping on to his fours as long as ever
he could. Tumbling Numnuddies startled him, calling in the
air. And once a clouded vulture with wings at least six
cudgels wide dropped like a stone upon a leafless Boobab-
branch, and watched him gloatingly go limping by.

He sat down in his loneliness and rested, and nibbled one
of Mishcha's nuts. But try as he might, he could not swallow much. When once more he set out, for a long way some

skulking beast which he could not plainly see stalked through the nodding grasses a few paces distant from him, but side by side. He flourished his cudgel, and sang softly the Mulla-Mulgar's Journey Song which Seelem had taught him long ago:

> That one
> Alone
> Who's dared, and gone
> To seek the Magic Wonderstone,
> No fear,
> Or care,
> Or black despair,
> Shall heed until his journey's done.
>
> Who knows
> Where blows
> The Mulgars' rose,
> In valleys 'neath unmelting snows –
> All secrets
> He
> Shall pierce and see,
> And walk unharmed where'er he goes.

Whether it was the Wonderstone under his breast-bone, or the sight of his cudgel, or a distaste for his shrill voice and skinniness, Nod could not tell, but in a little while, when he stopped a moment to peer between the thick streamers of Samarak, the secret beast was gone. Day drew on. He saw no tracks in the snow, except of wild pig and long-snouted Brackanolls. The only sound he heard was the falling of frosted clots of snow from the branches of the trees and the sad, continuous *'Oo-ee, oo-ee, oo-ee!'* of the little rust-coloured Bittock amid the sunlit snow. He did not dare now to rest, though his feet grew more painful at every step, and his poisoned shoulder itched and ached.

He stumbled on, scarcely heeding where his footsteps were leading him. Mulgar flies, speckled and humped,

roused by the cloudless sun, buzzed round his eyes and bit and stung him. And suddenly his heart stood still at sight of seven amber and spotted beasts standing amid the grasses, casting a league-long shadow with their necks – such beasts as he had never seen before. But they were busy feeding, their heads and tiny horns and lustrous eyes half hidden in the foliage of the branches. Nod stared in fear and wonder, and passed their arbour very softly by.

Night began to fall, and the long-beaked bats to flit in their leathery hoods, seeking small birds and beasts to quench their thirst. It seemed now to Nod, his brave heart fallen, that he was utterly forsaken. Darkness had always sent him scuttling home to the Portingal's hut when he was little. How often his mother had told him that Noomanossi with his luring harp-strings roamed these further forests, and strange beasts, too, that never show their faces to the sun! Worse still, as he lifted his poor wrinkled forehead to the tree-tops to catch the last beams of day, he felt a dreadful presence around him. Leopard it was not, nor Gunga, nor Minimul.

He stood still, his left hand resting on its knuckles in the snow, his right clutching his cudgel, and leaning his round ear sidelong, he listened and listened. He put down his cudgel, and stood upright, his hands clasped behind his neck, and lifting his flat nose, sniffed and sniffed again the scarcely stirring air. There was a scent, faint and strange. He turned as if to rush away, to hide himself – anywhere away from this brooding, terrifying smell, when, as if it were a little voice speaking beneath his ribs, he heard the words: 'Fear not. Ummanodda; press on, press on!'

He took up his cudgel with a groan, and limped quickly forward, and in an instant, before he could start back, before even he could cry out, he heard a click, his foot slipped, out of the leaves whipped something smooth and shining, and he was jerked into the air, caught, bound fast in a snare.

He writhed and kicked, he spat and hissed. But the more he struggled, the tighter drew the cord round his neck. Everywhere, faint and trembling, rose the strange and dreadful unknown smell. He hung quite still. And as he dangled in pain, a night-wandering Bittock on a branch above him called piteously: *'Oo-ee, oo-ee, oo-ee!'*

'Why do you mock me, my friend?' groaned Nod.

'Oo-ee, oo-ee, oo-ee!' wailed the Bittock, and hopping down slowly, perched herself before his face. Her black eye gleamed. She clapped her tiny wings above her head, and softly let them fold. *'Oo-ee, oo-ee, oo-ee!'* she cried again.

Nod stared in a rage: *'Oo-ee, oo-ee!'* he mocked her feebly. 'Who's caught me in this trap? Why do you come mocking me, swinging here to die? Put out my eyes, Bird of Sorrow. Nod's tired of being Nod.'

The little bird seemed to listen, with rusty poll poked forward. She puffed out her feathers, raised her pointed bill, and piercingly into the shadows rang out her trembling voice again, '*Oo-ee, oo-ee, oo-ee*,' she sang, spread her wings, and left Nod quite alone.

His thong twitched softly. He shut his eyes. And once again, borne on the faint cold wind, that smell came sluggishly to his nostrils. His fears boiled up. His hair grew wet on his head. And suddenly he heard a distant footfall. Nearer and nearer – not panther's, nor Gunga's, nor Ephelanto's. And then some ancient voice whispered in his memory: 'Oomgar, Oomgar!' Man!

CHAPTER NINE

The Solitary Sailor

There was only the last of day in the forest. But Nod, dangling in terror, could clearly see the Oomgar peering at him from beneath the unstirring branches – his colourless skin, his long yellow hair, his musket, his fixed glittering eyes. And there came suddenly a voice out of the Oomgar, like none the little Mulgar had ever heard in his life before. Nod screamed and gnashed and kicked. But it was in vain. It only noosed him tighter.

'So, so, then; softly now, softly!' said the strange clear voice. The Oomgar caught up the slack end of the noose and wound it deftly around his captive, binding him hand and foot together. Then he took a long steel knife from his breeches pocket, cut the cord round Nod's neck, and let him drop heavily to the ground. '*Poor* little Pongo! poor leetle Pongo!' he said craftily, and cautiously stooped to pick him up.

Nod could not see for rage and fear. He drew back his head, and with all his strength fixed his teeth in that white terrible thumb. The Oomgar sucked in his breath with the pain, and catching up the little Mulgar's own cudgel that lay in the snow, rapped him angrily on the head. After that Nod struggled no more. A thick piece of cloth was tied fast round his jaws. The Oomgar slipped the barrel of his musket through the Cullum-rope, lifting the little Mulgar on to his back, and strode off with him through the darkening forest.

They came out after a while from among the grasses, vines, and undergrowth. The Oomgar climbed heavily up a

rocky slope, trudged on over an open and level space of snow, across an icy yet faintly stirring stream, and came at length to a low wooden house, drifted deep in snow, in front of which a big fire was burning, showering up sparks into the starry sky. Here the Oomgar stooped and tumbled Nod over his shoulder into the snow at a little distance from the fire.

He bent his head to the flames, and examined his bitten thumb, rubbed the blood off with a handful of snow, sucked the wound, bound it roughly with a strip of blue cloth, and tied the bandage in a knot with his teeth. This done, making a strange noise with his lips like the hissing of sap from a green stick, he began plucking off the wing and tail feathers of a large grey bird. This he packed in leaves, and uncovering a little hole beneath the embers, raked it out, and pushed the carcass in to roast.

He squinnied narrowly over his shoulder a moment, then went into his hut and brought a cooking-pot, which he filled with water from the stream, and put into it a few mouse-coloured roots called Kiddals, which in flavour resemble an artichoke, and are very wholesome, even when cold. He hung his cooking-pot over the fire on three sticks laid cross-wise. Then he sat down and cleaned his musket while his supper was cooking.

All this Nod watched without stirring, almost without winking, till at last the Oomgar, with a grunt, put down his gun, and came near and stood over him, staring down with a crooked smile on his mouth, between his yellow hair and the short, ragged beard beneath. He held out his bandaged thumb. 'There, little master,' he said coaxingly, 'have an-other taste; though I warn ye,' he added, wagging his head, 'it'll be your werry last.' Nod's restless hazel eyes glanced to and fro above the stifling cloth wound round his mouth. He felt sullen and ashamed. How his brother Thimble would have scoffed to see him now, caught like a sucking-pig in a snare!

The Oomgar smiled again. 'Why, he's nowt but skin and bone, he is; shivering in his breeches and all. Lookee here, now, Master Pongo, or whatsomedever name you goes by, here's one more chance for ye.' He took out his knife and slit off the gag round Nod's mouth, and loosened the cord a little. Nod did not stir.

'And who's to wonder?' said the Oomgar, watching him. He began warily scratching the little Mulgar's head above the parting. 'It was a cruel hard rap, my son – a cruel hard rap, I don't gainsay ye; but, then, you must take Andy's word for it, they was cruel sharp teeth.'

Nod saw him looking curiously at his sheep's-jacket, and, thinking he would show this strange being that Mulla-Mulgars, too, can understand, he sidled his hand gently and heedfully into his pocket and fetched out one of the Ukka-nuts that old Mishcha had given him.

At that the Oomgar burst out laughing. 'Brayvo!' he shouted; 'that's mother-English, that is! Now we's beginning to unnerstand one another.' He poured a little hot water out of his cooking-pot into a platter and put it down in the snow. Nod sniffed it doubtfully. It smelt sweet and earthy of the root simmering in it. But he raised the platter of water slowly with his loosened hands, cooled it with blowing, and supped it up greedily, for he was very thirsty.

The Oomgar watched him with an astonished countenance. 'Saints save us!' he muttered, 'he drinks like a Christian!'

Nod wriggled his mouth, and imitated the sound as best he could. *'Krisshun, Krisshun,'* he grunted.

The stooping Oomgar stared across the fire at Nod in the shadow as a man stares towards a strange and formidable shape in the dark. 'Saints save us!' he whispered again, crossing himself, and sat down on his log.

He scraped back the embers and stripped the burnt skin and frizzled feathers off his roasted bird, stuck a wooden prong into a Kiddal, and, with a mouthful of bird and a mouthful of Kiddal, set heartily to his supper. When he had eaten his fill, he heaped up the fire with green wood, tied Nod to a thick stake of his hut, so that he could lie in comfort of the fire and to windward of its smoke; then, with a tossed-up glance at the starry and cloudless vault of the sky, he went whistling into the hut and noisily barred the door.

Softly crooning to himself in his sorrow and loneliness, Nod lay long awake. Of a sudden he would sit up, trembling, to glance as if from a dream about him, then in a little while would lie down quiet again. At last, with hands over his face and feet curled up towards the fire, he fell fast asleep.

When Nod woke the next morning the Oomgar was already abroad, and busy over his breakfast. The sun burned clear in the dark blue sky. Nod opened his eyes and watched the Oomgar without stirring. He stood in height by more than a hand's breadth taller than the Gunga-Mulgar. But he was much leaner. The Gunga's horny knuckles had all but brushed the ground when he stood, stooping and glowering, on legs crooked and shapeless as wood. The Oomgar's arms reached only midway to his knees; he walked straight as a palm-tree, without stooping, and no black, cringing cunning nor blood-shot ferocity darkened his face.

His hair dangled beaming in the sun about his clear skin. His hands were only faintly haired. And he wore a kind of loose jacket or jerkin, made of the inner bark of the Juzanda-tree (which is of finer texture than the Mulgars' cloth), rough breeches of buffskin, and monstrous boots. But most Nod watched flinchingly the Oomgar's light blue eyes, hard as ice, yet like nothing for strangeness Nod had ever seen in his life before, nor dreamed there was. But every time they wheeled beneath their lids piercingly towards him he closed his own, and feigned to be asleep.

At last, feeling thirsty, he wriggled up and crawled to the dish, which still lay icy in the snow, and raised it with both hands as far as his manacles would serve, and thrust it out empty towards the Oomgar.

The Oomgar made Nod a great smiling bow over the fire in answer, and filled it with water. Then, breaking off a piece of his smoking flesh, he flung it to the Mulgar in the snow. But Nod would not so much as stoop to smell it. He gravely shook his head, thrust in his fingers, and drew an Ukka-nut out of his pocket. 'And who's to blame ye?' said the Oomgar cheerfully. 'It's just the tale of Jack Sprat, my son, over again; only your little fancy's neether lean nor fat, but monkey-nuts!' He got up, and, screening his eyes from the sun, looked around him.

Then Nod looked, too. He saw that the Oomgar had built his hut near the edge of a kind of shelving rock, which sloped down softly to a cliff or gully. A little half-frozen stream flowed gleaming under the sun between its snowy banks, to tumble wildly over the edge of the cliff in blazing and frozen spray. Beyond the cliff stretched the azure and towering forests of Munza, immeasurable, league on league, flashing beneath the whole arch of the sky, capped and mantled and festooned with snow.

Near-by grew only thin grasses and bushes of thorn, except that at the southern edge of the steep rose up a little company or grove of Ukka-nuts and Ollacondas. Toward these strode off the Oomgar, with a thick billet of wood in his hand. When he reached them, he stood underneath, and flung up his billet into the tree, just as Nod himself had often done, and soon fetched down two or three fine clusters of Ukka-nuts. These he brought back with him, and held some out to the quiet little Mulgar.

'There, my son,' he said, 'them's for pax, which means peace, you unnerstand. I'm not afeard of you, nor you isn't afeared of me. All's spliced and shipshape.' So there they sat beneath the blazing sun, the dazzling snow all round them, the Oomgar munching his broiled flesh, and staring over the distant forest, Nod busily cracking his Ukka-nuts, and peeling out the soft, milky, quincey kernel. Nod scarcely took his bewitched eyes from the Oomgar's face, and the longer he looked at him, the less he feared him. All creatures else he had ever seen seemed dark and cloudy by comparison. The Oomgar's face was strange and fair, like the shining of a flame.

'Now, see here, my son,' said the Oomgar suddenly, when, after finishing his breakfast, he had sat brooding for

105

some time: 'I go there – *there*,' he repeated, pointing with his hand across the stream; 'and Monkey Pongo, he stay *here* – here,' he repeated, pointing to the hut. 'Now, s'posin' Andy Battle, which is *me*' – he bent himself towards Nod and grinned –'s'posin' Andy Battle looses off that rope's end a little more, will Master Pongo keep out of mischief, eh?'

Nod tried hard to understand, and looked as wise as ever he could. *'Ulla Mulgar majubba; zinglee Oomgar,'* he said.

Battle burst out laughing. *'Ugga, nugga, jugga, jingles!* That's it – that's the werry thing,' he said.

Nod looked up softly without fear and grinned.

'He knows, by gum!' said Battle. 'There be more wits in that leetle hairy cranny than in a shipload of commodores.' He got up and loosened the rope round Nod's neck. 'It's only just this,' he said. 'Andy Battle isn't turned cannibal yet – neither for white, black, nor monkey-meat. I wouldn't eat you, my son, not if they made me King of England to-morrow, which isn't likely to be, by the look of the weather, so *don't ee have no meddlin' with the fire!'*

'Middlinooiddyvire,' said Nod, mimicking him softly.

And at that Battle burst into such a roar of laughter the hut shook. He filled Nod's platter with water, and gave him the rest of the Ukka-nuts. He went into the hut and fetched musket, powder, and bullets. He put a thick-peaked hat on his head, then, with his musket over his shoulder, he nodded handsomely at the little blinking Mulgar, and off he went.

Nod watched him stride away. With a hop, skip, and a jump he crashed across the frozen water, and soon disappeared down the steep path that led into the forest. When he was out of sight, Nod lay down in the shadow of the log-hut. He felt a strange comfort, as if there was nothing in all Munza-Mulgar to be afraid of. His rage and sullenness were gone. He would rest here awhile with his Oomgar, if he were as kind as he seemed to be, and try to understand what he said. Then, when his feet were healed of their sores and blains, and his shoulder was quite whole again, he would set off once more after his brothers.

All the next day, and the day after that, Nod sat patient and still, tethered with a long cord round his neck to the Oomgar's hut. When Battle spoke to him he listened gravely. When he laughed and showed his teeth, Nod showed his cheerfully, too. And when Battle sat silent and cast down in thought, Nod pretended to be unspeakably busy over his nuts.

And soon the sailor found himself beginning to look forward to seeing the hairy face peering calmly out of the sheep's jacket on his return from his hunting. On the third evening, when, after a long absence, he came home, tired out and heavy-laden, with a little sharp-horned Impolanca-calf and a great frost-blackened bunch of Nanoes, he took off Nod's halter altogether and set him free.

'There!' said he; 'we're messmates now, Master Pongo. Andy Battle's had a taste of slavery himself, and it isn't reasonable, my son. It frets in like rusty iron, my son; and Andy's supped his fill of it. I takes to your company won-nerful well, and if you takes to mine, then that's plain-

sailing, says I. But if them apes and monkeys over yonder are more to yer liking than a shipwrecked sailor, who's to blame ye? Every man to his own, says I; breeches to breeches, and bare to bare. The werry first thing is for me and you to unnerstand one another.'

Nod listened gravely to all this talk, and caught the sailor's meaning, what with a word here, a nod, a wink, or a smile there, and the jerk of a great thumb.

'But as for Andy Battle,' went on the sailor, 'he never were much struck at a foreign lingo. So, says I, Andy shall learn Master Pongo his'n. And here goes! That,' said he, holding up a great piece of meat on his knife – 'that's *meat*.'

'*'Zmeat – ugh!*' said Nod, with a shudder.

'And this here's nuts,' said Battle.

'*'Znuts!*' repeated Nod, rubbing his stomach.

Battle rapped on his log. 'Excellentissimo!' he said. 'He's a scholard born. Now, monkeys like you,' he went on, looking into Nod's face, 'if I make no mistake, the blacka-moors calls "Pongoes".'

Nod shook his head.

'No? 'Njekkoes, then,' said the sailor.

Nod shook his head again. '*Me Mulla-Mulgar! Pongo – Jecco*' – he shook his head vehemently – '*me Mulla-Mulgar Ummanodda Nizza-neela.*'

The Oomgar laughed aloud. 'Axing your pardon, then, Master Noddle Ebenezer, mine's Battle – Andrew, as which is Andy Battle.'

'*Whizzizandy – Baffle,*' said Nod, with a jerk.

'Famous!' said the sailor. 'Us was a down-right dunce to you, my son. Now, then, hoise anchor, and pipe up! Andy Battle is an Englishman; hip, hooray! Andy Battle –'

'" *Andy Baffle –*" '

'"Is an –" '

'"*Izzn –*" '

'"Is an Englishman." '

108

' "*Izziningulissmum,*" ' said Nod very slowly.

' "Hip, hooray!" ' bawled Battle.

' "*Ippooray!*" ' squealed Nod. And Battle rocked to and fro on his log with laughter.

'That's downright rich, my son, that is! "Izzuninglushum!" As sure as ever mariners was born to be drownded,

> We'll sail away, o'er the deep blue say,
> And to old England we'll make our way.

A piece of silver for a paw-shake, and two for a good-e'en. Us'll make a fortune, you and me, and go and live in a snug little cottage with six palm-trees and a blackamoor down Ippleby way. Andrew Battle, knight and squire, and Jack Sprat, Prince of Pongo-land. Ay, and the King shall come to sup wi' us, comfortable-like, 'twixt you and me, and drink hisself thirsty out of a golden mug.'

And so it went on. Every day Battle taught Nod new words. And soon he could say a few simple things in his Mulgar-English, and begin to make himself understood. Battle taught him also to cook his meat for him, though Nod would never taste of it himself. And Nod, too, out of Sudd and Mambel-berries and Nanoes and whatever other dried and frosted fruits Battle brought home, made monkey-bread and a kind of porridge, which Battle at first tasted with caution, but at last came to eat with relish.

The sailor stitched his friend up a jacket of Juzanda cloth, with Bamba-shells for buttons, and breeches of buff-skin. These Nod dyed dark blue in patches, for his own pleasure, with leaves, as Battle directed him. Battle made him also a pair of shoes of rhinoceros-skin, nearly three inches thick, on which Nod would go sliding and tumbling on the ice, and a cap of needlework and peacocks' feathers, just as in his dream.

There were many things in Battle's hut gathered together for traffic and pleasure in his journey: a great necklace of Gunga's or Pongo's teeth; a bagful of Cassary beads, which changed colour with the hour, a bolt-eyed Joojoo head, a bird-billed throwing-knife, also beads of Estridges' eggs, as large as a small melon. There was also, what Battle cherished very carefully, a little fat book of 566 pages and nine woodcuts that his mother had given him before setting out on his hapless voyagings, with a tongue or clasp of brass to keep it together. Moreover, Battle gave Nod a piece of looking-glass, the like of which he had never seen before. And the little Mulgar would often sit sorrowfully talking to his image in the glass, and bid the face that there answered his own be off and find his brothers. And Nod, in return, gave Battle for a keepsake the little Portingal's left-thumb knuckle-bone and half the faded Coccadrillo saffron which old Mishcha had given to him.

Of an evening these castaways had music for their company – a bell of copper that rang marvellously clear across the frosty air, and would bring multitudes of night-birds hovering and crying over the hut in perplexity at the sweet and hollow sound. And besides the bell, Battle had a cittern, or lute, made of a gourd, with a Juggawood neck like a fiddle. Stretched and pegged this was, with twangling strings made of a climbing root that grows in the denser forests, and bears a flower lovelier than any to be seen on earth beside. With Battle thrumming on this old crowd or lute, Nod danced many a staggering hornpipe and Mulgar-jig. Moreover, Battle had taught himself to pick out a melody or two. So, then, they would dance and sing songs together – 'Never, tir'd Sailour', 'The Three Cherry-trees', 'Who's seene my Deere with Cheekes so redde?' and many another.

Battle's voice was loud and great; Nod's was very changeable. For the upper notes of his singing were shrill and trembling, and so the best part of his songs would go; but when they dipped towards the bass, then his notes burst out so sudden and powerful, it might be supposed four men's voices had taken up the melody where a boy's had ceased. It pleased Battle mightily, this night-music – music of all the kinds they knew, White Man's, Jaqqua-music, Nugga-music, and Mulla-Mulgars'. Nod, too, often droned to the sailor, as time went on, the evening song to Tishnar that his father had taught him, until at last the sailor himself grew familiar with the sound, and learned the way the notes went. And sometimes Battle would sit and, singing solemnly, almost as if a little forlornly, through his nose, would join in too. And sometimes to see this small monkey perched up with head in air, he could scarce refrain his laughter, though he always kept a straight face as kindly as with a child.

But the leopards and other prowling beasts, when they heard the sound of their strings and music, went mewing and fretting; and many a great python and ash-scaled poison-snake would rear its head out of its long sleep and sway with flickering tongue in time to the noisy echoes from the rocky and firelit shelf above. Even the Jack-Alls and Jaccatrays squatted whimpering in their bands to listen and would break when all was silent into such a doleful and dismal chorus that it seemed to shake the stars.

CHAPTER TEN

Immanâla

It was many a day after Nod had been taken in the sailor's snare, and one very snowy, when the little Mulgar, looking up over his cooking, saw Battle come limping white and blood-beslobbered across the frozen stream towards home. He carried nothing except his gun, neither beast nor bird. He stumbled over the ice, and walked crazily. And when he reached the fire, he just tumbled his musket against a log and sat himself down heavily, holding his head in his hands, with a sighing groan. Now, this was the fifth day or more that Battle had gone out and returned without meat, and Nod, in his vanity, thought the sailor was beginning to weary of flesh, and to take pleasure only in nuts and fruit, as the Mulla-Mulgars do. But when Battle had dried up the deep scratch in his neck, and eaten a morsel or two of Nod's fresh-baked Nano-cake, he told him of his doings.

Nod could even now, of course, only understand a little here and there of what Battle said. But he twisted out enough words to learn that the sailor was astonished and perplexed at finding such a scarcity of game, howsoever far or cautiously he roamed in search of it.

'Ay, and maybe that's no great wonder, neether, what with this everlasting snow and all. But tell me this, Nod Mulgar: Why does, whenever I spies a fine fat four-legged breakfast or two-winged supper feeding within comfortable musket-shot – why does a howl like a M'keeso's, dismal and devilish, break out not fifteen paces off, and scare away every living creature for leagues around? Why does leopards and Jack-Alls and Jaccatrays swarm round

112

Andy Battle when he goes a-walking, thick as cats round
cream? They've scotched me this once, my son – an old she-
leopard, black as pitch out of an Ollacondy. And I could
have staked a ransom I cast my eye over every bough.
Next time who's to know what may happen? Nizza-neela
will go on cooking his little hot niminy-cakes, and wait and
wait – only for bones – only for Battle's bones, Mulgar *mio*.
What I says is this-how: leopards and Jaccatrays, from
being what they once was, two or three, one to-day and
three to-morrow, now lurks everywhere, looking me in the
face as bold as brass, and sniffling at my very musket. But,
there! that's all plain-sailing. What Andy wants to know
for sartin sure is: what beast it is grinds out so close against
his ear that unearthly human howling. 'Twixt me and you
and Lord Makellacolongee, it criddles my very blood to
hear it. My finger begins tapping on the musket-trigger like
hail on a millpond.'

Nod listened, puckered and intent, and looked a good
deal wiser than he was. And when supper was done he
fetched out the thick rhinoceros-shoes which Battle had
made him, as if to go disporting himself as usual on the ice.
But, instead of this, he hid them behind a hummock of
snow, and, crossing over the stream, crept to the edge of the
snowy shelf, and sat under an Exxzwixxia-bush, gazing

113

down into the gloom, silently watching and listening. He heard soft, furtive calls, whimperings. A startled bird flew up on beating wings, and far and near the Jack-Alls were hollowly barking one to another in their hunting-bands. But he saw no leopards nor heard any voice or sound he knew no reason for, or had not heard before. Perhaps, he thought, his dull wits had misunderstood the Oomgar's talk.

He was just about to turn away, when he heard a little call often repeated, 'Chikka, chikka,' which means in Munza-Mulgar, 'Bide here', or 'Wait awhile'. And there, stealing up from under the longer grasses, came who but Mishcha, the old witch-hare. But very slowly and cautiously she came, pretending that she was searching out what poor fare she could find in the dismal snow.

When she was come close, she whispered: 'Move not; stir not a finger, Mulla-Mulgar; speak to me as I am. I have a secret thing to say to you. These seven long frozen evenings have I come fretting abroad in my forest and watched and watched, and chikka'd and chikka'd, but you have not come. Why, O Prince of Tishnar, do you linger here with this flesh-eating Oomgar, whose gun barks Noomanossi all day long? Why do you think no more of your brothers and of the distant valleys?'

Nod crouched in silence a little while, twitching his small brows. 'But this Oomgar took me in a snare,' he said at last. 'And he has fed me, and been like my own father Seelem come again to me, and we are friends – "messimuts", old hare. Besides, I wait only until I am healed of my blains and thorns, and my shoulder is quite whole again. Then I go. But even then, why has the old Queen Quatta come louping through Munza all these seven evenings past, only to tell me that?'

Mishcha eyed him silently with her whitening eyes. 'Not so blind am I yet, little Mulgar, as not to creep and creep a league for the sake of a friend. Be off to-morrow, Nizza-neela! What knows an Oomgar of friendship? *That* brings only the last sleep.'

'I mind not the last sleep, old hare,' said Nod in his vanity. 'Did I fear it when half-frozen in the snow? Besides, my friend, the Oomgar, whose name is Battle, he will guard me.'

Mishcha crept nearer. 'Has not the little Mulla-Mulgar then, heard Immanâla's hunting-cry?'

Now, Immanâla in Munza means, as it were, unstoried, nameless, unknown, darkness, secrecy. All these the word means. Night is Immanâla to Munza-Mulgar. So is sorcery. So, too, is the dark journey to death or the Third Sleep. And this *Beast* they name Immanâla because it comes of no other beast that is known, has no likeness to any. Child of nothing, wits of all things, ravenous yet hungerless, she lures, lures, and if she die at all, dies alone. By some it is said that this Immanâla is the servant of Noomanossi, and has as many lives as his white resting-tree has branches. And so she is born again to haunt and raven and poison Munza with cruelty and strife. All this Nod had heard from his father Seelem, and his skin crept at sound of the name. But he pretended he felt no fear.

'Who is this Immanâla, the Nameless,' he scoffed softly, 'that a Mulla-Mulgar should heed her yapping (*ugga-gugga*)?'

'Ah,' said the old hare, 'he boasts best who boasts in safety. Mishcha, little Mulgar, has met the Nameless face to face, and when I hear her hunting-cry I do not make merry. How could she all these days have given ear to the Oomgar's gun in the forest, and make no sign – she who has for her servants leopards and Jaccatrays of many years' hunting? Mark this, too,' said Mishcha, 'if the little Mulgar were not the chosen of Tishnar, his Oomgar would long ago have been nothing but a few picked bones.'

The old hare touched him with her long clawed foot, and

gazed earnestly into his face with her half-blind, whitening eyes. 'Yes, Mulgar,' she said at last, whispering, 'your brothers that rode on the Little Horses of Tishnar are none so far away. "Why," say they to each other, roosting half-frozen in their tree-huts – "why does Ummanodda betray all Munza-Mulgar to the Oomgar's gun? He is no child of Royal Seelem's now."'

Nod's heart stood still to hear again of his brothers, and that they were so near. And Mishcha promised if he would abandon the Oomgar, she would lead him to them. Nod gazed long into the gloom before he sadly answered:

'I cannot leave my master,' he said, 'who has fed and befriended me. I cannot leave him to be torn in pieces by this Beast of Shadows. He is wise – oh, he is wise! He was born to stand upright. He fears not any shadow. He walks with Noomas beneath every tree. He kills, old Mishcha – that I know well – and feeds like a glutton on flesh. But a she-leopard in one moon eats as many of the Munza-Mulgars as she has roses on her skin. As for the Nameless, my father Seelem told me many a time of *her* thirsty tongue.'

Then Mishcha whispered warily in Nod's ear in the shadow of the thorn-bush beneath which they sat, turning her staring stone-coloured eyes this way, that way. 'If the

Oomgar were safe from her,' she said, scarcely opening her thin lips above the lean curved teeth, 'would *then* the little Mulgar go?'

Nod laughed. 'Then would I go on all fours, O Mishcha, for I am weary of waiting and being far from my brothers, Thumb and Thimble. Then would I go at once if I could leave the

116

Oomgar quietly to his hunting, and safe from this Shadow-Beast and from more than three lean hunting leopards on the Ollaconda boughs at one time.'

Then Mishcha told him what he should do. And Nod listened, shivering, in part for the cold, and in part for dread of what she was saying. 'There are three things, Nizza-neela,' she said, when she had told him all her stratagem – 'there are three things even a Mulla-Mulgar must have who fights with Immanâla, Queen of Shadows: he must have Magic, he must have cunning, and he must have courage. Oh, little Prince of Tishnar, should I have physicked you and saved you from the sooty spits of the Minimuls if you had been neither wise nor brave?'

And Nod promised by his Wonderstone to do all that she had bidden him. And she crept soundlessly back into the gloom of the forest. Nod himself quickly hobbled home, took up his sliding-shoes again, and returned to the little hut and the Oomgar's red fire.

Battle sat there, stooping in the light of the rising moon and the ruddy glow over his little book. But he held it for memory's sake rather than to read it. His head was jerking in sleep when Nod sat himself down by the fire, and the little Mulgar could think quietly of all that the old hare had told him. He half-shut his eyes, watching his slow, curious Mulgar thoughts creep in and out. And while he sat there, lonely and wretched, struggling between love for his brothers and for the Oomgar, he heard a small clear voice within him speaking that said: 'Courage, Prince Ummanodda! Tishnar is faithful to the faithful. Who is this Nameless to set snares against her chosen? Fear not, Nizza-neela; all will be well!' Thus it seemed to Nod the inward voice was saying to him, and he took comfort. He would tell the poor sailor, perhaps, part of what he feared and knew, and with Tishnar to help him would seek out his Immanâla and meet her face to face.

Night rode in starry darkness above the great black forest. The logs burned low. Close before his fire sat Battle, his chin on his breast, his yellow-haired head rolling from side to side in his sleep. Thin clear flames, blue and sulphur, floated along the logs, and lit up his fast-shut eyes. Nod sat with his little chops in his hairy hands watching the sailor. Sometimes a solitary beast roared, or a night-bird squalled out of the gloom. At last the little book fell out of Battle's sleep-loosened fingers. He started, raised his head, and stared into the darkness, listening to howl answering to howl, shrill cry to distant cry. He yawned, showing all his small white teeth.

'Your friends are uncommonly fidgety to-night, Nod Mulgar,' he said.

Nod got up and threw more wood on the glowing fire. 'Not Mulla-Mulgar's friends. Nod's friends not hate Oomgar.' Up sprang the flames, hissing and crackling.

The sailor grinned. 'Lor' bless ye, my son; you talks wonnerful hoity-toity; but in *my* country they would clap ye into a cage.'

'Cage?' said Nod.

'Ay, in a stinking cage, with iron bars, for the rabble to jeer at. What would the monkeys do with a White Man, an Oomgar, if they cotched 'n?'

'In my father Seelem's hut over there,' said Nod, waving his long hand towards the Sulemnāgar, 'Oomgar's bones hanged click, click, click in the wind.'

Battle stared. 'They hates us, eh? Picks us clean!'

Nod looked at him gravely. 'Mulla-Mulgar – me – not hate Oomgar. All Munza' – he lifted his brows – 'ay! he kill and eat, eat, eat, same as leopard, same as Jaccatray.'

Battle frowned. 'It's tit for tat, my son. I kills Roses, or Roses kills me. Not a Jack-All that howls moon up over yonder that wouldn't say grace for a picking. But apes and monkeys, no; not even a warty old drumming Pongo that's twice as ugly as his own shadow in the glass. I never did burn powder 'gainst a monkey yet. What's more,' said Battle, 'who's to know but we was all what you calls Oomgars once? Good as. You've just come down in the world, that's all. And who's to blame ye? No barbers, no ships, no larnin', no nothing. Breeches? – One pair, my son, to half a million, as far as Andy ever set eyes on. Maybe you came from that wicked King Pharaoh over in Egypt there. Maybe you was one of the plagues, and scuttled off with all the fleas.' He grinned cheerfully. Nod watched his changing face, but what he said now he could not understand.

'There's just one thing, Master Mulgar,' went on Battle solemnly. 'Kill or not kill, hairy as hairy, or bald as a round-shot, God made us every one. And speakin' comfortable-like, 'twixt you and me, just as my old mother taught me years gone by, I planks me down on my knees like any babby this very hour gone by, while you was sliding in your shoes, and said me prayers out loud. I'm getting mortal sick of being lonesome. Not that I blames *you*, my son. You're better company than fifty million parakeets, and seven-and-seventy Mullagoes of blackamoors.'

Nod stared gravely. 'Oomgar talk; Nod unnerstand – no.' He sorrowfully shook his head.

'My case all over,' said Battle. 'Andy unnerstand – no. But there, we'll off to England, my son, soon as ever this mortal frost breaks. Years and years have I been in this here dismal Munza. Man-eaters and Ephelantoes, Portingals and blackamoors, chased and harassed up and down, and never a spark of frost seen, unless on the Snowy Mountains. What wouldn't I give for a sight of Plymouth now!'

He rose and stretched himself. Facing him, across the unstirring darkness of the forest, shone palely the great new-risen moon. ' "Hi, hi, up she rises," ' said Battle, staring over. ' "But what's to be done with a shipwrecked sailor?" Nobody knows, but who can't tell us. Now, just one stave, Nod Mulgar, afore we both turns in. Give us "Cherry-trees". No, maybe I'll pipe ye one of Andy's own, and you

119

shall jine in, same as t'other.' Nod climbed up and stood on
his log, his hands clasped behind his neck, and stamped
softly with his feet in time, while Battle, after tuning up his
great gourd – or Juddie, as he called it – plucked the sounding strings. And soon the Oomgar's voice burst out so loud
and fearless that the prowling panthers paused with cowering head and twitching ears, and the Jaccatrays out of the
shadows lifted their cringing eyes up to the moon, dolefully
listening. And when the last two lines of each verse had
been sung, Battle plucked more loudly at his strings, and
Nod joined in.

Once and there was a young sailor, yeo ho!
    And he sailèd out over the say
For the isles where pink coral and palm-branches blow,
    And the fire-flies turn night into day,
                Yeo ho!
    And the fire-flies turn night into day.

But the *Dolphin* went down in a tempest, yeo ho!
    And with three forsook sailors ashore,
The Portingals took him where sugar-canes grow,
    Their slave for to be evermore,
                Yeo ho!
    Their slave for to be evermore.

With his musket for mother and brother, yeo ho!
    He warred wi' the Cannibals drear,
In forests where panthers pad soft to and fro,
    And the Pongo shakes noonday with fear,
                Yeo ho!
    And the Pongo shakes noonday with fear.

Now lean with long travail, all wasted with woe,
    With a monkey for messmate and friend,
He sits 'neath the Cross in the cankering snow,
    And waits for his sorrowful end,
                Yeo ho!
    And waits for his sorrowful end.

120

This song sung, Nod danced the Jaqquas' War-Dance, which Battle had taught him, stooping and crooked, 'wriggle and stamp', gnashing his teeth, waving a club – which waving, indeed, always waved Nod sprawling off his log before long, and set Battle rolling with laughter, and ended the dance.

That dance danced, they sat quiet awhile, Battle softly, very softly, thruming on his Juddie, gazing into the fire. And suddenly in the silence, out of the vast blackness of the moonlit leagues beneath them, broke a strange and dismal cry. It rose lone and hollow, and yet it seemed with its sound to fill the whole enormous bowl of star-be-dazzling sky above the forest. Then down it lingeringly fell, note by note, wailing and menacing, an answering song of hatred against the solitary Oomgar and his gun.

Battle caught up his musket and stood erect, facing with scowling eyes the vast silence of the forest. And instantly from far and near, solitary and in hunting-bands, deep and shrill, every beast that slinks and lies in wait beneath the moon broke into its hunting-cry.

Battle stood listening with a savage grin on his face, until the last echo had died away. Then, throwing down his musket, he hitched up the cloth bandage on his shoulder, lifted his great Juddie, and strode out from the fire a few paces till he stood black and solitary in the moonlight of the snow. And he plucked the girding strings and roared out with all his lungs his mocking answer:

Voice without a body,
Panther of black Roses,
Jack-Alls fat on icicles,
Ephelanto, Aligatha,
Zevvera and Jaccatray,
Unicorn and River-horse;
      Ho, ho, ho!
Here's Andy Battle,
Waiting for the enemy!

Imbe Calandola,
M'keeso and Quesanga,
Dondo and Sharammba,
Pongo and Enjekko,
Millions of monkeys,
Rattlesnake and scorpion,
Swamp and death and shadow;
      Ho, ho, ho!
Come on, all of ye,
Here's Andy Battle,
Waiting and – alone!

He swept his great scarred thumb over the strings with a
resounding flourish, and burst into a laugh. Then he turned
his back on the unanswering forest, and sat down by the
fire again, wiping the sweat from his face and combing out
his tangled beard. Nod drew a little away from the fire, and
sat softly watching him. The Oomgar was muttering with
wide-open lids. He snatched up a lump of the cold Mulgar-
bread that Nod had cooked for his supper, and gnawed it
with twitching fingers. He glanced over it with bright blue
glittering eyes at his little hunched-up friend.

'Don't you have no shadow of fear, my son. If they come,
come they must. Just you skip off into the forest with your
courage where your tail ought to be. I care not a pinch of
powder for them or'nery beasts. It's that there Shadowlegs
that beats me with her mewling. I've heard it down on the

coast; I've heard it with the Portingals; I've heard it with the Andalambandees; I've heard it wake and sleep. But witch-beast or no witch-beast, and every skulk-by-night that creeps on claws, I'll win home yet!' He kicked a few loose smoking logs into the blaze. 'More fire, my son! I like a light to fight by when fighting comes.'

The darkness was clear as glass. The sky seemed shaken as if with fire-flies. Not a sound stirred now, not even a hovering wing. Nod heaped high the huge fire, and followed the Oomgar into his hut.

But not to sleep. He crouched on his snug dry bed of moss, and waited patiently till Battle's snores rose slow and mournful beneath the snow-piled roof. Then very quickly he put on his sheep's-coat over his Juzanda jacket and breeches. He crawled out, and lifted down with both hands the heavy bar of the door, and stole out into the moonlight again. He thrust his puckered hand under his jacket, and touched his skinny breast-bone, beneath which, ever since the Little Horse of Tishnar had toppled him into the snow, he had felt the slumbering Wonderstone strangely burning. And, as if even Oomgar magic, too, might help him, he hobbled back into the hut and put Battle's little dog's-eared book into his pocket. Then, before his heart could fail him, he ran out as fast as his stumpy legs would carry him to where he had heard rise up in the night the Hunting-Song of Immanâla.

On the extreme verge of the steep, opposite Battle's hut, stood a solitary flat-headed rock beside the frozen stream. Here the water burst in a blaze of moonlight into a cascade of icicles and foam. Nod stood there in the rock's shadow awhile, looking down into the forest. And as if a little cloud had come upon the glittering moon, he felt, as it were, a sudden darkness above his head, and a cold terror crept over his skin.

Then he stepped, trembling, out of the shadow of the

rock into the moonlight,
and gazed up into the
shadowy countenance of
Immanâla. She lay gaunt
and spare, her long neck
touching the snow, her
eye-balls beneath their
wide lids fixed glassily on
Nod. He gazed and gazed, until it seemed he was sinking
down, down into those wide unstirring eyes.

His heart seemed to rise up into his mouth. He coughed,
and something hard and round and tingling slid on to his
tongue. He put up his hand to his thick lips, and, like
courage that steals into the mind when all else is vain, fell
into his hand, milk-pale and magical, the long-hidden
Wonderstone.

'I couch here, Ummanodda,' said the Nameless, without
stirring, 'night after night, hungry and thirsty, waiting for
the Oomgar's head. Why does the Mulla-Mulgar keep me
waiting so long for my supper?'

'Because, O Queen of Shadows,' said Nod as calmly as
he could – 'because the head of the Oomgar refused to come
without his legs – and his gun.'

'Nay,' said she, 'there must be many a shallow gourd in

the Oomgar's hut. Cut off the head, and bring it hither yourself in that.'

'*Ohé*,' said Nod, 'the Nameless has sharp teeth, if all that is said be true. She shall cut, and I will carry. Princes of Tishnar have no tongue for blood.'

Immanâla crouched low, with jutting head. 'Who is this Prince of Tishnar that, having no tongue for blood, roasts meat with fire for an Oomgar, the enemy of us all?'

'I, Nameless, am Nod,' said he softly. 'But meat dead is dead meat. What against *me* is it if this blind Oomgar hungers for scorched bones? It is a riddle, Immanâla. Come with me now, then; let us palaver with him together.'

'Yea, together!' snarled the Nameless – 'I to ride and thou to carry.' She gathered herself as if to spring.

Nod whispered, 'O Tishnar!' and he stood stock-still.

Immanâla drew back her flat grey head from the snow, and shook it, softly glancing at the moon.

'Why, O Prince of Tishnar, should we be at strife one with another? We hate the Oomgar. And if it were not for this magic that is yours, my servants would have slain him long since in his hunting.'

'Ah, me!' said Nod, sighing it in Mulgar-Royal, as if to himself alone, 'I myself love this Oomgar none too much. Did he not catch me walking lonely in Munza in a wild pig snare? If he is to die, let him die, says Nod. But I like not your fashion of hunting, Beast of Shadows, skulking and creeping and scaring off his wandering supper-meat. Bring your hunting-dogs into the open snow here out of their dens and lairs and shadows. Then shall the Oomgar fight like an Oomgar, one against a hundred, and Nod can go free!'

Immanâla rose bristling against the clearness of the moon.

'Tell me, Prince of Tishnar, what is this story you seem to be whispering about my hunting-dogs?'

And Nod, with his Wonderstone clipped tight in his hot

palm, bethought him of all Mishcha's counsel, and promised Immanâla he would come down the next night following. And if she would call her packs into the ravine, he would lead them, and open the door of the hut and lure out the Oomgar. 'Then you, O fearless Queen of Shadows, shall watch the hunt in peace,' he said. 'One forsaken Oomgar without his gun against nine-and-ninety Jack-Alls and Jaccatrays, and perhaps a Roses or two, famished and parched with cold. Ay, but before I whistle them up,' he muttered, as if to himself, 'I must steal the Oomgar's M'Keeso's coat, which is drenched through with magic.'

Immanâla peered gloatingly from her rock. 'The little Mulla-Mulgar has a cunning face,' she said, 'and a heart of many devices. I have heard of his comings and goings in Munza-Mulgar. But if he deals falsely with me, though Tishnar came herself in all her brightness, I would wait and wait. Not an Utt nor a Nikka-nikka but should be his enemy, and as for those magicless Mulla-Mulgars, his brothers, who even now squat sullen and hungry in their leafy houses, they shall lie cold as stones before the morning light.'

'Why,' said Nod softly, 'he must be frightened who begins to threaten. I have no fear of you, O Nameless, who are but a creeping candle-fly at twilight to the blaze of Tishnar's moon. Come hither to-morrow with your half-starved hunting-dogs, and I'll show you good hunting, will I.'

Without another word, with every hair on end, he ran swiftly back to the hut by the way he had come. But even now his night's doings were not ended, for in a while, by which time the Immanâla should have returned from her watching-rock into the shadows of the forest, he ran out again, and, crouching beneath the old Exxzwixxia-bush under the Sulemnāgar, he called softly: 'Mishcha, old hare! Mishcha!'

When he had called her many times, she came slowly and

warily limping across the chequered snow. And Nod told her of all he had done that night, and of how he had met and abashed the Nameless face to face. The old hare watched dimly his flashing eyes and the vainglory of the face of the young Mulgar Prince boasting in his finery, and she grimly smiled.

'*Chakka, chakka*,' says she; '*tchackka, tchackka*: you bleed before you're wounded, Mulgar-Royal.'

But Nod in the heat of his glory cared nothing for what his old friend said to quench it. And he told her to bring his brothers to the great Ukka-tree that stood over against the shadow, where they talked, there to wait and watch till morning. 'By that time,' he said, 'I shall have finished my supper with the Nameless, and the Oomgar will know me for the Prince I am.'

Mishcha wagged slowly her old head. She hated the Oomgar, but she hated the Beast of Shadows more, and off she hopped again, stiff and cold, to seek out Thimble and Thumb.

CHAPTER ELEVEN

Jack-Alls

Battle went out hunting as usual the next morning. Tracks of leopards were everywhere in the night's thin snow. He ventured not far into the forest, and returned with only a poor old withered bird, too cold and weak to fly off from his gun.

'It's this way, my son,' he said; 'I've heard the thing before. The howl brings half the forest against me, like blue-flies to meat. So all I does is to keep a weather-eye open, and musket a-cock. One of these days, Mulgar *mio*, Shadow or no Shadow, she shall have a brace of bullets in her vitals, as sure as my name's Battle.' But in spite of his fine words, he crouched gloomy and distracted beside his fire all day, casting ever and anon a stealthy glance over his shoulder, and lifting his eye slowly above the flames, to survey the clustering fringe of the forest around his hut.

But Nod told Battle nothing of his talk with the old hare. He did not as much as tell him even that his brothers were near, or that he had seen Immanâla. He cleaned his master's gun. He busied himself over his Nano-cakes and nuts, and prevailed on Battle to eat by making him laugh at his antics. The more he thought of leaving him, and of the danger of the coming night, and the stony cruelty of Immanâla's gloating eyes, his heart fell deeper and deeper into trouble and dismay. But each time when it seemed he must run away and hide himself he gulped his terror down, and touched his Wonderstone.

He himself lugged out Battle's Juddie when evening fell. But Battle had no mind for merriment and braveries that night. He picked out idly on the strings old mournful chanties that sailors sometimes sing; and he taught Nod a new song to bray out in his queer voice, 'She's me forgot':

> Me who have sailèd
>   Leagues across
> Foam haunted
>   By the albatross,
> Time now hath made
>   Remembered not:
> Ay, my dear love
>   Hath me forgot.
>
> Oh, how should she,
>   Whose beauty shone,
> Keep true to one
>   Such long years gone?
> Grief cloud those eyes! –
>   I ask it not:
> Content am I –
>   She's me forgot.
>
> Here where the evening
>   Ooboë wails,
> Bemocking
>   England's nightingales,
> Bravely, O sailor,
>   Take thy lot;
> Nor grieve too much,
>   She's thee forgot!

But even between his slow-drawled shakety notes of deep and shrill Nod listened for the least stir in the forest, and seemed to hear the low, hungry calls and scamperings of Immanâla's hunting pack which she had summoned from far and near to the tangled ravine beneath the rock.

He got Battle early to bed by telling him he would dress his wounded shoulder, which was angry and inflamed, with a poultice of leaves such as his mother, Mutta-matutta, had taught him to make. 'Now,' says he, 'it is broad full-moontime, master, and all Munza-Mulgar will be gone hunting. But wake not. Nod, Prince of Tishnar, will watch'; and even as he said it came remembrance of the Pigs to mind.

Battle laughed, thinking what wondrous good sense these two-legged monkeys seemed to have, concerning which King Angeca had yet himself often assured him that it is all nothing but a show and pretence, since man alone has wisdom and knowledge, and little remains over for the beasts' share.

The warmth and sleepiness of his big poultice soon set him snoring. And in a blaze of moonlight Nod warily opened the door, and stood in the squat black shadow of the hut, looking out over the forest. He had bound himself up tight. He had wound up his Wonderstone in a piece of lead that he had found in the hut to keep it from hopping in his pocket, and had stuck the sailor's sharp sheath-knife down the leg of his breeches.

Then, like but an Utt or a gnome in that great waste of whiteness he sallied out to destroy the Nameless. He came to the rock, but no shadow couched there now in the sheen. He crept on all fours, and between two great frost-lit boulders peeped into the ravine. There, changing and stir-

130

ring, shone the numberless small green lanterns of the eyes of Immanâla's hunting-pack. He heard their low whinings and the soft crunch of their clawed feet in the snow. Else all was still.

And Nod called in a low voice: 'Why do you hide from me, Immanâla, Queen of Shadows?'

He waited, but no answer came. 'Venture out, mistress,' cried Nod louder, 'and we will be off together to the Oomgar's hut. You shall sit on the roof and watch the hunting-dogs at their supper.'

At that, up by a narrow path from the ravine stole Immanâla, and all the Jack-Alls and Jaccatrays fell silent, staring with blazing eyes out of the darkness.

'Call not so lustily, Prince of Tishnar,' she said, fawning; 'we shall awake the Oomgar.'

'*Ohé*,' said Nod boldly; 'he sleeps deep. He fears neither beast nor Meermut in all this frozen Munza. Bid your greedy slaves stand ready, Immanâla. When I whistle them supper is up.'

Immanâla lifted her flat grey head, and seemed to listen. 'I hear the harps of Tishnar in the forest. The leaves of the branches of the trees of my master Noomanossi stir, and yet there moves no wind.'

She fixed her colourless eyes on Nod, with her ears on her long, smooth forehead pricked forward. 'What is the cunning Mulgar thinking beneath all he says? Like fine sand in water, I hear the rustling of his thoughts.'

Nod took a long breath and shut his eyes. 'I was thinking,' he said, 'what stupid fellows must be these dogs of yours, seeing that each and every one keeps whimpering "The head – the head for me!" But they must wait in patience yet a little longer, if even a knuckle-bone is to be a share. I will go forward and choose out all that I and the Mulla-Mulgars, my brothers, want of the Oomgar's house-treasures before the Jaccatrays tear everything to pieces.'

'Softly, now, softly,' said Immanâla. 'You think very little of me, Nizza-neela. Do you dream I came from far to protect you from my slaves, Roses and Jaccatray, and now am to get nothing for my pains? What of that stiff coat drenched with magic? That is mine. No, no, little greedy Mulgar; we share together, or I have all.'

'Well, well,' said Nod, as if unwilling, 'you shall take part, mistress, though all that's there is truly Tishnar's. Follow quietly! I will see if my Zbaffle be still asleep.'

Immanâla crouched snarling in the moonlight, and Nod ran swiftly to the hut. The moon streamed in on the sailor's upturned face, where, lying flat on his back, he snored and snored and snored. Then Nod very quietly took down from its wooden hook the sailor's great skin coat, his belt of Ephelanto-hide, his huge hair hat, all such as in his wanderings he had captured from black Kings and men of magic. He filled the pockets, he stuffed them with bullets and copper rings and stones and lumps of ice – everything heavy that he could find. At the rattling of the stones Battle rolled over, muttering hoarsely in his sleep. Nod stopped instantly and listened. No words he understood. Then once more he set to work and soon had dragged the huge stiff coat and hat and belt one by one over the door-log into the snow.

'Hither, come hither! Hasten, mistress!' he called softly, capering round about them. 'Here's a sight to cheer your royal heart! Here's riches! What have we here but the magic coat which the Oomgar stripped from the M'keeso of the old Lord Shillambansa, that feeds a hundred peacocks on his grave?'

Softly as a shadow, and crouching low on her belly in the snow, Immanâla drew near; paused; sniffed; and sniffed again.

'Fear not, Beast of Shadows,' cried Nod softly, 'the Oomgar sleeps like moss on the Tree of Everlasting.'

And all her vanity and greed welled up in the heart of the creature; for whosoever her dam may be, and all her lineage of solitude and strangeness, she has more greed than a wolf, more vanity than a vixen. She thrust her long lean head into the Cap.

'Do but now let me help you, mistress,' said Nod, 'as I used to help the Oomgar. Stand upright, and I will thrust your arms into the sleeves. We must hasten, but we must be quiet.' At every glance her smouldering eyes grew brighter. Nod heaved and tugged till his thick fur lay dank on his poll, and at last the dreadful Beast was draped and mantled from ears to tail in the Oomgar's coat.

'Now for the Dondo's belt of sorcery,' said Nod. 'Sure, none will dare sneeze in Munza-Mulgar when the sailorman is gone.' He put the thick belt round her lean body, though his head swam with her muskiness, and drew it tight beneath the buckle.

'Gently, gently, little brother!' sighed Immanâla. 'It is heavy, and I scarce can breathe.'

'The very Oomgar himself used often to snort,' said Nod.

'But why does he keep so many stones in his pocket?' pined Immanâla.

'Why, Queen of Wisdom! What if the wind should blow and all his magic flit away? Ay, ay, ay! stripped from the M'keeso of the dead Lord Shillambansa came this coat into my Messimut's hands, who feeds five hundred peacocks on his grave! And now his wondrous Cap of Hair! Nine Fulbies, as I live, were flayed to skin that cap withal,' said Nod, 'and seven rogue Ephelantoes gave the Oomgar of their tails.'

'Ah yes, ah yes!' groaned Immanâla; 'but what are seventy Ephelantoes compared with Immanâla, Queen of All?'

'Now,' said Nod, 'I will weary myself no more with speeches. Is it warm?'

133

'I am in a furnace; I burn.'

'Is it too loose? Does it wrinkle? Does it sag?'

'Oh, but I can breathe but a mouthful at a time!'

'Last and last again, then,' said Nod, packing into the pockets one or two of the stones and bullets and lumps of ice that had fallen out, 'is it comfortable?'

'O my friend, my scarce-wise Mulgar-Royal, when did you ever hear that grand clothes were comfortable?'

'Wait but a little moment, then, while I go in to fetch the magic-glass, that will show you your face, Immanâla, handsome and lovesome.'

The Beast struggled faintly in her magic coat. 'Have a care – oh, have a care, Ummanodda! The gun, the gun! The Oomgar might wake. Let me creep swiftly to my stone, and bring the glass to me there.'

'The Oomgar will not wake,' said Nod; 'he sleeps as deep as the Ghost of the Rose upon the bosom of Tishnar.'

'But, O Mulgar, think again. Strip off from my body this grievous belt,' she pleaded; 'you will keep nothing for yourself.'

'Have no fear, friend,' said Nod shakily; 'I will keep' – and his eyes met hers in the shadow of the hat, stony and merciless and ravenous – 'I will keep,' he grunted, 'my Zbaffle.'

He went into the hut and seated himself on a little stool. Then very carefully he took the Wonderstone out of his pocket and unwrapped it. Its pale gleam mingled softly with the moonlight, as a rainbow mingles with foam. Wetting his left thumb with spittle, he rubbed it softly, softly, Samaweeza, three times round. And distant and clear as the shining of a star a voice seemed to cry 'The Spirit of Tishnar answers, Prince Ummanodda Nizza-neela; what dost thou require of me?'

'Oh, by Tishnar, only this,' said Nod, trembling, 'that the nine-and-ninety hunting-dogs in their hunting mistake the ravening Beast of Shadows, Immanâla, for the sailor-man, Zbaffle, my master and friend.'

And surely, when Nod looked out from the doorway, it seemed that, strange and terrible, the shape muffled within the Oomgar's coat was swollen out, stretched lean and tall, Oomgar-like, that even lank gold hair dangled on her shoulders from beneath the furry cap. It seemed he heard a faraway crying and crying, out of that monstrous bale, as the creature within, standing hidden from the moonlight, began to sway and stir and totter over the snow. And Nod, choking with terror, called one word only – *'Sulâni!'* Then, with all his force, he whistled once, twice, thrice, clear and loud and long and shrill; then he shut fast the door and barred it, and went and crouched beside the Oomgar's bed.

Already Battle was wide awake. 'Ahoy!' said he, and started up and thrust out his hand for his gun.

'Steady – oh, steady, Oomgar Zbaffle!' said Nod. 'It is dogs of the Immanâla only, that soon will be gone.'

Even as he spoke rose out of the distance a dreadful bay-ing and howling. Battle leapt up out of his bed to the window-hole. But Nod squatted shivering, his face hidden in his hands.

'Ghost of me! What is it?' said Battle to himself. 'What beast is this they're after – M'keeso, or Man of the Woods?'

It reeled, it fell, it rose up; it wheeled slowly, faintly weeping and whining, and then stood still, with arms lifted high, struggling like a man with a great burden. But over the crudded snow, like a cloud across the moon, streamed with brindled hair on end, jaws gaping and flaming eyes, the hungry pack of the Shadow's hunting-dogs. 'Oomgar, Oomgar, Oomgar, Oomgar!' they yelled one to another. 'Immanâla, Immanâla, death, death, death!' And pre-sently, while Battle in amazement watched, there came one miserable cry of fear and pain. The tottering shape seemed to melt, to vanish.

Then Nod scampered and opened the door.

'What say you now, hunting-dogs? Was the Oomgar tender or tough?'

'Tough, tough!' they yelled.

'Go, then, and tell your mistress, Queen of Shadows, Immanâla, that you have supped with the Prince of Tishnar, and are satisfied.'

'Why lurks the little Mulgar in the Oomgar's hut?' yelped a lank hoary Jaccatray.

'I guard her treasures for the Nameless,' said Nod; but he had hardly said the word when he heard Battle striding to the door.

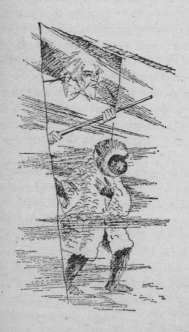

'It's no good prattling and blabbing, my son,' he was saying. 'If come it be, it's come. Off now, while your skin's whole, and let me give the rogues a taste of powder.'

Two or three of the hunting-dogs yelped aloud. 'What, my brothers!' said Nod. 'Did you hear the Oomgar's Meermut calling for his gun?'

A few of the meaner dogs scampered off a few paces at this, sniffing and cocking their ears.

'Out of the way, Pongo,' whispered the Englishman through the doorway, and the next moment there fell a crash that nearly toppled Nod into the snow, and Battle strode out of the hut with his smoking musket. But the cowardly Jack-Alls, at sound of his gun and at sight of the ghost of the Oomgar they had torn to pieces, lifted up their voices in a howl of terror, and in an instant over the snow they swept off at a gallop, and soon were lost in the moonless silence and shadowiness of Munza.

Nod turned towards the hut. Battle stood in his breeches, his gun in his hand, his blue eyes wide open as if in fear.

CHAPTER TWELVE

Good-bye: and On

'What's these, what's these?' he muttered, for there, on the farther bank of the stream, stood in the twilight of the sinking moon two strange, solitary figures, motionless, staring. Nod ran to Battle, and laid his long, narrow hand on the glimmering gun-barrel. 'Oh, not shoot, not shoot!' he said, 'black Oomgars – no; Mulla-Mulgars, too. Nod's friends, Nod's brothers!'

'What's he jabbering about?' said Battle, with eyes fixed brightly on the two gaunt shapes.

'Nod's brothers, there,' said Nod – 'Thumb, Thimble, Thimble, Thumb. Nod show Oomgar. Oh, wait softly!' He ran swiftly over the snow till he came to the frozen bank of the stream. But still his brothers never stirred, ragged and hollow-eyed with hunger and cold.

'Come,' said Nod, lifting up his hands in salutation; 'there is no fear, no danger! Here is Nod, my brothers.'

'What voice was that we heard?' said Thumb, trembling. 'Can the mouth of the Oomgar speak after it is shut in death?'

'The Oomgar is not dead, Thumb, my brother; the hunting-packs killed only that Beast of Shadows, Immanâla, who hoped to kill us all, and the Oomgar too. Come over, my brothers! Every day, every night, Nod has talked in his quiet with you.'

'We do not understand the little Oomgar,' said Thimble angrily. 'Who are you, the youngest of us all, to lie and make cunning against the people of the forest? Let your master, the blood-spilling Oomgar, shoot us, too. What are we in such a heap of bones? We have no fear of him. On all fours, back, parakeet; tell him where the Mulgars' hearts lie hid. Maybe he'll fling his Nizza-neela a bone.'

'O Thimble, Mulla-Mulgar, why do you seek out all the black words for me? Haven't I done all for the best? Did I play false with you when I saved you from the spits of the Minimuls? The Little Horse of Tishnar smelt out my wounded shoulder. And the Oomgar's strangling trap caught me. But he did not kill me. He took me, and was kind to me, fed me and shared his fire with me, and we were "messimuts". Yet all day, all night, moon and no-moon, I have talked in myself with you, and run looking for you in my dreams, while I slept in the hairless Oomgar's hut. The Nameless is gone for a little while. The Oomgar is wise with his hands and in little things. Now I may go. He kills only for meat, Mulla-Mulgars. He will do no harm to Ummanodda's brothers. Come over with me!'

Thumb and Thimble, with toes a little turned in, and heads bent forward, stood listening in the snow.

'Why, then,' said Thumb, muttering, 'if he kills only for food, and relishes not his own flavour in the pot, let him hobble out here to us now and greet us, like with like – Oomgar-Mulgar with Mulla-Mulgar – and leave his spit-fire and his magic behind him. But into his hut, nor stum-

bling among his Munza bones, we will *not* go. And if he will not come, brother to brother, then it is *"Gar Mulgar dusangee"* between us three, O youngest son of Seelem. Go back to your cooking-pots. I and Thimble will journey on alone. All day would the Harp-strings be twangling over Mulgars smelling of blood.'

So Nod, cold with misery, went back to Battle, who sat yawning, gun on knee, beside his fire.

'Oomgar!' he said, leaning a little on one small hand, and standing a few paces distant from the sailor, 'my brothers, the Mulla-Mulgars, sons of Seelem, brother of Assasimmon, Prince of the Valleys of Tishnar, are here. They say Nod is not true, speaks lies, eater-of-flesh, no child of Tishnar.' He stared forlornly into Battle's face. 'Tired of his living is Nod now. Shoot straight with Oomgar Zbaffle's gun. Nod will be still.'

The Englishman crinkled up his eyelids, opened his mouth, and burst out laughing.

'To tell ye sober truth, my son,' he said, 'bullets and powder Battle haven't much left to waste. And what's lark-pie to a hungry sailor! As for them hunched-up hobba-goblins over younder, don't 'ee heed what envy has to say. Battle is hands down on your side, my son, and let 'em meddle if they dare! But mercy on us,' he added under his breath, 'what wouldn't my old mother have said to hear these Pongoes chatter? "Shoot straight!" says he. "Tired of his living!" says he. Button up your sheep's-jacket, my son.

140

We'll home to England yet. And, what's more' – he waved his hand towards the lonely figures still standing motionless in the silvery dusk – 'Andy Battle's best respects to the hairy gentlemen, and there's a warm welcome and fresh-picked bones for breakfast. But the night's creeping cold, and bed's bed, old friend, and Andy's eyes was never made for moth-hunting. So here goes.' He went in with his gun, and Nod heard him shut and bar the door.

Nod listened awhile, with eyes fixed sorrowfully on the fast-shut door; then, having heaped more logs on to the fire, he went slowly back to his brothers.

Now that the moon was down, and night at its darkest, the frost hardened. And Thumb and Thimble, when they were sure the Oomgar was asleep in his hut, were glad enough to hobble across the ice and to sit and warm themselves before the fire. Their jackets hung in tatters. Thumb's left second toe was frost-bitten, and Thimble's eyes were so sore from the glaring whiteness of the snow he could only dimly see. Moreover, they were weary of living and sleeping in their tree-houses among the scatter-brained Forest-Mulgars, and though at first they sat shaky and sniffing, and started if but a dry leaf snapped in the fire, they listened in silence to Nod's long story of his doings, and began to see at last that what he had done by Mishcha's counsel had been for the best, and not for his own sake only.

'But we cannot stay here, Ummanodda,' said Thumb. 'We could not rub noses with the Oomgar. His voice, his smell! He is not of our kind, little brother. And now that all the peoples of Munza-Mulgar are our enemies, we must press on, with no more idling and fine eating and sitting shanks to fire, or we shall never reach the Valleys alive.'

'I am ready, Thumb, my brother,' Nod answered. 'The Oomgar has been kind to me, his own kind's kind. It was my Tishnar's Wonderstone that saved him from the teeth of the Nine-and-ninety, and from Immanâla's magic, though why should I tell it is so? Now they will think it is his skin-bonneted Meermut that stalks to and fro with the ghost-gun of a ghost. They will forsake this place, every one – claw and talon, upright and fours, everyone. How long shall a flesheater, hungry and gluttonous, live on dried berries and nuts? Me gone; unless the frost flies soon, or a great Bobberie, as he does say, comes up from that strange water, the Sea, over yonder, the Oomgar will die. O brothers, just as that Oomgar, the Portingal, died whose bones dangled over us when we stood by Mutta's knee and listened to them clicking. Do but let me stay to say good-bye, and we will go together at morning!'

So, when day began to break, Thumb and Thimble hastened away and hid themselves in the Ukka-trees till Nod should come out to them. Nod busied himself, and baked his last feast with his master. He broiled him some bones – they were little else – of the Jack-All the sailor had shot in the moonlight. And when Battle – strange and solitary as he seemed to Nod now, after talking with and looking on his brothers – when Battle opened the door and came out, Nod told him as best he could, in the few words of his English, of Immanâla and her hunting-dogs, and of his brothers. And he told him that he must leave him now, and go on his travels again.

Battle listened, scratching his head, and with a patient, perplexed grin on his face, but he could understand only very little of what Nod meant. For even a Mulla-Mulgar, though he can repeat like a child, or like a parrot, by rote, has small brains for really learning another language, so that it may be a telling picture of his thoughts. Indeed, Battle thought that poor Nod had fallen a little crazy with the cold. He fondled him and scratched his head – this Prince of Tishnar – as if he were at his hearth at home, and Nod his parlour cat. But at least he knew that the little

Mulgar wished to leave him, and he made no hindrance except his own sadness to his going.

He gave him out of his own pocket a silver groat with a hole in it, and a large piece of fine looking-glass, besides the necklet of clear blue Bamba-beads, and three rings of copper. He gave him, too, one leaf of his little fat book, and in this Nod wrapped his Wonderstone. Nor even in his kindness did Battle say the least word about his big coat and Ephelanto-belt and his Fulby's hairy hat – all which things he supposed (Mulgars being by nature thieves and robbers in his mind) Nod's brothers had stolen.

'Good-bye, my son,' he said. ' "Bravely, ole sailor, take your lot!" There, there; I make no dwelling on fine words. Good-bye, and don't forget your larnin'. There's many a full-growed Christian Battle's come acrost in his seafarin' – but there, flattery butters no parsnips. Good-bye, once more, Mulgar *mio*, and thankee kindly.'

Nod raised his hands above his head. '*Oomgar, Oomgar*,' he said, with eyes shut and trembling lips, '*ah-mi, ah-mi; sulâni ghar magleer*.' Then, with a heavy heart, he turned away, and without looking back ran scampering as fast as he could to the five Ukka-trees. His brothers had long been awaiting him, and swung down gladly from their sleeping bowers in the trees. Then with the hut and the Oomgar's pillar of smoke upon their cudgel-hand they set out once more, all but due north, towards the Valleys of Assasimmon.

CHAPTER THIRTEEN

The Quarrel

The sun rose and beat down on the bare expanse of snow. But soon they lurched headlong down again into the forest. But it was forest not so dense as the forest of the Minimul mounds, nor by a tenth part as dark as the forest where haunts the Telateuti. At scent of Nod every small beast and bird scuttled off or flew away. And it was dreary marching for the travellers where all that lived feared even their savour on the wind. But by evening they had pushed on past Battle's farthest hunting, and being wearied with their long day's march, nor any tracks of leopards to be seen, they made no fire with their fire-sticks, but gathered a big heap of dry leaves scattered in abundance by this strange cold, this Witzaweelwnllah, and huddled themselves close for warmth in sleep.

Next day they broke out into the open again, and before them, clear as amber or coral, still and beautiful in the sunrise, rose afar off upon the horizon the solitary peaks, which are seven – Kush, Zut, Kippel, Solmi, Makkri, Moot, and Mulgar-meerez – the Mountains of Arakkaboa.

All this day they trudged on in difficulty and discomfort, for the ground was sharp and stony, and sloped now perpetually upward. And though at first sight of them it had seemed they need but stretch out a finger to touch the mountain-tops, they found now that the farther they journeyed towards them, the more distant seemed these wonderful peaks to be. And their spirits began to sink within them.

On the evening of the fifth day Thumb and Thimble

were stooping together over their firesticks in a great waste of bare rocks, while Nod was pounding up a sweet but unknown fruit they had found in their day's march growing close upon the ground, when suddenly they heard in the distance a hubbub of shouts and cries the like of which they had never heard in their lives before. They hastily concealed their small bundles of food in a crevice of the rocks, and, creeping cautiously, peered out in the last rays of the sun in order to discover the cause of this prodigious uproar.

And they saw advancing towards them a vast host and multitude of the painted Babbabooma-Mulgars, travelling, as is their custom, in company across these desolate wastes. On they came rapidly, the biggest males on the margins. But presently, while they were yet some little way off, at the sound of a great shout all came to a standstill (the sun now being set) to take up their night-quarters. Even in the fading light their body-colours glowed, scarlet and purple, and bright Candar blue, where, squatting in their hundreds at supper (some meanwhile pacing sedately on the outskirts of the company like watchmen, to and fro on all fours, with long, doglike snouts and jutting teeth) they made their evening encampment.

All that night our Mulla-Mulgars never ventured to kindle a fire. They huddled together as best they could in a crevice in the rocks, warmed only by their own hairy bodies. For they had heard of old from Seelem how these Babbabooma troops resent with ferocity the least meddling with them. They will speedily stone to death any intruder, and will tear a leopard in pieces with their teeth. But the travellers, all three, curiously, cautiously peeping out, watched their doings while there was the least light left, taking good care that not a spark of their jackets should be seen, for these Babbaboomas fret more fiercely even than our bulls at the colour red.

They watched them sprinkling, scratching themselves,

like the Mullabruks, with their feet, and dusting their great bodies with dry snow, rubbing it in with their hands, though for what purpose, seeing that snow had never whitened their pilgrimages before, who can say? The children, the Karakeena-Babbaboomas, squealed and frisked and gambolled in the last sunshine together, quarrelling and at play. The old men sat silent, munching with half-closed eyes, and watching them. And it seemed that the big shes of the Babbaboomas had brought some small tufty, goatlike animals with them, which they now sat milking into pots or gourds. And with this milk they presently fed the littlest of the young ones.

For many hours after the sun had gone down the three brothers sat wide awake, whispering together, listening to the talk and palaver of the chiefs of the Babbaboomas. Sometimes they seemed to be clamouring, fifty together; then presently a great still voice would be lifted over them, and all would fall silent; while of his calm authority the master-voice said, 'So shall it be,' or 'Thus do we make it.' Then once more the clamour of the rabble would break out again. But what its meaning was, and whether they were merely gossiping together, or quarrelling, or holding consultation, or whether it was that the loud voice gave law and justice to the rest, Nod tried in vain to discover.

So at last, though much against his brothers' counsel, very curious to see what could occasion all this talk, he crept gradually, boulder by boulder, nearer to their great rocky bivouac. And there, by the silvery lustre of a dying moon, he peeped and peered. But though he plainly saw against the whiteness the pacing sentinels, and others of the Babbaboomas, huddling close by families for warmth in sleep beneath the rocks, he could not discover where their parliament or talkers were assembled. But still he heard them gabbling, and still, ever and anon, the great harsh voice sounding above all until at last this, too, ceased, and save for the befrosted watchmen, the whole innumerable horde of them lay – with the peaks of Arakkaboa to north of them, and Sulemnāgar to south – in that still dying moon-light fast asleep. Then he, too, scuttled softly back by the way he had come.

By morning (for the Babbaboomas are on the march before daybreak), when the brothers awoke, cold and cramped, in their rocky cavern, the whole concourse was gone, and not a sign of them except their scattered shells and husks, their innumerable footprints, and the stones they had rooted up in search of whatever small creeping food might lurk beneath. Else they seemed a dream – Meermuts of the moonlight!

By noon of next day the travellers approached the mountain-slopes. They crossed down into a valley, and now the farther they went the steeper rose the bare, snow-flecked mountain-side, and beyond and around them loftier heights yet, while in the midst spired into the midday Kush, the first of the seven of the sacred peaks of Tishnar. Ever and again they were startled by the sudden crash of the snow sweeping in long-drawn avalanches from the steeps of the hills. And though it was desolate to see those towering and unfriendly mountains, their snowy precipices and dazzling peaks, yet their hearts came back to them, for a warm

wind was blowing through
the valley, and they knew the
white and cold of the snow
would soon be over, and the
forest be green again, and
once more would come the
flowering of the fruit-trees,
and the ripening of the nuts.

But here it was that a bitter quarrel began between
the brothers that might have
ended in not one of them
ever seeing Tishnar's Valleys
alive. It was like this: Not
knowing in which direction
to be going in order to seek
for a path or pass whereby to scale Arakkaboa, they were at
a loss what to be doing. Even the Munza-Mulgars detest
being more than the height of the loftiest forest-tree above
their shadows on the ground; more especially therefore
did these Mulla-Mulgars, who never, or very rarely, as I
have said many times already, climb trees at all. So they
determined to stay awhile here and rest and eat until
some Mulgar should come along of whom they could ask
the way.

It was a valley rich with the sweet ground-fruit I have
already mentioned, whose spikes of a faint and thorny blue
just pierce the crispèd snow, and whose berries, owing to
their sugary coats or pods, resist all coldness. So that, without mention of Ukka-nuts, of which a grove grew not far
beyond the bend of the valley, the travellers had plenty to
eat. They had also an abundance of water, because of a
little torrent that came roaring through its ice near by the
trees they had chosen for their lodging. The wind that softly
blew along this low land was warmer, or, at least, not so

keen and fitful as the forest wind, and they were by now growing accustomed to the cold. For the night, however, they raised up for themselves a kind of leaning shelter, or huddle, of branches to be moved against the wind according as it blew up or down the valley.

But idleness leads to mischief. And not to press on is to be sliding backward. And to wait for help is to let help limp out of sight. And overcome, perhaps, by the luscious fruit, of which they ate far too much and far too often, and growing sluggardly with sleep, the travellers soon went on to bickering and scuffling together. With all this food, too, and long sleep and idleness, their courage began to droop. And if they heard any sound of living thing, even so much as a call or crackling branch, they would sneak off and hide in their night-shelter, not caring now for any kind of boldness nor to think of venturing over these homeless mountains.

So it came about that one night, as they were sleeping together under their huddle, as was their custom, Thumb, who had been nibbling fruit nearly all day long, cried out in a loud and terrible voice in his sleep, till Thimble, half awakened by his raving, picked up his thick cudgel and laid it soundly across his brother's shoulders where he lay. Thumb started up out of his sleep, and in an instant the two brothers were up and at each other, wrestling and kicking, gnashing their teeth, and guzzling through their throats and noses like mere Gungas, Mullabruks, or Manquabees. Poor Nod, not knowing what was the cause of all the trouble, got a much worse drubbing than either, till at last, in their furious struggling, all three brothers rolled from under the wattles into the pale glimmering of the stars and snow. For in this valley, after the sun goes, moves a phantom light or phosphorescence over the snow. Brought suddenly to their senses by the chill dark air, the travellers sat dimly glaring one at another, hunched, bruised, and breathless. And Nod, seeing his brothers so enraged, and preparing to fight again, and having had half his senses battered out by their rough usage, asked what was amiss.

'Ask him, ask him!' broke out Thimble, 'the fat and stupid, who deafens the whole forest with his gluttonous screams.'

' "Glutton, glutton!" ' shouted Thumb. 'How many nights, my brother Ummanodda, have we lain awake comforting one another that this dismal grasshopper has only one nose to snore through! I'll teach you, graffalegs, to break my ribs with a cudgel! Wait till a blink of morning comes! Oh, grammousie, to think I have put up with such a Mullabruk so long!' He lifted a frozen hunch of snow and flung it full in Thimble's face, and soon once more they were scuffling and struggling, cuffing and kicking in the silence that lay like a cloak upon all the sacred Valleys of Tishnar. They fought till, broken in wind and strength, they could fight no more. And Nod was kept busy all the rest of the darkness of that night mending the wounds of, and trying to make peace with, now one brother, now the other.

As soon as daybreak began to stir between the hills, Thumb and Thimble rose up together, and without a word, with puffed and sullen faces, went off on their fours and began gathering a good store of fruit and Ukka-nuts, each very cautious of approaching too near the other in his search. Nod skipped drearily from one to the other, pleading with them to be friends. But he got only hard words for his pains, and even at last was accused by both of them of stirring up a quarrel between them for his own pride and pleasure. He edged sadly back to the huddle, and sat gloomily watching them, wondering what next they would be at. He was soon to know, for first Thimble came back to him where he sat beside their night-hut and bade him help tie up his bundle.

'Where are you going to, Thimble?' said Nod. 'O

Thimble, think a little first! All these days we have journeyed in peace together. What would our father, Royal Seelem, say to see us now fighting and quarrelling like Mullabruks, and all because you cudgelled Thumb in his sleep?'

'In his sleep!' screamed Thimble. 'Tell that to your flesh-eating Oomgar, Prince of Bonfires! How could he be asleep, when he was squealing like a Boobab full of parakeets? I go back – back *now*. Who can climb mountains with a fat hulk who takes two breaths to an Ukka-nut? Come, if you dare! But I care not, whether or no.' And with that, catching up bundle and cudgel, with a last black look over his shoulder at Thumb, Thimble started off down the valley towards the forest they had so bravely left behind.

Not a moment had he been gone when Thumb came limping and waddling back to the shelter, loaded with nuts and berries.

'Sit here and sulk, if you like, Nizza-neela,' he growled angrily. 'Come with me, or traipse back with that scatter-brains. Whichever you please, I care not. I am sick of the glutton that eats all day and cannot sleep of nights for thinking of his supper.'

'How can I go with you,' said Nod bitterly, 'when I would not go with Thimble? O Mulla-Mulgar Thumb, you who are the eldest and strongest and wisest of us, be now the best, too! Hasten after Thimble, and bring him back to be friends. How can we show our faces to our Uncle Assa-simmon, even if we get over these dreadful mountains, say-ing we wrangled and gandered all one cold night together simply because you screamed out with fear in your sleep?'

'Thumb scream! Thumb afraid! Thumb sweat after Lean-legs! If you had not been my mother's youngest son, Ummanodda, you should never open that impudent mouth again!' And with that, off went Thumb, too, not caring whither so long as it led him farthest away from Thimble.

Now, not to make too much ado about this precious quar-

rel, this is what befell the travellers: Thimble, face toward
Munza, trotted – one, two, three; one, two, three – stonily
on. But in a while solitude began to gather about him, and
the cold after the heat of the fight struck chill and woke
again his lazy senses. He sat down to wrap up his bruises,
wondering where to be going, what to be doing. The Oomgar, the Nameless, the Minimuls, the River, the Gunga –
even if, he thought, he should escape again all the dangers
they had so narrowly but just come through together, what
lay at the end of it all? A little blackened heap of ashes, the
mockery of Munza-Mulgar, and his mother's speechless
and sorrowful ghost. What's more, while he sat idly nibbling his nuts, for his tongue had suddenly wearied of the
luscious ground-fruit, he saw moving between the rocks no
sweeter company than a she-leopard gazing grinningly on
him where he sat beneath his rock.

Now, these leopards, made cunning by experience, and
knowing that a Mulla-Mulgar will fight long and bravely
for his life, if, when they are hunting alone, they spy out
such a one alone, too, they trot softly back until they meet
with another of their kind. Then, with purring and clashing of whiskers, they come to a sworn and friendly understanding together, sharing out
their supper-meat before they
have so much as sharpened

their claws. Then at nightfall both go hunting their prey in harmony together.

Thimble well knew this crafty and evil practice, and when dusk fell, he listened and watched without stirring. And soon, over the snow, he heard the faint mewings and coughings of his enemies, both shes, of wonderful clear, dark Roses, coming on as thievishly and as softly towards him as a cat in search of her kittens. So he tore off a little strip of his tattered red jacket and laid it in the snow. Then away he scuttled till he must needs pause to breathe himself beneath a farther rock.

Meanwhile the ravenous huntress, having come to the strip of Mulgar-scented rag, of their natures had to stop and sniff and to disport themselves with that awhile, as if to smell a dinner cooking is to ensure enjoying it more when cooked. This done, they once more set forward with sharper hunger along Thimble's track. Three times did Thimble so play with them, and at the third appetizing rag the leopards, famished and over-eager, hardly paused at all over his keepsake, but came swiftly coursing after him. And the first, that (of her own craft) was much the younger and fleeter, soon outdistanced her hunting-mate, the which was exactly the reason for Thimble's trickery with his red flag. For when, panting and alone, the first Roses had got well ahead of the other, Thimble dashed suddenly out upon her from a rock, and before she could bare her teeth, he had caught her forefoot between his grinding jaws and bitten it clean to the bone. It spoilt poor Roses' taste for supper, and, seeing now that her sister was past fighting, and only too eager to leave the Mulgar to his lone, her mate slunk off without more ado to her own lair, to feast on the morning's bones of a frost-bitten Mullabruk.

But Thimble, though he had worsted the leopards, hadn't much liking or stomach for nights as wild as this. Thumb's nightmares were sweet peace to it. All the next day he wandered about, not heeding whither his footsteps led him. And so it came about that just before evening he stumbled upon the very same valley he had left in his sulks the morning before. There, indeed, sat Nod, fast asleep in the evening light from sheer weariness of watching for his brothers, who, some faint hope had told him, would return.

As for Thumb, after limping on up the valley a little more than a league, he soon grew ashamed and sick at heart at having so easily become a silly child again. He sat down under a great boulder, humped round with ants' nests, too desolate to go on, too proud to turn back. All that day and the next he sat moodily watching these never-idle little creatures, that, afraid of nothing, are feared of all. They had tunnelled and walled, and wherever sunbeams fell had cast back the snow that hung above the galleries, and all day long they kept going and coming, carrying syrup and eggs and meat, and all this with endless palaver of their waving horns, as if there were nothing else that side of Arakkaboa but the business of their city. Thumb alive they paid no heed to, but Thumb dead they would have picked to the bare bones before sunset.

The next evening Thumb's better head overcame him, and back he went to his brothers, sitting miserable and forlorn in the new moonlight beneath their shelter. Nothing

was said. They dared scarcely look into each other's faces awhile, until Thumb caught Nod's bright, anxious little eyes glancing under his puckered forehead from brother to brother, in mortal fear they would soon be breaking out again. And Nod looked so queer, and small, and anxious, and loving, and all these things so much at once, that Thumb burst out into a roar of laughter. And there they sat all three, rocking to and fro, holding their sides beneath the gigantic steeps of Arakkaboa, happy and at peace together again, while tears ran down their nose-troughs, with their shouts on shouts of laughter.

CHAPTER FOURTEEN

The Men of the Mountains

Next day the travellers were about very early, combing and
grooming themselves in the dawn-mist for the first time
these many days, and, before the sun had shot his first
colours across Arakkaboa, they had eaten and drunk and
set out from the valley of the languid and luscious fruits
that had been the chief cause of all their folly.

They pushed up the valley, searching anxiously the hillside for sign of any track or path by which they might
ascend. The day was crisp and golden with sunlight. And
that evening they made their night-quarters beside a vast
frozen pool in a kind of cup of the overhanging cliffs. Here
every word they said came hollowly back in echo.

They cried, 'Seeleem!' 'Seeleem, Seeleem!' replied the
mocking voices.

'*Ummani nâta?* Still we go on?' shouted Thumb hoarsely.

'*Nâta, nâta!* On, on, on!' sang echo hoarselier yet.

Wind had swept clean the glassy floor. In its black lustre
gleamed the increasing moon. And after dark had fallen,
mists arose and trailed in moonlit beauty across the granite
escarpments of the hills. So that night the travellers lay in a
vast tent of lovely solitude, with only the strange noises of
the ice and the whisperings of the frost to tell poor wakeful
Nod he was anything more than a little Mulgar in a dream.

Next morning early they met one of those crack-brained
Môh-Mulgars that wander, eat, sleep, live, and die alone,
having broken away from all traffic and company with their
friends and kinsmen. He wore about his neck a double-
coiled necklet of little bones, and wound round his middle a

plait of Cullum. He was dirty, bowed, and matted, and his
eyes were glazed as he lifted them into the sunlight in
answer to Thumb's shout:

'Tell us, O Môh-Mulgar, we beseech you, how shall three
travellers to the Kingdom of Assasimmon find a pathway
across these hills?'

The Môh-Mulgar lifted both gnarled hands above his
head.

'*Geguslar, nooma gulmeta mūh!*' replied a thick, half-
brutal voice.

'What does he say?' said Nod, wondering to see him
wave his spotted arms as he wagged his crazy head.

'Well,' says Thumb, 'what he says is this: 'Death's at
the end of all paths.'

Thimble coughed. 'So it is,' he said solemnly.

'Ay,' said Thumb; 'but what *I* was asking was the longest
way round ... A track, a path to the beautiful Valleys of
Tishnar,' he shouted across to the solitary Môh-Mulgar.
Sorrowfully he waved his bony arms about his head, and
stooped again. '*Geguslar, nooma gulmeta mūh!*' came back
his dismal answer.

Thimble, with a sign to him, laid gravely down a little
heap of nuts in the snow. And the three travellers left the

old pilgrim still standing desolate and unquestionable in the snow, watching them till they were gone out of sight.

Coming presently after to some trees with tough, straight branches, the travellers made themselves fresh cudgels. After which, to raise their fallen spirits, they played hoppole awhile in the sunshine, just as they used to in the first days of the snow before they set out on their travels. And about noon, when the sun stood radiant above them, they met three Men of the Mountains, with shallow baskets on their heads, coming down to gather Ukka-nuts in the valley. These Mulgars have long silken black-and-white hair and very profuse whiskers. They are sad in face, with pouting lips, have but the meanest of thumbs, and turn their toes in as they walk, one behind another, and sometimes in chains of a hundred together. Thumb stood in their path, and inquired of the first of them, as before, which way they must follow to cross the mountains.

The voice of the Man of the Mountains who answered them was so high and weak Nod could scarcely hear his whisper. 'There is no way over,' he said.

'But over we must go,' said Thumb.

The other shook his head, and looked sadder than ever. And on they all three went again, lisping softly together, but without another word to Thumb.

'What's to be done now?' said Nod.

'Where they came down we can go up,' said Thumb.

So, the Men of the Mountains being now hidden from sight by the rocks below, Thumb and his brothers turned up the narrow track between great boulders of stone, by which they had come down. And glad they were of the new staves or cudgels they had broken off. Even with the help of these, so steep was the path that they had often to pull themselves up by roots and jutting rocks. And gradually, besides being steep, the way grew so narrow that they were simply walking on a ledge of rock not more than two Mul-

159

gar paces wide. And for giddiness Nod nearly fell flat when by chance he turned his eyes and looked down to where, far below, a frozen torrent gleamed faintly amid huge boulders that looked from this height no bigger than pebble-stones.

It made him giddy even to keep his eyes fixed on the narrowing path before him, and shuffle up, up, up.

Suddenly, Thumb, who was wheezing and panting a few paces in front, came to a standstill.

'What is it, Thumb?' said Nod.

'Why do you stop, Nod?' said Thimble, who was last of all.

'Look, look!' said Thumb.

They slowly raised their eyes, and not a hundred paces beyond them, on the same narrow ledge of rock against the deep blue sky, came slowly winding down thirty at least of these same meagre and hairy Men of the Mountains, a few with long staves in their hands, and every one with his long tufted tail over his shoulder and a round shallow basket on his head. These Men of the Mountains have very weak eyes; and it was not until they were come close that they perceived the three travellers standing on their mountain-path. The first stopped, then he that was next, and so on, until they looked like a long black-and-white caterpillar, clinging to the precipice with tiny tufts waving in the air.

Thumb raised his hand as if in peace. 'We are, sirs, strangers to these rocks and hills. After the shade of Munza, our eyes dizzy with the heights. And we walk, journeying to the Courts of Assasimmon, in great danger of falling. How, then, shall we pass by?'

They heard a faint, shrill whispering all along the hairy row. Then the first of the Men of the Mountains came quite close, and told the three brothers to lie down flat on their faces, and he and his thirty would all walk gently over them. 'But to go on has no end,' he said, 'and the travellers had better far turn back.'

161

At this Thumb grew angry. 'What does the old grey-beard mean?' he coughed out of the corner of his mouth. 'Mulla-Mulgars stoop on their faces to no-one. Do you lie down on yours.'

The old Mountain-Mulgar blinked. 'We are thirty; you are three,' he said. Thumb laughed.

'We are strangers to Arakkaboa, O Man of the Mountains. And we fear to lie down, lest we never rise up again.' At this civil speech the old Mulgar went shuffling back to the others.

And, to Nod's astonishment, he presently saw him take his long staff of tough, sinewy wood, and thrust it into a little crevice of the rock, even with the path, so that about a third of its length overhung the precipice. Meanwhile, another of these Mountain-Mulgars had in the same way thrust his staff into the rock a little farther down. The first Man of the Mountains, who was, perhaps by half a span, taller than the rest, took firm hold of the end of his staff with his long-fingered but almost thumbless hands, and lightly swung himself down over the precipice. The next scrambled down over his shoulders until he swung by his leader's heels; the next followed, and so on. Three such Mulgar strings presently hung down from their staves over the abyss. And there being thirty Men of the Mountains in all, each string consisted of ten. [For this reason some call these Mountain-Mulgars Caterpillar- or Ladder-Mulgars.]

When they were all thus quietly dangling, their leader bade Thumb advance. Stepping warily over the little heaps of baskets, this the brothers did. But as Nod passed each string in turn, and saw it swinging softly over the sheer precipice, and all the ten faces with pale eyes blinking sadly up at him out of their fluff of hair, he thought he should certainly be toppled over and dashed to pieces. At last, however, all three were safely passed by. But the rocky ledge was here so narrow that Thimble could not even turn himself about to thank the Mountain-Mulgars for their courtesy, nor to watch them climb back one by one to their mountain-path again.

On and on, up, ever up, climbed the ribbon-like path winding about the granite flanks of Kush. Once Nod lifted up his face, and saw in one swift glimpse the glittering peaks and crest of the mountains rising in beauty, crowned with snow, out of the vast sun-shafted precipices. He hastily shut his eyes, and his knees trembled. But there could be no turning back now. He followed on close behind his fat panting brother, until suddenly Thumb leapt back to a standstill, shouting in a voice of fear: '*O ho, ho! Illa ulla, illa ulla! O ho, ho!*'

'O Thumb, why do you call "*ho!*" like that?' said Nod anxiously.

'Back, back!' Thumb cried; '*du steepa datz.*'

Nod stooped low on the smooth rock, and under the tatters of Thumb's metal-hooked coat stared out between his brother's bandy legs. He simply looked out of that hairy window straight into the empty air. They stood like peering cormorants at the cliff's edge. The path had come to an end.

Thumb whined softly and coughed, and a faint steam rose up from his body. 'We must go back,' he barked huskily.

'Yes, brother,' said Thimble softly; 'but I cannot go

back. If I turn, down I go. But if you two can turn, down go will I.'

'Tishnar, O Tishnar,' cried Nod in terror, 'the hills are dancing.'

'Softly, softly, child!' said Thumb. 'It is only your giddy eyes rolling. What's more,' he said, pretending to laugh, 'those old hairy Men of the Mountains, even if only Meermuts, *must* have come from somewhere. Where they came from we can go to. *O and Ahôh!*' he called.

'Why do you call *"Ahôh!"* Thumb?' whispered Nod, with tight-shut eyes.

'Both together, Thimbulla,' muttered Thumb. '*Ahôh, ahôh, ahôh!*' they bawled.

Their voices sounded small and far-away. Only a bird screamed in answer from the chasm beneath. The sun blazed shadowlessly over the peak of Kush upon the three Mulgars, standing motionless, pressed close against the steaming rock. To Nod the minutes crawled like hours, while he crouched sick and trembling, clutching Thumb's rags to keep him from falling.

'Thimble, my brother,' at last called Thumb softly, 'could you, if little Nod twisted himself round, straddle your legs enough to let him creep through? We old gluttonous fellows were never meant for mountain-climbing. And standing here over the great misty pot –' But just then it seemed to Thumb he felt, light as the wind, something softly pluck at his wool hat. Very, very slowly, and without a word, he lifted his head and looked up – looked straight up into the sorrowful hairy face of a Man of the Mountains dangling, the last of a long chain, from a rocky parapet above.

'Why?' says Thumb, looking into his face. 'What then?'

'Up, up!' said he, in a thin, lisping Munza-tongue, making a step or loop of his long fringed arms.

This, then, was the stairs or ladder on which the travellers must climb into safety. But Thumb could barely touch him with the tips of his fingers. He stood in doubt, staring up. And presently down that living rope of Mulgars yet another Man of the Mountains softly descended, and his arms just reached Thumb's elbows.

'Tread gently, Mulla-Mulgar,' said this last, with a doleful smile. 'You are fat, and our ladder is slender.'

Thumb, with one white, doglike glance into the deeps, took firm hold, and slowly, heavily, he climbed on from trembling Mulgar to trembling Mulgar till at length he reached the top.

'Now, Nizza-neela,' said the last Man of the Mountains, 'it is your turn.' Up clambered Nod after Thumb, groping carefully with the palms of his feet from hairy loop to loop. But he was glad that the Men of the Mountains, as their custom generally is, dangled with their faces to the rock, and could not see into his eyes.

At last all three were safely up, and found themselves on a wide, smooth, shelving ledge of the mountain, about fifty Mulgar paces wide, with here and there a tree or tuft of grass, and to the right a cascade of ice, roped with icicles, streaming from the heights above. But what most Nod blinked in wonder at were the small white mushroom houses of these Mountain-Mulgars. More than a hundred of them were here, standing like snow-white beehives in the glare of the sun, each with its low round door, from which, here and there, a baby Mulgar, with short, fleecy, and cane-coloured whiskers, stood on its fours, peeping at the strangers.

When they were all three safely landed, one of the Men of the Mountains led them between the beehive houses to a cool, shadowy cavern in the mountain-side. There he bade them sit down, while others brought them a kind of thin, sour cheese and a mess of crushed and mouldy Ukka-nuts. For these Arakkaboan Mulgars will not so much as look at a nut fresh and crisp; it must be green and furred to please their taste. And while the travellers sat nibbling a little meanly of the nuts and cheese, Thumb told the Men of the Mountains as best he could in the Munza tongue who they were, and why they were come wandering in Arakkaboa.

When Thumb in his talk made mention of the name of Tishnar, the Mountain-Mulgars that sat round them in a circle bobbed low, till the hair of their faces touched the cavern floor.

'The Valleys of Assasimmon lie far from here,' said the first Mountain-Mulgar in a shrill, thin voice. 'And the Men of the Mountains walk no mountain-paths beyond the peak of Zut; nor have we ever dangled our ropes into the Ummuz-groves of Tishnar. I do not even know the way thither. It would have been go thin and come back fat, O Mulla-Mulgars, if I did. Rest and sleep now, travellers. We will bring you to the Mulla-Moona-Mulgars [that is, Lord, or Captain] of Kush when he awakes from his "glare".'

This 'glare', or 'shine', is the name the Mountain-Mulgars give to the sleep they take in the middle of the day. Some little while before 'no-shadow', as they call it, or noonday, they creep into their mushroom houses and sleep till evening begins to settle. So weak have their eyes become (or are, by nature) that they rarely venture out in full daylight to go nut-gathering in the valleys. And often then, even, many go bandaged, keeping touch merely with their tails. It was in the midst of this noonday sleep or glare that the travellers had rousted them with their halloo. At evening they awake, and when the moon is clear their ladders may be seen near and far drooping over the precipices. And they go walking with soft, shambling steps from ledge to ledge. Even the least of them have no fear of any height. Their children of an evening will sit and eat their suppers, their spindle legs dangling over a depth so extreme that no Munza-Mulgar could see to the bottom.

Left alone, the Mulla-Mulgars, who had been climbing many hours now, and felt stiff in legs and back, were glad to roll themselves over in the flealess sand of the cavern, and soon were all three asleep.

CHAPTER FIFTEEN

Ghibba and the Secret 'Walks'

When Nod opened his eyes beneath the vast blue arch of the cavern, not a sign of the Man of the Mountains was to be seen. He sat for awhile watching his brothers humped up in sleep on the floor, and wondering rather dismally when they should have done with their troubles and come to the palace of their Uncle Assasimmon. He was blained and footsore; his small bones stuck out beneath his furry skin, his hands were cracked and scorched. And the keen high air of Arakkaboa made him gasp at every breath.

When Thumb awoke they sat quietly mumbling and talking together awhile. Beyond the mouth of the cavern stood the beehive-houses of the Mountain-Mulgars, each in its splash of lengthening shadow. Day drew on to evening. An eagle squalled in space. Else all was still; no living thing stirred. For these Men of the Mountains have no need to keep watch. They sleep secure in their white huts. None can come in, and none go out but first they must let down their ladders. Thumb scrambled up, and he and Nod hobbled off softly together to where the cataract hung like a shrine of hoar-frost in pillars of green ice from the frozen snows above.

The evening was filled with light of the colour of a flower. Even the snow that capped the mountains was faintest violet and rose, and far in the distance, between the peaks of Zut and misty Solmi, stretched a band of darkest purple, above which the risen moon was riding in pale gold. And Nod knew that there, surely, must be Battle's Sea. He pointed Thumb to it, and the two Mulgars stood, legs bandy, teeth shining, eyes fixed. Nod gazed on it bewitched, till it seemed he almost saw the foam of its league-long billows rolling, and could catch in his thin round ear the roar and surge Battle had so often told him of. '*Oché!* if my Oomgar were but with me now!' he thought. 'How would his eyes stare to see his friend the sea!'

But the Men of the Mountains were now bestirring themselves. They came creeping, lean and hairy, out of their mushroom houses. Some fetched water, some looped down over the brink by which the travellers had come up. Some clambered up into little dark horseshoe courts cut in the rock like martins' holes in sand, and came down carrying sacks or suchlike out of their nut pantries and cheeserooms. Some, too, of the elders sat combing their long beards with a kind of teasel that grows in the valleys, while their faint voices sounded in their gossiping like hundreds of grasshoppers in a meadow. Nod watched them curiously. Even the faces of the quite puny Mountain-Mulgars were sad, with round and feeble eyes. And he couldn't help nudging Thumb to look at these tiny creatures gravely combing their hairy chops – for all had whiskers, from the brindled and grey, whose hair fell below their knees, to the mouse and cane coloured babies lying in basins or cradles of Ollaconda-bark, kicking their toes towards the brightening stars.

The moonlight dwelt in silver on every crag. And like things so beautiful that they seem of another world, towered the mountains around them, clear as emeralds, and crowned with never-melting snow.

Thimble, when he awoke, was fevered and aching. The heights had made his head dizzy, and the mountain cheese was sickly and faint. He lay at full length, with wandering eyes, refusing to speak. So when the Mulla-Moona sent for the three travellers, only Thumb and Nod went together. He was old, thin-haired and thick-skinned, and rather fat

169

with eating of cheese; he wore a great loose hat of leopard-skin on his head. And he looked at them with his eyes wizened up as if they were creatures of no account. And he asked one of the Mountain-Mulgars who stood near, who were these strangers, and by whose leave they had come trespassing on the hill-walks of the Mountain-Mulgars. 'Munza is your country,' he said. 'The leaves are never still with you, thieves and  gluttons, squealing and fighting and swinging by your tails!'

Thumb opened his mouth at this. 'We are three, and you are many, Old Man of the Mountains,' he barked, 'but keep a civil tongue with us, for all that. We are neither thieves nor gluttons. We fight, oh yes, when it pleases us. But having no tails, we do not swing by them. We are Mulla-Mulgars, my brothers and I, and we go to the kingdom of our father's brother, Assasimmon, Prince of the Valleys of Tishnar. He is a Prince, O Mulla-Moona, who has more slaves in his palace and more Ukka-trees in the least of his seventy-seven gardens than your royal whiskers have hairs! On, then, we go! But be not afraid, Mulla-Moona-Mulgar. We will leave a few small stones of Arak-kaboa behind us. But whether you will or whether you won't, on we go until the Harp sounds. Then our Meer-muts will Tishnar welcome, and bid wander over these her mountains, never hungry, never thirsty, never footsore, with sweet-smelling lanterns to light us, and striped Zevveras to carry us, and gongs to make music. But if we live, Chief Mulgar of Kush, we will remember your words, I and my

170

brother Ummanodda Nizza-neela for he shall breathe them into a little book in the Zbaffli, Oomgar's tongue for Prince Assasimmon to mock at in his Ummuz-fields.'

Nod listened in wonder to this harangue. Had he, then, been talking in his sleep, that Thumb knew all about the Oomgar's little fat magic-book? The old Mountain-Mulgar sat solemnly blinking, fingering the tassel of his long tail. He was a doleful and dirty fellow, and very sly.

'Why,' he said at last, 'I did but speak Munza fashion. Scratch if you itch, traveller. Even an Utt can grow angry. As for writing my words in the Oomgar's tongue, that is magic, and I understand it not. Rest in the cool of the shadow of Kush a little, and to-morrow my servants shall lead you as far across Arakkaboa as they know the way. But this I will tell you: Beyond Zut my paths go not.' He raised his pale eyes softly. 'But then, Meermuts need no paths, Mulla-Mulgars.'

Thumb laughed. 'All in good time, Prince,' he said, showing his teeth. 'I begin to get an itching for this Zut. We will rest only one day. The Mulla-Mulgar Thimbulla has a poor stomach for your green cheese. We will journey on to-morrow.'

The Mulla-Moona then called an old Mulgar who stood by, whose name was Ghibba, and bade him take a rope [that is, twenty or more] of the Mountain-Mulgars with him to show the travellers the secret 'walks' and passes across their country to the border round Zut. 'After that,' he said, turning sourly to Thumb, 'though your Meermuts were three hundred and not three, and your Uncle, King Assasimmon, had more palaces than there are nuts on an Ukka-tree, I could help you no more. *Sulâni*, O Mulla-Mulgars, and may Tishnar, before she scatters your dust, sweeten your tempers!'

And at that the old Mountain-Man curled his tail over his shoulder and shut his eyes.

171

When Thumb and Nod came into the great cavern again to Thimble, they found him helpless with pain and fever. He could not even lift his head from his green pillow. His eyes glowed in their bony hollows, and when Thumb stooped over him he screamed, *'Gunga! Gunga!'* as if in fear.

Thumb turned and looked at Nod. 'We shall have to carry him, Ummanodda,' he said. 'If he eats any more of their mouldy nuts and cheese our brother will die in these wild mountains. They must be sad stomachs that thrive on meat gone green with age. And now the physic is gone, and where shall we find more in these great hills of ice? We must carry him – we must carry him, Nodnodda.'

Then Ghibba, who was standing near, understanding a little of what Thumb said, though he had spoken low in Mulgar-Royal, called four of his twenty. And together they made a kind of sling or hammock or pallet out of their strands of Cullum, and cushioned it with hair and moss. For once every year these Mulgars shave all the hair off their bodies, and lie in chamber until it is grown again. By this means even the very old men keep sleek and clean. With this hair they make a kind of tippet, also cushions and bedding of all sorts. It is a curious custom, but each,

growing up, follows his father, and so does not perceive its oddness. Into this litter, then, they laid Thimble, and lifted him on to their shoulders by ropes at the corners, plaited thick, so as not to chafe the bearers. Then, the others laden with great faggots of wood and torches, bags of nuts and cheese, and skin bottles of milk, they passed through an arch in the wall of the cavern, and the travellers set out once more. All the Men of the Mountains came out with their little ones in the starlight and torch-flare to see them go. Even the old chief squinnied sulkily out of his hut, and spat on the ground when they were gone.

The Mulgar-path on the farther side of this arch was so wide that here and there trees hung over it with frost-tasselled branches. And a rare squabbling the little Mountain-owls made out of their holes in the rock to see the travellers' torches passing by. First walked six of the Men of the Mountains, two by two. Then came Thimble, tossing and gibbering on his litter. Close behind the litter followed Ghibba, walking between Thumb and Nod. And last, talking all together in their thin grasshopper voices, the rest of the Mountain-Mulgars with more bags, more faggots, and more burning torches. It was, as I have said, clear and starry weather. Far below them the valleys lay, their blackness fleeced with mist; high above them glittered the quiet ravines of ice and snow. So cold had it fallen again, Nod huddled himself close in his sheep's-jacket, buzzing quiet songs while he waddled along with his staff. So all night they walked without resting, except to change the litter-bearers.

When dawn began to stir, they came to where the Mulgar-path widened awhile. Here many rock-conies dwelt that have, as it were, wings of skin with which they leapt as if they flew. And here the travellers doused their torches, set Thimble down, and made breakfast. While they all sat eating together, on a narrow pass beneath them wound by another of the long-haired companies of the Men of the Mountains. From upper path to lower was about fifteen Mulgars deep, for that is how they measure their heights. All these Mulgars were laden with a kind of fresh green seaweed heaped up on their shallow head-baskets, and were come three days' journey from the sea from fetching it. This seaweed they eat in their soup, or raw, as a relish or salad. Perhaps they pit it against their cheese. Whether or no, its salt and refreshing savour rose up into the air as they walked. And Nod sniffed it gladly for simple friendship and memory of his master, Battle.

Breakfast done, the snow-bobbins hopped down to pick up the crumbs. These little tufty birds, of the size of a plump bullfinch, but pure white, with coral eyes, hop among the Mountain-Mulgar troops wheresoever they go, having a great fancy for their sour cheese-crumbs.

The Men of·the Mountains then hung up on their rods or staves a kind of thick sheet or shadow-blanket, as they call it, woven of goats' wool and Ollaconda-fibre, under which they all hid themselves from the glare of the over-riding sun. Nod, too, and Thumb sat down in close shade beside Thimble's litter, and slept fitfully, tired out with their night-march, but anxious in the extreme for their brother.

Towards about three, as we should say, or when the sun was about three parts across his bridge, having wound up their shadow-blankets and made all shipshape, the little company of grey and brown Mulgars set out once more. Thimble, who had lain drowsy and panting, but quiet, during the day, now began to toss and rave as if in terror. His cries rang piercing and sorrowful against these stone walls, and even the hairy Mountain-Men who carried him in such patience slung between them, grew at last weary of his clamour, and shook his litter when he cried out. As if, indeed, that might quiet him!

Nod stumped on for a long time in silence, listening to his brother's raving. 'O Thumb, what should we do,' he broke out at last – 'what should we do, you and me, if Thimble died?'

Thumb grunted. 'Thimble will not die, little brother.'

'But how can you know, Thumb? Or do you say it only to comfort me?'

'I never could tell how I know, Ummanodda; but know I do, and there's an end.'

'I suppose we shall get to Tishnar's Valleys – in time,' said Nod, half to himself.

'The Nizza-neela is downcast with long travel,' said Ghibba.

'Ay,' muttered Thumb, 'and being a Mulla-Mulgar, he does not show it.'

Nod turned his head away, blinked softly, shrugged up his jacket, but made no answer. And Thumb, in his kindness, and perhaps to ease his own spirits, too, broke out in his great seesaw voice into the Mulgar Journey Song. High above the squabbling of the little Mountain-owls, high above the remote thunder of the surging waters in the ravine, into the clear air they raised their hoarse voices together:

In Munza a Mulgar once lived alone,
And his name it was Dubbuldideery, O;
With none to love him, and loved by none,
His hard old heart it grew weary, O,
    Weary, O weary, O weary.

So he up with his cudgel, he on with his bag
Of Manaka, Ukkas, and Keeri, O;
To seek for the waters of 'Old-Made-Young'
Went marching old Dubbuldideery, O,
    Dubbuldi-dubbuldi-deery.

The sun rose up, and the sun sank down;
The moon she shone clear and cheery, O,
And the myriads of Munza they mocked and mopped
And mobbed old Dubbuldideery, O,
      Môh-Mulgar Dubbuldideery.

He cared not a hair of his head did he,
Not a hint of the hubbub did hear he, O,
For the roar of the waters of 'Old-Made-Young'
Kept calling of Dubbuldideery, O,
      Call – calling of Dubbuldideery.

He came to the country of 'Catch Me and Eat Me' –
Not a fleck of a flicker did fear he, O,
For he knew in his heart they could never make mince-meat
Of tough old Dubbuldideery, O,
      Rough, tough, gruff Dubbuldideery.

He waded the Ooze of Queen Better-Give-Up,
Dim, dank, dark, dismal, and dreary, O,
And, crunch! went a leg down a Cockadrill's throat,
'What's *one*?' said Dubbuldideery, O,
      Undauntable Dubbuldideery.

He cut him an Ukka crutch, hobbled along,
Till Tishnar's sweet river came near he, O –
The wonderful waters of 'Old-Made-Young,'
A-shining for Dubbuldideery, O,
      Wan, wizened old Dubbuldideery.

He drank, and he drank – and he drank – and he – drank:
No more was he old and weary, O,
But weak as a babby he fell in the river,
And drowned was Dubbuldideery, O,
      Drown-ded was Dubbuldideery!

It was a long song, and it lasted a long time, and so many were the verses, that at last even the Men of the Mountains caught up the crazy Mulgar drone and wheezily joined in, too. A very dismal music it was – so dismal, indeed, that many of the eagles who make their nests or eyries in the crevices and ledges of the topmost crags of Arakkaboa flew screaming into the air, sweeping on their motionless wings between the stars over the echoing precipices.

The travellers had set to the last verse of the Journey Song more lustily than ever, when of a sudden one of these eagles, crested, and bronze in the torchlight, swooped so close in its anger of the voices that it swept off Thumb's wool hat. In his haste he heedlessly struck at the shining bird with his staff or cudgel. Its scream rose sudden and piercing as it soared, dizzily wheeling in its anger, at evens with the glassy peak of Kush. Shrilly the Men of the Mountains cried out on Thumb to beware. In an instant the night was astir, the air forked with wings. From every peak the eagles swooped down upon the rock-ledged Mulgars, now fighting wildly and desperately to beat them off. They had

laid poor Thimble down in his sling and covered up his
eyes from the tumult with a shadow-blanket. And with
sticks and staves and flaring torches they turned on the
fierce birds that came sweeping and swirling out of the dark
upon them on bristling feathers, with ravening beaks and
talons.

But against Thumb the eagles fought most angrily for
his insult to their Prince, hovering with piercing battle-
cry, their huge wings beating a dreadful wind upon his
cowering head. Nod, while he himself was buffeting, duck-
ing and dodging, could hear Thumb breathing and coughing
and raining blows with his great cudgel. The moon was

now sliding towards the mouth of Solmi's Valley, and her beams streamed aslant on the hosts of the birds. Wherever Nod looked, the air was aflock with eagles. His hand was torn and bleeding, a great piece of his sheep's-jacket had been plucked out, and still those moon-gilded wings swooped into the torchlight, beaks snapped almost in his face, and talons clutched at him.

Suddenly a scream rose shrill above all the din around him. For a moment the birds hung hovering, and then Nod perceived one of the biggest of the eagles struggling in mid-air with something stretched and wrestling upon its back. It was a Man of the Mountains floating there in space, while the maddened eagle rose and fell, and poised itself, and shook and beat its wings, vainly striving to tear him off. And now many other of the eagles wheeled off from the Mulgars and swept in frenzy to and fro over this struggling horse and rider, darting upon them, beating the dying Mul-

gar with their wings, screaming their war-song, until at last, gradually, lower and lower they all sank out of the moonlight into the shadow of the valley, and were lost to sight.

The few birds that remained were soon beaten off. Five lay dead in their beautiful feathers on the pass. And the breathless and bleeding Mulgars gathered together on this narrow shelf of the precipice to bind up their wounds and rest and eat. But three of them were nowhere to be found. They made no answer, though their friends called and called, again and again, in their shrill reedy voices. For one in fighting had stumbled and toppled over, torch in hand, from the path, one had been slit up by an eagle's claw, and one had been carried off by the eagles.

CHAPTER SIXTEEN

The Prince of
Tishnar's Dream

And now that the moon was near her setting, dark grew the air. The Men of the Mountains had at last ceased to call their lost companions, and on either side of the path were breaking up their faggots and building fires, leaving two wide spaces beneath the beetling rock for their encampment between the fires. Nod, sitting beside Thimble's litter, watched them for some time, and presently he fancied he heard a distant howling, not from the darkness below, but seemingly from the heights above the Mulgar-pass. He rose and limped along to Ghibba, who was busy about the fires. 'Why are you heaping up such large fires,' he said 'and whose, Man of the Mountains, are those howlings I heard from the mountain-tops?'

Ghibba's face was scorched and bleeding; one of his long eyebrows was nearly torn off. 'The fires and the howls are cousins, little Mulgar,' he said. 'The screams of the golden-folk have roused the wolves, and if we do not light big fires they will come down in packs along their secret paths to devour us. It is a good thing to fight bravely, but it's a better thing not to have to fight at all.'

Nod came back and told this news to Thumb, who was sitting with a great strip of his jacket bound round his head like a Turk's turban. 'It is good news, brother,' he said – 'it is good news. What stories we shall have to tell when we are old!'

'But two of the hairy ones are dead,' said Nod, 'and one is slipping, they say, from his second sleep.'

'Then,' said Thumb, looking softly over the valley, 'they need fight no more.'

Nod sat down again beside Thimble's litter and touched his hand. It was dry and burning hot. He heard him gabbling, gabbling on and on to himself, and every now and again he would start up and gaze fixedly into the night. 'No, Thimble, no,' Nod would say. 'Lie back, my brother. It is neither the Harp-strings nor our father's Zevveras; it is only the little mountain-wolves barking at the icicles.'

On either side of their camping-place he heard yelp answering yelp, and then a long-drawn howl far above his head. He began to think, too, he could see, as it were, small green and golden marshlights wandering along the little paths. And, watching them where he sat quietly on his heels in a little hollow of the rock, it brought back, as if this were but a dream he was in, the twangle of Battle's Juddie, the restless fretting and howling of Immanâla's Jaccatrays. As the Moona-Mulgar's fires mounted higher, great shadows sprang trembling up the mountains, and tongues of flame cast vague shafts of light across the shadowy abyss; while, stuck along the wall in sconces of the rock, a dozen torches smoked.

Thumb grunted. 'They'd burn all Munza up with fires like these,' he muttered. 'Little wolves need only little fires.' But Thumb did not know the ferocity of these small mountain-wolves. They are meagre and wrinkle-faced, with prick ears and rather bushy tails. In winter they grow themselves thick coats as white as snow, except upon their legs, which are short-haired and grey, with long tapping claws. And they are fearless and very cunning creatures. Nod could now see them plainly in the nodding flamelight, couched on their haunches a few paces beyond the fires, and along the galleries above, with gleaming eyes, scores and scores of them. And now the eagles were returning to their eyries from their feasting in the valley, and though they swept up through the air mewing and peering, they dared not draw near to the great blaze of fire and torch, but screamed as they ascended, one to the other, until the wolves took up an answer, barking hard and short, or with long mournful ululation.

When at last they fell quiet, then the Men of the Mountains began wailing again for their lost comrades. They sit with their eyes shut, resting on their long, narrow hands, their faces to the wall, and sing through their noses. First one takes up a high lamentable note, then another, and so on, faster and faster, for all the world like a faint and distant wind in the hills, until all the voices clash together, *'Tishnaehr!'* Then, in a little, breaks out the shrillest in solo again, and so they continue till they weary.

Nod listened, his face cupped in his hands, but so faint and fast sang the voices he could only catch here and there the words of their drone, if words there were. He touched Thumb's shoulder. 'These hairy fellows are singing of Tishnar!' he said.

Thumb grunted, half-asleep.

'Who taught them of Tishnar?' Nod asked softly.

Thumb turned angrily over. 'Oh, child!' he growled, 'will you never learn wisdom? Sleep while you can, and let Thumb sleep too! To-morrow we may be fighting again.'

But though the Ladder-Mulgars soon ceased to wail, and, except for those who were left to keep watch and to feed the fires, laid themselves down to sleep, Nod could not rest. The mountains rose black and unutterably still beneath the stars. Up their steep sides enormous shadows jigged around the fires. Sometimes an eagle squawked on high, nursing its wounds. And whether he turned this way or that way he still saw the little wolves huddled close together, their pointed heads laid on their lean paws, uneasily watching. And he longed for morning. For his heart lay like a stone in him in grief for his brother Thimble. A little dry snow harboured in the crevices of the rocks. He filled his hands with it, and laid it on poor Thimble's head and moistened his lips. Then he walked softly along past the sleeping Mulgars towards the fire.

Where should we all be now, he thought, if the eagles had come in the morning? On paths narrow as those there was not even enough room to brandish a cudgel. The fire-watcher raised his sad countenance and peered through his hair at Nod.

'What is it in your mouldy cheese, Man of the Mountains, that has poisoned my brother?' said Nod.

The Mulgar shook his head. 'Maybe it is something in the Mulla-Mulgar,' he answered. 'It is very good cheese.'

'Will morning soon be here?' said Nod, gazing into the fire.

The Mulgar smiled. 'When night is gone,' he answered.

'Why do these mountain-wolves fear fire?' asked Nod.

The Mulgar shook his head. 'Questions, royal traveller, are easier than answers,' he said. 'They *do*.'

He caught up a firebrand, and threw it with all his strength beyond the fire. It fell sputtering on the ledge, and instantly there rose such a yelping and snarling the chasm re-echoed. Yet so brave are these snow-wolves one presently came venturing pitapat, pitapat, along the frosty gallery, and very warily, with the tip of his paw, poked and pushed at it until the burning stick toppled and fell over, down, down, down, down, till, a gliding spark, it vanished into the torrent below. The Mountain Mulgar looked back over his shoulder at Nod, but said nothing.

Nod's eyes went wandering from head to head of the shadowy pack. 'Is it far now to my uncle, Prince Assasimmon's? Is it far to the Valleys?' he said in a while.

'Only to the other side of death,' said the watchman. 'Come Noomanossi, we shall walk no more.'

'Do you mean, O Man of the Mountains,' said Nod, catching his breath, 'that we shall never, never get there

185

alive?' The watchman hobbled over and threw an armful of wood on to the fire.

'"Never" shares a big bed with "Once", Mulla-Mulgar,' he said, raking the embers together with a long forked stick. 'But we have no Magic.'

Nod stared. Should he tell this dull Man of the Mountains to think no more of death, seeing that *he*, Ummanodda himself, had Magic? Should he let him dazzle his eyes one little moment with his Wonderstone? He fumbled in the pocket of his sheep-skin coat, stopped, fumbled again. His hair rose stiff on his scalp. He shivered, and then grew burning hot. He searched and searched again. The Mulgar eyed him sorrowfully. 'What ails you, O nephew of a great King?' he said in his faint, high voice. 'Fleas?'

Nod stared at him with flaming eyes. He could not think or speak. His Wonderstone was gone. He turned, dropped on his fours, sidled noiselessly back to Thimble's litter, and sat down.

How had he lost it? When? Where? And in a flash came back to his outwearied, aching head remembrance of how, in the height of the eagle-fighting, there had come the plunge of a lean, gaping beak and the sudden rending of his coat. Vanished for ever was Tishnar's Wonderstone, then. The Valley's faded. Noomanossi drew near.

He sat there with chattering teeth, his little skull crouch-

ing in his wool, worn out with travel and sleeplessness, and the tears sprang scalding into his eyes. What would Thumb say now? he thought bitterly. What hope was left for Thimble? He dared not wake them, but stooped there like a little bowed old man, utterly forlorn. And so sitting, cunning Sleep, out of the silence and darkness of Arakkaboa, came softly hovering above the troubled Nizza-neela; he fell into a shallow slumber. And in this witching slumber he dreamed a dream.

He dreamed it was time gone by, and that he was sitting on his log again with his master, Battle, just as they used to sit, beside their fire. And the Oomgar had a great flat book covering his knees. Nod could see the book marvellously clearly in his dream – a big book, white as a dried palm-leaf, that stretched across the sailor knee to knee. And the sailor was holding a little stick in his hand, and teaching him, as he used in a kind of sport to do, his own strange 'Ningllish' tongue. Before, however, the sailor had taught the little Mulgar only in words, by sound, never in letters, by sight. But now in Nod's dream Battle was pointing with his little prong, and the Mulgar saw a big straddle-legged black thing in the book strutting all across the page.

'Now,' said the Ooomgar, and his voice sounded small but clear, 'what's that, my son?'

But Nod in his dream shook his head; he had never seen the strange shape before.

'Why, that's old "A", that is,' said Battle; 'and what did old straddle-legs "A" go for to do? What did "A" do, Nod Mulgar?'

And Nod thought a voice answered out of his own mouth and said: ' "A" ... Yapple-pie.'

'Brayvo!' cried the Oomgar. And there, sure enough, filling plump the dog's-eared page, was a great dish something like a gourd cut in half, with smoke floating up from a little hole in the middle.

' "A" – Apple-pie,' repeated the sailor; 'and I wish we had him here, Master Pongo. And now, what's this here?' He turned the page.

Nod seemed in his dream to stand and to stare at the odd double-bellied shape, with its long straight back, but in vain. 'Bless ye, Nod Mulgar,' said Battle in his dream, 'that's old Buzz-buzz; that's that old garden-robber – that's "B".'

' "B",' squealed Nod.

'And "B" – he bit it,' said Battle, clashing his small white teeth together and laughing, as he turned the page.

Next in the dream-book came a curled black fish, sitting looped up on its tail. And that, the Oomgar told him, leaning forward in the firelight, was 'C'; that was 'C' – crying, clawing, clutching, and croaking for it.

Nod thought in his dream that he loved learning, and loved Battle teaching him, but that at the word 'croaking' he looked up wondering into the sailor's face, with a kind of waking stir in his mind. What was this 'IT'? What could this 'IT' be – hidden in the puffed-out, smoking pie that 'B' bit, and 'C' cried for, and swollen 'D' dashed after? And . . . over went another crackling page . . . The Oomgar's face seemed strangely hairy in Nod's dream; no, not hairy – tufty, feathery; and so loud and shrill he screamed 'E'. Nod all but woke up.

' "E",' squeaked Nod timidly after him.

'And what – what – what did "E" do?' screamed the Oomgar.

But now even in his dream Nod knew it was not the beloved face of his sailor Zbaffle, but an angry, keen-beaked, clamouring, swooping Eagle that was asking him the question, ' "E", "E", "E" – what did "E" do?' And clipped in the corner of its beak dangled a thread, a shred of his sheep's-jacket. What ever, ever did 'E' do? puzzled in vain poor Nod, with that dreadful face glinting almost in touch with his.

'Dunce! Dunce!' squalled the bird. '"E" eat it . . .'

'"E" . . . eat it,' seemed to be faintly echoing on his ear in the darkness when Nod found himself wide awake and bolt upright, his face cold and matted with sweat, yet with a heat and eagerness in his heart he had never known before. He scrambled up and crept along in the rosy firelight till he came to the five dead eagles. Their carcasses lay there with frosty feathers and fast-sealed eyes. From one to another he crept slowly, scarcely able to breathe, and turned the carcasses over. Over the last he stooped, and – a flock, a thread of sheep's wool dangled from its clenched black beak. Nod dragged it, stiff and frozen, nearer the fire, and with his knife slit open the deep-black, shimmering neck, and there, wrapped damp and dingily in its scrap of Oomgar-paper, his fingers clutched the Wonderstone. He hastily wrapped it up, just as it was, in the flock of wool, and thrust it deep into his other pocket, and with trembling fingers buttoned the flap over it. Then he went softly back to his brothers, and slept in peace till morning.

CHAPTER SEVENTEEN

The Long-nosed Obobbomans

When he awoke, bright day was on the mountains. The little snow-wolves had slunk back to their holes and lairs. The fires burned low. And Thimble lay in a sleep so quiet and profound it seemed to Nod the heart beneath that sharp-ribbed chest was scarcely stirring. It was bitter cold on these heights in the sunlessness of morning. And Nod was glad to sit himself down beside one of the wood-fires to eat his breakfast of nuts, and swallow a suppet or two of the thawed Mulgar-milk. But the Men of the Mountains had plucked and roasted the eagles, and were squatting, with not quite such doleful faces as usual, picking with pointed, rather cat-like teeth, the bones.

Nod could not help watching them under his eyebrows, where they sat, with tail-tufts over their shoulders, in their fleecy hair, blinking mildly from their pale pink eyes. For, though here and there may be seen a Mountain-Mulgar with eyes blue as the turquoise, by far the most of them have pink, and some (but these are what the Oomgar-Nuggas would call Witch-doctors, or Fulbies) have one of either. They looked timid and feeble enough, these Moona-Mulgars, yet with what fearless fury had they fought with the eagles! How swiftly they shambled dim-sighted along these wrinkling precipices! Some even now were seated on the rocky verge as easily as Skeeto in its tree-top, their lean shanks dangling over. But they nibbled and tugged at their slender bird-bones, and peered and waved their long arms in faint talk; though, as their watchman had told Nod in the firelight, they knew they were all within earshot of the Harp.

Ghibba was sitting a little away from the others, eating with his eyes shut.

'Are you so sleepy, Prince of the Mountains, that you keep your eyes shut in broad day?' said Nod.

Ghibba wagged his head. 'No, Mulla-Mulgar, I am not sleepy; but one eye is scorched with the fire and one a little angry with the eagles, so that I can scarcely see at all.'

'Not blind?' said Nod.

Ghibba opened his eyes, red and glittering. 'Nay, twilight, not night, little Mulgar,' he answered cheerfully. 'I see no more of you than a little brown cloud against black mountains.'

'But how will you walk on these narrow, icy shelves?' said Nod.

'Why,' says he, 'I have a tail, Mulgar-Royal; and my people must lead me ... What of the morning, Nizza-neela?'

'It is bright as hoar-frost on the slopes and tops there,' said Nod, pointing. 'It dazzles Ummanodda's eyes to look. But the sun is behind this huge black wall of ours, so here we sit cold in the shadow.'

'Then we will wait,' said Ghibba, 'till he comes walking a little higher to melt the frost and drive away the last of the wolves.'

'Man of the Mountains,' said Nod presently, 'would you hold me if I crept close and put my head over the edge? I would like to see how many Mulgars-deep we walk.'

Ghibba laughed. 'This path is but as other Mulgar-paths, Mulla-Mulgar; no traveller need stumble twice. But I will do as you ask me.'

So Nod lay down flat on his stomach, while two of the Mountain-Mulgars clutched each a leg. He wriggled forward till head and shoulders hung beyond the margent of the rock. He shut his eyes a moment against that terrific steep of air, and the huge shadow of the mountain upon the deep blue forest. All far beneath was still dark with

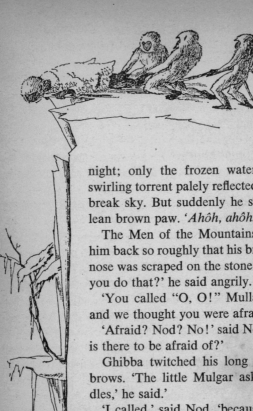

night; only the frozen waters of the swirling torrent palely reflected the daybreak sky. But suddenly he shot out a lean brown paw. '*Ahôh, ahôh!* I say!'

The Men of the Mountains dragged him back so roughly that his broad snub nose was scraped on the stone. 'Why do you do that?' he said angrily.

'You called "O, O!" Mulla-Mulgar, and we thought you were afraid.'

'Afraid? Nod? No!' said Nod. 'What is there to be afraid of?'

Ghibba twitched his long grey eyebrows. 'The little Mulgar asks us riddles,' he said.'

'I called,' said Nod, 'because I spied something jutting there with a fluff of hair in the wind that leaps the chasm, and with thin ends that look to me like the arms and legs of a Man of the Mountains lying caught in a bush of Tummusc.'

At the sound of Nod's '*Ahôh!*' Thumb had come scrambling along from the other fire, and many of the

Mountain-Mulgars fell flat on their faces, and leaned peering over the precipice. But their eyes were too dim to pierce far. They broke into shrill, eager whisperings.

'It is, perhaps, a wisp of snow, an eagle's feather, or maybe a nosegay of frost-flowers.'

'What was the name of him who fell fighting?' said Nod eagerly.

'His name was Ubbookeera,' said Ghibba.

'Then,' said Nod, 'there he hangs.'

'So be it, Eyes-of-an-Eagle,' said Ghibba; 'we will go down before he melts and fetch him up.' So they drove two of their long staves into a crevice of the rocks. And Ghibba, being one of the strongest of them, and also nearly blind, crept to the end and unwound himself down; then one by one the rest of the Mountain-Mulgars descended, till the last and least was gone.

'Hold my legs, Thumb, my brother, that I may see what they're at,' said Nod. Thumb clutched him tight, and Nod edged on his stomach to the end of the bending pole. He saw far down the grey string of the Men of the Mountains dangling, but even the last of them was still twenty or thirty Mulgars off the Tummusc-bush. He heard their shrill chirping. And presently the first sunbeam trembled over the wall of the mountain above them, and beamed clear into the valley. Nod wriggled back to Thumb. 'They cannot reach him,' he said. 'He lies there huddled up, Thumb, in a Tummusc-bush, just as he fell.'

'Why, then,' said Thumb, 'he must have hung dead all night. The eagles will have picked his eyes out.'

In a little while the last and least of the Mountain-Mulgars crept back over Ghibba's shoulders and scrambled on to the path. He was a little blinking fellow, and in colour patched like damask.

'Is he dead? Is he dead? Is thy "Messimut" dead?' said Nod, leaning his head.

'He is dead, Mulla-Mulgar, or in his second sleep,' he answered.

Now, all the Mulgar beads on that strange string stood whispering and nodding together. Ghibba presently turned away from them, and began raking back the last smoulderings of their watch-fire.

'What will you do?' said Nod. 'Why do you drag back the embers?'

'The swiftest of us is going back to bring a longer "rope" and stronger staves and Samarak, and, alive or dead, they will drag him up. But we go on, Mulla-Mulgar.'

'*Ohé*,' said Nod softly; 'but will he not be lifeless by then, Prince of the Mountains? Will not the eagle's feather be blown away? Will not the frost flowers have melted from the bush?'

Ghibba turned his grave, hairy face to Nod.

'The Men of the Mountains will remember you in their drones, Mulla-Mulgar, for saving the life of their kinsman; they will call you in their singing "Mulla-Mulgar Eengenares" ' – that is, Royal-Mulgar with the Eyes of an Eagle.

Nod laughed. 'Already am I in my brothers' thoughts, Prince of Bonfires, Noddle of Pork; if only I could see through Zut, they also might call me Eengenares, too!'

All were in haste now, binding up what remained of faggots and torches, combing and beating themselves, and quenching the fires. Soon the Mulgar who had been chosen to return had rubbed noses and bidden them all farewell, and had set out on his lonely journey home. Thimble still lay in a deep sleep, and so cold after the heats of fever that they had to muffle him twice or thrice in shadow-blankets to regain his warmth.

When they had trudged on a league or so the day began to darken with cloud. And a thin smoke began to fume up from below. The travellers pressed on in all haste, so fast that the tongues of the bearers of Thimble's litter lolled between their teeth. Wind rose in scurries, and every peak was shrouded. Unnatural gloom thickened around the lean, straggling troop of Mulgars. And almost before they had time to drive in their long poles, as shepherds drive in posts for their wattles, and to swathe and bind themselves close into the sloping rock, the tempest broke over them. A dense and tossing cloud of ice-motes beat up on the wind, so that soon the huddled travellers looked like nothing else than a long low mound on the Mulgar pass, heaped high with the drifting crystals. On every peak and crest the lightning played blue and crackling. In its flash the air hung still, bewitched with snowflakes. Thunder and wind made such a clamour between them that Nod could scarcely hear himself think. But the travellers sat mute and glum, and moved never a finger. Such storms sweep like wild birds through these mountains of Arakkaboa, and, like birds, are as quickly flown away. For in a little while all was peace again and silence. And the sun broke in flames out of the pale sky, shining in peaceful beauty upon the mountains, as if, indeed, the snow-white Zevveras of Tishnar had passed by.

The travellers soon beat each other free of their snow, and danced and slapped themselves warm. And now they were rejoiced to see in the distant clearness peeping above the shoulder of Makkri that league-long needle, Moot. The pass now began to widen, and a little before noonday they broke out into a broad and steep declivity of snow. And, seeing that they had but lately rested themselves, and soon would be journeying in shelter from the sun, they did not tarry for their 'glare', or middle-day sleep.

Their breath hung like smoke on the icy air. They sank at every step wellnigh up to their middles in snow, and were all but wearied out when at last they climbed up into a gorge cut sheer between bare walls of rock, and so lofty on either hand that daylight scarcely trembled down to them at the bottom.

So steep and glazed with ice was this gorge or gully that they were compelled to tie themselves together with strands of Cullum. They laid Thimble's litter on three long pieces of wood strapped together. Then, Ghibba going foremost, one by one they followed the ascent after him, stumbling and staggering, and heaving at the Cullum-rope to drag up poor Thimble on his slippery bed.

The Men of the Mountains have bristly feet and long, hairy, hardnailed toes. But Thumb and Nod, with their naked soles and shorter toes, could scarcely clutch the icy path at all, and fell so often they were soon stiff with bruises. Worse still, there frequents in the upper parts of these mountains a kind of witless or silly Mulgars, who are called Obobbomans, with very long noses. And just as men use a spyglass for sight, to magnify things and to bring things at a distance nearer, so these Obobbomans use their prolonged noses for smell. Long before Thumb and his company were come to their precipitous gully they had sniffed them out. And, being as mischievous as they are dull-witted, they had already scampered about, gathering together great heaps of stones and had now set themselves in a row, sniffing and chattering, along the edge of the rock on both sides, and waited there concealed in ambush.

When the Men of the Mountains had climbed up some little way into the gorge, and were scrambling and stumbling on the ice, these Obobbomans began pelting them as fast as they could with their stones and snowballs and splinters of ice. These missiles, though not very large, fell heavily down the walls of the precipice. And soon the whole caravan of Mulgars was brought to a standstill, they were so battered and bewildered by the stones.

As soon as the travellers stopped, these knavish Long-noses ceased to pelt them. So cautious and furtive are they that not a sign of them could be distinguished by the Mulgars staring up from below, though, indeed, a hundred or more of their thin snouts were actually protruded over the sides of the chasm, sniffing and trembling.

'Does it always rain pebble-stones and lumps of ice in these miserable hills?' said Thumb bitterly.

And Ghibba told him that it was the Long-nose Mulgars who were molesting them. They squatted down to breathe themselves, hoping to tire out the Obobbomans. But the instant they stirred, down showered snowball, ice, and stones once more. The travellers bound faggots and blankets over their heads, and struggled on, but the faggots kept slipping loose, and did not cover their stooping backs and buttocks. They shouted, threatened, shook their hands towards the heights; one or two even flung pebbles up that only bounced down upon their own heads again. It was all in vain. They halted once more, and squatted down in despair.

To add to their misery, it was so cold in this gorge that the breath of the Hill-Mulgars froze in long icicles on their beards, and whensoever they turned to speak to one another, or if they sneezed (as they often did in the cold, and with the snuff-like ice-dust), their fringes tinkled like glass. At last Ghibba, who had been sitting lost in thought of what to be doing next, suddenly groped his way forward, and bade two of his people sit down to their firesticks to make fire.

'What is this Whisker-face tinkering at now?' muttered

Thumb. 'What is he after now? We had best have come alone.'

'I know not,' said Nod; 'but if he can fight Noses, Thumb, as well as he can fight Beaks, we shall soon be getting on again.'

They crouched miserably in the snow, huddled up in shadow-blankets. The Obobbomans peeped farther into the ravine, chattering together, at a loss to understand why the travellers were sitting there so still. But at last fire came to the firesticks, and Ghibba then bade two or three of his Mountaineers kindle torches. Whereupon he gave to each a bundle of the eagle feathers which they had plucked from the five carcasses on the pass, and told them to burn them piecemeal in their torches.

'Ghost of a Môh-Man!' grunted Thumb sourly; 'he has lost his cheesy wits!'

With feathers fizzling, away they went again, slipping, staggering, and straining at the rope. Down at once hailed the stones again, the Obobbomans gambolling and squealing with delight in their silly mischief. And now no longer little were the snowballs, for the Long-noses all this time had been busy making big ones. These, four or five of them shoving together, with noses laid sidelong, rolled slowly to the edge, and pushed over. Down they came, bounding and rebounding into the abyss, and broke into fragments on the travellers' heads. Some, too, of the craftier of the Long-noses had mingled stones and ice in these great balls.

Thumb groaned and sweated in spite of the cold, for he, being by far the fattest and broadest of the travellers, received the most stones, and stumbled and fell far more often than the rest on his clumsy feet on the ice. Now, however, the smoke of the burning bunches of eagles' feathers was mounting in pale blue clouds through the gorge. It was enough. At the first sniff and savour of this evil smoke the Long-noses paused in their mischief, coughing and sneezing. At the next sniff they paused no longer. Away they scampered headlong, higgledy-piggledy, toppling one over another in their haste to be gone, squealing with disgust and horror; and the travellers at last were left in peace.

'I began to fear, O Man of the Mountains,' grunted Thumb to Ghibba, 'that your wits had got frostbitten. But I am not too old nor fat to learn wisdom.'

Ghibba lifted his face and peered from under the bandage he had wound over his sore eyes into Thumb's bruised face. 'Munza or Mountains, there's wisdom for all, brave traveller,' he said. 'They are very old friends of ours, these Long-noses; they could smell out a mouse's Meermut in the moon.'

CHAPTER EIGHTEEN

On Again

The icy pass grew ever steeper, but now that the travellers were no longer pestered by the Obobbomans they managed to struggle slowly on. And near about sunset they had tugged their way to the top, and come out again upon the open mountainside. They spread their blankets and threw themselves down, panting, bruised, and outwearied. But they made no fire here yet, because their wood was running short, and all that they had would be needed against the small hours of the night. They nibbled at their blue cheese and a few cold eagle-bones, and, having cut one of their skin-bags to pieces, broke up the frozen milk and shared the lumps between them.

Thumb and Nod crouched down beside Thimble, who was now awake and in his own mind. And they told him all that had happened since his megrims had come on. He was still weak and fretful, and turned his eyes hastily from sight of the mouldy cheese the Mountain-Mulgars were nibbling. But he sucked a few old Ukka-nuts. Then they lifted him gently, and with an arm round Thumb's neck and a hand on Nod's shoulder, they walked him awhile quietly in the snow.

While the brothers were thus walking friendly together, Ghibba groped his way up to them.

'I come, Royal Travellers,' he said, 'to tell you that here our country ends. Zut lies now behind us. Yonder stretches the Shadow Country, and my people know the way no farther.'

The three brothers turned their heads to look, and on

their cudgel-hand, about two leagues distant, stood Solmi; to the west, and a little in front of them, Moot and Makkri. Upon the topmost edge of the snow-slope at the foot of which they were now encamped ran a long, low border of a kind of thorn-bush, huddling among great rocks and boulders, resembling a little the valleys of the Babba-boomas.

'You mean, O Man of the Mountains, whose friendship has been our very lives to us,' said Thumb, 'that now we must journey on alone?'

'No, Mulla-Mulgar; I mean only that here the Moona country, my people's country, ends, and therefore that I cannot now be certain of the way to the Valleys of Tishnar. But this I do know; that beyond here is thick with the snares of Noomanossi. But if the Mulgar Princes and the Nizza-neela Eengenares, who saved my kinsman's life, would have it so, and are not weary of our company, then I and my people will journey on with them till they come to an end. We know from childhood these desolate mountains. They are our home. We eat little, drink little, and can starve as quietly as an icicle can freeze. If need be (and I do not boast, Mulla-Mulgars), we Thin-shanks can march

201

softly all day for many days, and not fall by the way. We are, I think, merely Leather-Men, not meant for flesh and blood. But the Mulla-Mulgars have fought with us, and we are friends. And I myself am friend to the last sleep of the small Prince, Nizza-neela, who has the colour of Tishnar in his eyes. Shall it be farewell, Travellers, or shall we journey on together?'

The brothers looked long at the black and thorn-set trees, at the towering rocks, at the wastes of the beautiful snows, then turned with astonishment to this old, half-blind mountaineer with his lean, sinewy arms, and hill-bent legs and his bandaged eyes. And Thumb lifted his hands in salutation to Ghibba, as if he were a Mulla-Mulgar himself.

'Why should we lead you into strange dangers, O Man of the Mountains,' he grunted – 'maybe to death? But if you ask to come with us, if we have only to choose, how can I and my brothers say no? We will at least be friends who do not part while danger is near, and though we never reach the Valley, Tishnar befriends the Meermuts of the brave. Let us, then, go on together.'

So Ghibba went back to his people, and told them what Thumb had said. And being now agreed together, they all hobbled off but three, who were left to guard the bundles, to break and cut down wood, and to see if perhaps among the thorns grew any nut-trees. But they found none; and for their pains were only scratched and stung by these waste-trees which bear a deadly poison in their long-hooked thorns. This poison, like the English nettle, causes a terrible itch to follow wherever the thorns scratch. So that the travellers could get no peace from the stinging and itching except by continually rubbing the parts in snow wherever the thorns had entered.

And Nod, while they were stick-gathering, kept close to Ghibba.

'Tell me, Prince of the Mountains,' he said, 'what are

these nets of Noomanossi of which you spoke to my brother Thumb? What is there so much to fear?'

Ghibba had sat himself down in the snow to pluck a thorn out of his foot. 'I will tell the Prince a tale,' he said, stooping over his bundle.

'Long time ago came to our mountains a Mulgar travelling alone. My kinsmen think oftener of him than any stranger else, because, Mulla-Mulgar, he taught us to make fire. He was wayworn and full of courage, but he was very old. And he too was journeying to the Valleys of Tishnar. And he, too, was a silent Mulgar, never stirred his tongue unless in a kind of drone at evening, and told us little of himself except in sleep.'

'What was he like?' said Nod. 'Was he mean and little, like me, tall and bony, like my brother Thimble, or fat, like the Mulla-Mulgar, my eldest brother, Thumb?'

'He was,' said Ghibba, 'none of these. He was betwixt and between. But he wore a ragged red jacket, like those of the Mulgars, and on his woman-hand stood no fourth finger.'

'Was the little woman-finger newly gone, or oldly gone?' said Nod.

'I was younger then, Nizza-neela, and looked close at everything. It was newly gone. The stump was bald and pale red. He was, too, white in the extreme, this old Mulgar travelling out of Munza. Every single hair he carried had, as it were, been dipped in Tishnar's meal.'

'I believe – oh, but I do believe,' said Nod, 'this poor old traveller was my father, the Mulla-Mulgar Seelem, of the beautiful Valleys.'

'Then,' said Ghibba, jerking his faggot on to his back, and turning towards the camp, 'he was a happy Mulgar, for he had brave sons.'

'Tell me more,' said Nod. 'What did he talk about? Did he speak ever of Ummanodda? How long did he stay with the Mulla-Moonas? Which way did he go?'

'Lead on, then,' said Ghibba, peering under his bandage.

'Here go I,' said Nod, touching his paw.

'He followed the mountain-paths with my own father,' said Ghibba, 'and lived alone for many days in one of our Spanyards,* for he was worn out with travel, and nearly dead from lying down to drink out of a Quickkul-fish pool. But after five days, while he was still weak, he rose up at daybreak, crying out in Munza-Mulgar he could remain with us no longer. So my people brought him, as I have brought you, to this everlasting snow-field, where he said farewell and journeyed on alone.'

'Had he a gun?' said Nod.

'What is a gun, Nizza-neela?'

'What then – what then?' cried Nod impatiently.

'Two nights afterwards,' continued the old Mulgar, 'some of my people came up to the other end of the gorge of the Long-noses. There they found him, cold and bleeding, in his second sleep. The Long-noses had pelted him with stones till they were tired. But it was not their stones that had driven him back. He would not answer when the Men of the Mountains came whispering, but sat quite still, staring under his black arches, as if afraid. After two days more he rose up again, crying out in another voice, like a Môh-Mulgar. So we came again with him, two "ropes" of us, along the walks the traveller knows. And towards evening, with his bag of nuts and water-bottle, in his rags of Juzana, he left us once more. Next morning my father and my

---

* I suppose, huts or burrowings.

people came one or two together to where we sit, and – what did they see?'

'*What* did they see?' Nod repeated, with frightened eyes.

'They did see only this,' said Ghibba: 'footsteps – one-two, one-two, just as the Mulla-Mulgar walks – all across the snow beyond the thorn-trees. But they did see also other footsteps, slipping, sliding, and here and there a mark as if the traveller had fallen in the snow, and all these coming *back* from the thorn-trees. And at the beginning of the ice-path was a broken bundle of nuts strewn abroad, but uneaten, and the shreds of a red jacket. Water-bottle there was none, and Mulgar there was none. We never saw or heard of that Mulgar again.'

'O Man of the Mountains,' cried Nod, 'where, then, is my father now?'

Ghibba stooped down and peered under his bandage close to Nod's small face. 'I believe, Eengenares, your father – if that Mulgar was your father – is happy and safe now in the Valleys of Tishnar.'

'But,' said Nod, 'he must have come back again out of his wits with fear of the Country of Shadows.'

'Why,' said Ghibba, 'a brave Mulgar might come back once, twice, ten times; but while one foot would swing after the other, he might still arise in the morning and try again. "On, on," he would say. "It is better to die, going, than to live, come-back."'

And Nod comforted himself a little with that. Perhaps he would yet meet his father again, riding on Tishnar's leopard-bridled Zevveras; perhaps – and he twisted his little head over his shoulder – perhaps even now his Meermut haunted near.

'But tell me – tell me *this*, Mountain-Mulgar: What was the fear which drove him back? What feet so light ran after him that they left no imprint in the snow? Whose shadow-hands tore his jacket to pieces?'

Ghibba threw down his bundle of twigs, and rubbed his itching arms with snow.

'That, Mulla-Mulgar,' he said, smiling crookedly, 'we shall soon find out for ourselves. If only I had the Wonderstone hung in my beard, I should go singing.'

Nod opened his mouth as if to speak, and shut it again. He stared hard at those bandaged eyes. He glanced across at the black, huddling thorn-trees; at the Mountain-Mulgars, going and returning with their faggots; at Thimble lying dozing in his litter. All the while betwixt finger and thumb he squeezed and pinched his Wonderstone beneath the lappet of his pocket.

Should he tell Ghibba? Should he wait? And while he was fretting in doubt whether or no, there came a sharp, short yelp, and suddenly out of the thorn-trees skipped a

Mountain-Mulgar, and came scampering helter-skelter over the frozen snow, yelping and chattering as he ran. Following close behind him lumbered Thumb, who hobbled a little way, then stopped and turned back, staring.

'Why do you dance in the snow, my poor child? What ails you?' mocked Ghibba, when the Mountain-Mulgar had drawn near. 'Have you pricked your little toe?'

The Mountain-Mulgar cowered panting by the fire which Ghibba had kindled. And for a long while he made no answer. So Nod scrambled on his fours up the crusted slope of snow. He passed, as he went, two or three of the Men of the Mountains whimpering and whispering. But none of them could tell him what they feared. At last he reached Thumb, who was still standing, hunched solitary amid the snow, gazing in silence at the clustering thorn-trees.

'What is it, brother?' said Nod, as he came near. 'What is it, brother? Why do you crouch and stare?'

'Come close, Ummanodda,' said Thumb. 'Tell me, is there anything I see?' They hobbled a little nearer, stayed again; and stood motionless.

These thorn-trees, as dense as holly, but twisted and huddled, grew not close together, but some few paces apart, as if they feared each other's company. Between them only purest snow lay, on which evening shed its light. And now that the sun was setting, leaning his beams on them from behind Moot, their gnarled and spiny branches were aflame with scarlet. It was utterly still. Nod stood with wide-open eyes. And softly and suddenly, he hardly knew how or when, he found himself gazing into a face, quiet and lovely, and as it were of the beauty of the air. He could not stir. He had no time to be afraid. They stood there, these clumsy Mulgars, so still that they might have been carved out of wood. Yet, thought Nod afterwards, he was not afraid. He was only startled at seeing eyes so beautiful beneath hair faint as moonlight, between the thorn-trees, smiling out at

him from the coloured light of sun-
set. Then, just as suddenly and as
softly, the face was gone, vanished.

'Thumb, Thumb!' he whispered,
'surely I have seen the eyes of a
wandering Midden of Tishnar?'

'Hst!' said Thumb harshly; 'there,
there!' He pointed towards one of
the thorn-trees. Every branch was
quivering, every curved, speared leaf
trembling, as if a flock of silvery
Parrakeetoes perched in the upper
branches, where there are no thorns, or as if scores of the
tiny Spider-Mulgars swung from twig to twig. The next
moment it was still – still as all the others that stood around,
afire with the last sunbeams. Yet nothing had come, nothing
gone.

'*Acch magloona nani, Nod,*' called Thumb, afraid, '*lago-
osla sul majeela!*'

They scuttled back, without once turning their heads, to
the fire, where all the Hill-Mulgars were sitting. Whispering
together they were, too, as they nibbled their cheese and
sipped slowly from their gurgling, narrow-mouthed bags or
bottles. They had carried Thimble close to the fire, and
Ghibba was roasting nuts for him. Thumb and Nod came
down and seated themselves beside Ghibba, but they had
agreed together to say nothing of what they had seen, for
fear of affrighting Thimble, who was still weak in head and
body, and continually shivering. And Nod told his brothers
all that Ghibba had told him concerning the solitary traveller. And Thumb sat listening, heavy and still, with his great
face towards the huddling thorns that wooded the height.

So they talked and talked, sitting together, round about
their fire. The twigs of these thorns burn marvellous clear
with colours, and at each thorn-tip, as the flame licks near,

wells out and gathers a milk-pale globe of poison that, drying, bursts in the heat. So all the fire is continually a-crackle, amidst a thin smoke of a smell like nard. Never before had so bright a bonfire blazed upon these hills. For the Men of the Mountains never camp beyond the pass, and the Long-noses have not even the wits to keep a fire fed with fuel. But as the day wore on, and when all the feather-smoke had dispersed, they assembled in hundreds upon hundreds, sitting a long distance off, all their noses stuck out towards the blaze, snuffing the cloudy fragrance of the nard. But they were too much afraid of the travellers to venture near now that they were free men and out of the pass.

The sun had set, but the moon was at full, and the travellers determined to go forward at once. It was agreed

that every one should carry a bundle of sticks on his shoulders, also a stout cudgel or staff; that they should march close in rows of four, with Thimble's litter in their midst; and that the Mulgar at each corner should carry a burning torch. They made what haste they could to tie up their bundles, bottles, and faggots, so as to lose nothing of the moon's brilliance during the long night. She rode unclouded above the snow-fields when the little band of Mulgar travellers set out. As soon as they were gone, down trooped the long-nosed Obobbomans to the fire, sniffing and scuffling, to fall asleep at last, higgledy-piggledy, in a great squirrel-coloured ring around the glowing embers, their noses towards the fire.

CHAPTER NINETEEN

The Phantoms and the Feast

The travellers marched slowly, keeping sharp watch, their cudgels ready in their hands. Behind them, paled by the moonlight, shook the fiery silver of the Sulemnāgar. With this at their backs and that North Pole, Moot, in huge concealment, a little to their left, they made their way at an angle across the open snow, and approached the tangled thickets. Here they walked more closely together, with heads aslant and tails in air, like little old men, like pedlars, blinking and spying, wishing beyond measure they were sitting in comfort around their watch-fire. The farther they zig-zagged betwixt the thorn-trees, the more doubtful grew the way. For these trees rise all so equal in height and thickness they often with their tops shut out the stars, and there was nothing by which the travellers could mark what way they went.

Still they pressed on, their hairy faces to the night-wind, which Ghibba had observed before starting was drifting from the north. They shuffled crisply over the snow, coughing softly, and gurring in their throats, winding in and out between the trees, and casting lean, gigantic shadows across the open spaces. For so dazzling bright the moon gleamed, she almost put out the smoky flare of their torches. But it gave the Mulgars more courage to march encompassed with their own light. Their packs were heavy, the thickets sloped continually upward. But the poison-thorns curl backward beneath the drooping hood of their leaves by night – in the hours, that is, when, it is said, they distil their poison – so the travellers were no longer fretted by their stings. Thus,

211

then, they gradually advanced till Moot was left behind them, and out of the grey night rose Mulgarmeerez, mightiest of Arakkaboa's peaks, whose snows have known no Mulgar footprints since the world began.

Only the whish of the travellers' feet on the snow was to be heard, when suddenly all with one accord stopped dead, as if a voice had cried, 'Halt!'

Their torches faintly crackled, their smoke rising in four straight pillars towards the stars. And, listening, they heard, as if from all around them in the air, clear yet strangely small voices singing, with a thin and pining sound like glass. It floated near, this tiny, multitudinous music – so near that the travellers drew back their faces with wide-open eyes. Then it seemed out of the infinite distance to come, echoing across the moonlit spars that towered above their heads.

And Ghibba said softly, jerking up his bundle and peering around him from beneath his eye-bandage: 'Courage, my kinsmen! It is the Danger-Song of Tishnar we hear, who loves the fearless.'

At this one of the Men of the Mountains thrust up his pointed chin, and said, wagging his head: 'Why do we march like this at night, Mulla-Moona? These are not our mountain-passes. Let us camp here while we are still alive, and burn a great watch-fire till morning.'

'You have faggots, Cousin of a Skeeto,' said Ghibba. 'Kindle a fire for yourself, and catch us up at daybreak.'

The Mountain-Men laughed wheezily, for now the singing had died away. On they pushed again. But now the thorn-trees gathered yet closer together, so that the Mulgars could no longer walk in company, but had to straggle up by ones or twos as best they could. Still up and up they clambered, laying hold of the thick tufts of leaves sticky with poison to drag themselves forward. Many times they were compelled to pause for breath, and to gaze back in wonder on the moon-dappled forest through which they had so heavily and toilfully ascended.

Thus they continued, until, without any warning, Thumb, who was leading the straggling troop, broke out into a loud, hard, dismal bark of fear, on suddenly finding himself beneath contorted branches facing the frozen verge of yet another and wider plateau of snow. He stood motionless, leaning heavily on his cudgel, the knuckles of his other hand resting in the snow, his breath caught back, and his head stooping forward between his shoulders, staring on and on between astonishment and dread.

For there, ranged along the opposite ridge, as it were on the margin of an enormous platter, stood as if frozen in the moonlight the monstrous silver-haired Meermuts of Mulgarmeerez, guarding the enchanted orchards of Tishnar. Thumb stood in deep shadow, for instantly, at sight of these shapes, as one by one the travellers came straggling up together, they quenched their hissing torches in the snow. No sign made the Meermuts that they had seen the little quaking band of lean and ragged Mulgars. But even a squirrel cracking a nut could have been heard across these windless and icy altitudes. And on and on it seemed that bark of fear went echoing from spur to spur. The wretched Mulgars could only stand and gaze in helpless confusion at the phantoms, whose eyes shone dismally in the moonlight from beneath their silver hair and great purple caps. The Meermuts stood, as it were, for a living rampart all down the untrodden snow towards the great Pit of Mulgarmeerez till lost in the faint grey mists of the mountains.

'What's to be done now, Prince of Ladder-makers?' said Thumb presently. 'Are we not weary of wandering? There's room for us all in those great shadowy bellies.'

'*Itthiluthi thoth "Meermut" annoth anoot oonoothi,*' lisped one of the Moona-Mulgars – that is to say, in their own language, 'But maybe these Meermuts gnaw before swallowing.'

As for Ghibba, he feigned that his eyes were too weak and sore, and peered in vain beneath his bandages. 'Tell me what's to be seen, Mulla-Mulgar,' he said. 'Why do we linger? The frost's in my toes. Up with fresh torches and go forward.'

Thumb grunted, but made no answer. Then Ghibba drew softly back into the deeper shadow, and the rest of the Mulgars, who by now were all come up, stood whispering, some in perplexity, not knowing what to do; some itching and sniffing to go forward, and one or two for turning back. One Moona-Mulgar, indeed, mewing like a cat in his extreme fear, when he had heard Thumb's sudden bark, had turned lean shanks and hairy arms and fled down by the way they had come. Fainter and fainter had grown the sounds of snapping twigs, until all again was silent.

'What wonder our father Seelem stumbled as he ran?' muttered Nod to Thumb.

But Ghibba stood thinking, the skin of his forehead twitching up and down, as is the habit of nearly all Mulgars high and low. 'This is our riddle, O Mulla-Mulgars,' he said : 'If we turn back and continue slowly upward, so as to creep round in hiding from these giant Meermuts, we shall

214

only come at last to batter our heads against the walls of Moot. And Moot I know of old: there the Gunga-Moonas make their huddles. And the other way, under the moon, there juts a precipice five thousand Mulgars deep, through which, so the old news goes, creeps slowlier than moss Tishnar's never-melting Obea of ice. Here, then, is our answer, Princes: The valleys must be yet many long days' journey. Either, then, we go straight forward beneath the feet of Tishnar's Orchard-Meermuts, like forest-mice that gambol among a Mutti of Ephelantoes, or else, like shivering Jack-Alls, we go back, to live out the rest of this littlest of lives itching, but having nowhere to scratch. What thinks the Mulgar Eengenares?'

And at that Nod remembered what the watchman had said, when they were talking together by the eagles' watchfires. He touched Thumb, speaking softly in Mulgar-Royal. 'Thumb, my brother, what of the Wonderstone? what of the Wonderstone? Shall we tell this Moona-Mulgar of that?'

Thumb laughed sulkily. 'Seelem kept all his wits for you, Jugguba,' he answered; 'rub and see!'

So Nod spread open his pocket-flap and fetched out the Wonderstone, wrapped in its wisp of wool and the stained leaf of paper from Battle's little book. He held it out in his brown, hairless palm to Ghibba beneath the thorn. 'What think you of that, Mulla-Moona?' he said. And even Ghib-

ba's dim eyes could discern its milk-pale shining. They talked long together in the shadow of the thorns, while the rest of the skinny travellers sat silent beside their bundles, coughing and blinking as they mumbled their mouldy cheese-rind.

Ghibba declared that, Nod

being a Nizza-neela, they two should venture on alone to-gether. 'I am nothing but a skin of bones – nothing to pick,' he said, 'and all but sandblind, and therefore could not see to be afraid.'

'No, no, no, Mulla-Moona,' Thumb grunted stubbornly. 'If mischief came to my brother, how could I live on, listen-ing to the chittering of his mother's Meermut asking me, "Where is Nod?" Stay here and guard my brother, Thim-bulla, who is too sick and weak to go with us; and if we neither of us return before morning, deal kindly with him, Mulla-Moona, and have our thanks till you too are come to be a shadow.'

So at last it was agreed between them. And Thumb and Nod returned together to the edge of the wood and peered out once more towards the phantom-guarded orchards. Nod waited no longer. He wetted his thumb once more, and rubbed thrice, droning or crooning, and stamping nimbly in the snow, till suddenly Thumb sprang back clean into the midst of a thorn-tree in his dismay.

'*Ubbe nimba sul ugglourint!*' he cried hollowly. For the child stood there in the snow, shining as if his fur were on fire with silver light. About his head a wreath of moon-coloured buds like frost-flowers was set. His shoulders were hung with a robe like spider-silk falling behind him to his glistening heels. But it was Nod's shrill small laughter that came out of the shining.

'Follow, oh follow, brother,' he said. 'I am Fulby, I am Oomgar's M'keeso; it is a dream; it is a night-shadow; it is Nod Meermut; it is fires of Tishnar. Hide in my blaze, Thumb Mulgar. And see these Noomas cringe!'

Thumb grunted, beat once on his chest like a Gunga, and they stepped boldly out together, first Nod, then black Thumb, into the wide splendour of the waste. And the Men of the Mountains watched them from between the spiky branches, with eyes round as the Minimuls', and mouths

ajar, showing through their whiskers their catlike teeth.

Out into the open snow that borders for leagues the trees of Tishnar's orchard stepped Nod, with his Wonderstone. And, as he moved along, the frost-parched flakes burned with the rainbow. But if the phantoms of Mulgarmeerez were not blind, they were surely dumb. They made no sign that they perceived this blazing pigmy advancing against them. Nod's light heels fell so fast Thumb could scarcely keep pace with him. He came on grunting and coughing, plying his thick cudgel, his great dark eyes fixed stubbornly upon the snow. And lo and behold! when next Nod lifted his face he saw only moonlight shining upon the smooth trunks of trees, which in the higher branches were stooping with coloured fruit. He laughed aloud, 'See, Thumb,' he said, 'my magic burns. M'keeso chatters. These Tishnar Meermuts are naught but trunks of trees!'

But Thumb stared in more dismal terror still, for he saw plainly now their huge and shadowy clubs, their necklets of gold and ivory, and the hideous, purple-capped faces of the ghouls gloating down on him. 'Press on, Ummanodda; your

eyes burn magic, and trees to you are sudden death to me.'
His hair stood out in a grisly mantle around him, for sheer
fear and horror of these gigantic faces as they passed. But
Nod edged lightly through, like mantling swan or peacock,
seeing only Tishnar's lovely orchards. No snow lay here in
these enchanted glades, but the grass was powdered with
pure white flowers that caught the flame of him in their
beauty as he passed. The strange small voices the travellers
had heard on the hillside seemed haunting the laden boughs
of the orchard. But to Thumb all was darkness, and frozen
snow, spiked thorn-trees, a-roost with evil birds, and the
horror of the motionless phantoms behind him. He seemed
ever and again to hear their stride between the twigs, and to
feel a terrific thumb and finger closing over his matted scalp.

In a little while the path the two Mulgars thridded led
out from under the boughs, and they found themselves at
the foot of the great peak they had all night been approaching. And Nod saw fountains springing in foam amid the
flowery grasses, and all about them were trees laden with
fruit, and the music of instruments and distant voices. But
not on these near things was his mind set, but on the secret
paths of Mulgarmeerez, winding down from the crested
peak above.

'O brother, my brother! Tishnar is walking on the hills,'
he said. But Thumb, though he rubbed his eyes, could see
nothing but the towering and desolate scaurs of ice and
snow and a kind of snow-choked ridge girdling the abrupt
mountainside. But Nod came to a stand, half-crouching,
amazed, and watched, as it seemed to him, the Middens of
Tishnar riding more beautiful than daybreak in the moonlight of her hills. And he heard a clear voice within him
cry: 'Have no fear, *Nizza-neela, Mulla-Mulgar jugguba
Ummanodda, neddipogo, Eengenares;* feast and be merry.
Tishnar watches over the brave.' And he told Thumb what
the voice had said to him.

And Thumb grew angry, for he was tired out of his courage. 'Have it as you will,' he said. 'It is easy to fear nothing and to see what is not here when you meddle with magic, and shine like a fish out of water. But as for me, I go back to my brother Thimble, and to my friends, the Men of the Mountains.' And he stumped sullenly off, crouching low over his cudgel.

Then Nod said softly: 'Wonderstone, Wonderstone! call back my brother and open his eyes.' Instantly Thumb stopped and stood upright. Thorn and snow, blain and ache and bruise were gone. He saw the meadows alight with starry flowers, the fountains and the fruit. And he smelled the smoke of nard and soltiziphal burning in the cressets of the servants of Tishnar. Nod laughed silently, and said: 'Bring, too, O Wonderstone, my brother Thimbulla on his litter, and the Prince Ghibba, and his kinsfolk to feast with me.'

For there, in the midst between the fountains, was a long low table spread with flowers and strange fruits and nuts, and lit with clear, pear-shaped flames floating in the air like that of the Wonderstone, but of the colours of ivory and emerald and amethyst; with nineteen platters of silver and nineteen goblets of gold. And presently they heard in the distance the grasshopper voices of the Hill-Mulgars, as they came stubling along with Thimble's litter in their midst, carrying their heavy faggots and bottles and bundles, their pink eyes blinking, their knees trembling, not knowing whether to be joyful or afraid.

CHAPTER TWENTY

The Fishing Mulgars

They cast off their burdens into the flowery meadows and besprinkled themselves with the pools of crystal water beneath the fountains. And Nod himself bathed Ghibba's eyes in the fountain-pool, so that he, too, could see, looking close, the wandering flames lighting the platters and goblets and fruits and nuts and flowers.

The travellers sat down, all the nineteen of them, Nod at the head of the table – that is, looking towards Mulgar-meerez – and Thumb at the foot, with Thimble propped up on the one side and Ghibba on the other. Many of the Mountain-Mulgars, however, who eat always sitting on the ground, soon found this perching on stools at a table irksome for their pleasure, and squatted themselves down in the thick grasses for Tishnar's supper. And they feasted on fruits they never before had tasted nor knew to grow on earth: one, rosy and red and round and small, with a long, slender stalk and a little pale hard stone, of the colour of amber, in the middle; one very sweet and globular, jacketed in a yellow rind, the inside divided into little juicy wedges as if for a mouthful each; another rough like lichen, with a tuft of leaves in a spike, rusty without and pale within; yet another with a hard, smooth coat like faded copper, but inside a houseful of hundreds of tiny fruits like seeds of the colour of blood, and running over with pleasant juices; also Manakin-figs, keeries, and love-apples, quinces, juleeps, xandimons, and grapes.

There were nuts also – green, coral, and cinnamon, long and little, hairy, smooth, crinkled, rough, in pairs, dark and double, round-ribbed and nuggeted – every kind of nut the

pouch of Mulgar knows. And they drank from their goblets
thin sweet wine, honey-coloured and lilac. And while they
ate and drank and made merry, lifting their cups, cracking
their nuts, hungrily supping, a distant and barbaric music
clashed in the air around the feasting travellers, like the
music of cymbal and dulcimer. Nod sat silken-silvery, with
every hair enlustred, his wrinkles gone, his small right hand
feeding him, while with his woman-hand he clasped his
Wonderstone, his little face bright as a child's, with topaz
eyes. Rejoiced were the sad-faced Mountain-Mulgars that
they had not forsaken the wandering Princes and gone
home. They feasted like men.

And at last, when all were refreshed, they rose and raised
their voices to Tishnar, hoarse and shrill, turning their
faces towards the vast and silent peak of Mulgarmeerez,
that jutted to the stars above their heads. Then they laid
themselves down in the sweet Immanoosa-scented meadow,
and soon, lulled by the noise of the fountains and the faint,
wandering orchard music, they fell asleep. Nod too, lay
down, ruffled with fire, burning like touchwood, amid the
enchanted flowers. But as deeper and deeper he sank to
sleep, his small brown fingers loosened and unclasped about
his Wonderstone; it fell to the bottom of his sheep-skin
pocket, and then, like a dream, vanished, gone, were fountain, feast, and music. And deep in snow, encircled by
poison-thorns, slumbered the nineteen travellers in their
rags and solitude, come out of magic, though they knew it
not.

One by one they awoke, stiff and dazed from so heavy a

221

sleep. They made no stay here, lest Tishnar should be angered with them. And to some the night seemed a dream. Some even whispered, 'Noomanossi'. And all, turning their faces, with daybreak broadening on their cheek-bones, hastily took up their workaday bundles again and hurried off.

But when Nod lifted his eyes to Mulgarmeerez, it seemed as if many phantom faces were looking down on them as they hastened, like some small company of hares or coneys, straggling across the whiteness. Being refreshed with sleep and Tishnar's phantom supper, the Mountain-Mulgars did not stay to take their 'glare', but just screened their feeble eyes against the sunbeams with eagle feathers, and, with Thimble swinging in his litter, scurried on across these smoother slopes. By night Mulgarmeerez, last of the seven peaks of Arakkaboa, was left behind them, and it seemed the wind blew not so sharply out of the haze on this side of the haunted woods. The travellers towards evening slept in a dry cavern. But it was a shallow, fidgety sleep, this cave being the haunt of a sharp-nosed wily sand-flea that made the most of a Mulgar-supper, more tooth-some than anything it had feasted on for many a moon.

Near about the middle of the next morning the travellers came in their descent to a river rushing swiftly but smoothly in the channel it had, ages gone, graven for its waters out

of the rock. The torrent was green, icy, and deep. On its farther side the rock rose steep and smooth. There, first they kindled themselves a fire, and warmed their cold bones. Then, having emptied their skin-bottles, they set off along the bank, or as near to it as they could walk at ease. Thimble's shivering was now gone, and he shanked along with his brothers, rather hobbledy, but in very good spirits. He took good care, however, to keep well in front of the Mountain-Mulgars, for if he even so much as faintly sniffed their cheese, he wambled. Steadily downward now they were marching. A warm wind was blowing out of the valley, the snows were melting, and rills trickling everywhere into the green and swirling water. And after a long march they came to a village of the Fishing-Mulgars.

These are a peaceable but ugly tribe of Mulgars, with extremely lean and sinewy tails, which are tufted at the tip, like those of the Moona-Mulgars, with a bunch of fine silky hair. They smear upon this tuft the pulp of a fruit that grows on a bush hanging over the water, called Soota, which the fish that swim in this torrent never weary of nibbling. Then, sitting huddled up and motionless in some little inlet or rocky hole in the bank, the Fishing-Mulgar pays out his long tail and lets it drift with the stream. By-and-by, maybe, some hungry fish comes swimming by that way and smells the pounded Soota. He softly stays, nibbling and tasting. Very slowly the Fishing-Mulgar, who instantly perceives the least commotion in his tail-tuft, draws back his bait without so much as blinking an eyelid. And when he has enticed the fish quite close to the bank, still all intent on its feeding, he stoops in a flash, and, plunging his sharp-nailed hands in the water, hooks the struggler out.

They swarm about water, these Mulgars, and teach their tiny babies to fish, too, by scooping out a hole or basin in the rock, which they fill from the torrent. In this they set free two or three little half-grown fish. These, with their infant tails, the children catch again and again, and are rewarded at evening, according to their skill, with a slice of roe or a backbone to pick.

An old and crafty Fishing-Mulgar will sit happy all day in some smooth hollow, and, having snared perhaps four or five, or even, maybe, as many as nine or twelve fat fishes, home he goes to his leaf-thatched huddle or sand-hole, and eats and eats till he can eat no more. After which his wife and children squat round and feed on what remains. Some eat raw, but those of less gluttony cook their catch at a large fire, which they keep burning night and day. Here the whole village of them may be seen sitting of an evening toasting their silvery supper. But, although they are such greedy feeders, there is something in the fish that keeps these Mulgars very lean. And the more they eat the leaner they get!

Sometimes, Ghibba told Nod, Fishing-Mulgars, who have given up all fruits and nuts to gluttonize, and live only on fish, have been known by much feeding to waste quite away. Moreover, a few years of this cold fishing paralyses their tails. And so, many go misshapen. On being questioned as to where they had learned to make fire, the Fishing-Mulgars told Ghibba that a certain squinting Môh-Mulgar had come their way once along the torrent, tongue-tied and trembling with palsy. By the fire he had made for himself the

224

Fishing-Mulgars, after he was gone, had stacked wood, and this was the selfsame fire that had been kept burning ever since. Did once this fire die out, not knowing of, nor having any, fire-sticks, it would be raw fish for the tribe for ever after. On hearing this, the travellers looked long at one another between gladness and dismay – gladness to hear that their father Seelem (if it was he) had come alive out of the Orchards, and dismay for his many ills.

They made their camp for two nights with these friendly people. They are as dull and stupid in most things as they are artful at fishing. But they are, beyond even the Munza-Mulgars, mischievous mimics. Even the little ones would come mincing and peeping with wisps of moss and grass stuck on their faces for eyebrows and whiskers, their long tails cocked over their shoulders, their eyes screwed up, in imitation of the Men of the Mountains. Lank old Thimble laughed himself hoarse at these piccaninnies. At night they beat little wood drums of different notes round their fires, making a sort of wearisome harmony. They also play at many sports – 'Fish in the Ring', 'A tail, a tail, a tail!' and 'Here sups Sullilulli'. But I will not describe them, for they are just such games as are played all the world over by Oomgar and Mulgar alike. They are all, however, young and old, hale and paralysed, incorrigible thieves and gluttons, and rarely comb themselves.

All along the rocky banks of the torrent the travellers passed next day the snug green houses of these Fishing-Mulgars. Nod often stayed awhile to watch their fishing and almost wished he had a tail, so that he too might smear and dangle and watch and plunge. But their language Nod could not in the least understand. Only by the help of signs and grimaces and long palaver could even Ghibba himself understand them. But he learned at least that, for some reason, the travellers would not long be able to follow the river, for the Fishing-Mulgar would first point to the travellers, then to the water, and draw a great arch with their finger in the air, shaking their little heads with shut eyes.

Ghibba tried in vain to catch exactly what they meant by these signs, for they had no word to describe their meaning to him. But after he had patiently watched and listened he said: 'I think, Mulla-Mulgars, they mean that if we keep walking along these slippery high banks, one by one, we shall topple head over heels into the torrent, and be drowned – over like that,' he said, and traced with his finger an arch in the air.

But this was by no means what the Fishing-Mulgars meant. For, about three leagues beyond the last of their houses, the travellers began to hear a distant and steady roar, like a faint, continuous thunder, which grew as they advanced ever louder and louder. And when the first faint flowers began to peep blue and yellow along the margin where the sun had melted the snow, they came to where the waters of the torrent widened and forked, some, with a great boiling of foam and prodigious clamour, whelming sheer down a precipice of rock, while the rest swept green and full and smooth into a rounded cavern in the mountain-side.

Here, as it was now drawing towards darkness, the travellers built their fire and made their camp. Next morning Ghibba decided, after consultation, to take with him two or three of the Mountain-Mulgars to see if they could in any wise clamber down beyond the cataract, and discover what kind of country lay beneath. Standing above, and peering down, they could see nothing, because, with the melting of the snow, a thick mist had risen out of the valley, and swam white as milk beneath them, into which great dish of milk the cataract poured its foam. Ghibba took at last with him five of the nimblest and youngest of the Moona-Mulgars, not knowing what difficulties or dangers might not beset them. But he promised to return to the Mulla-Mulgars before nightfall.

'But if,' he said, 'the first star comes, but no Ghibba, then do you, O Royalties, if it please you, build up a big fire above the waters, so that we may grope our way back to you before morning.'

So, with bundles of nuts and a little of the mountain cheese that was left, when the morning was nigh, Ghibba and his five set off. The rest of the travellers sat basking in the sunshine all that day, dressing their sores and bruises, dusting themselves, and sleeking out their matted hair. Some even, so great was the neglect they had fallen into, took water to themselves to ease their labour. But for the most part Mulgars use water for their *in*sides only (and that not often, so juicy are their fruits), never for their out. But dusk began to fall, the stars to shine faintly, darkness to sally out of the forest upon the mountain-side, and Ghibba had not returned. The travellers heaped on more wood, of which there was abundance, and lit a fire so fiery bright that to the Rock-folk looking down – wolf, and fox, and eagle, and mountain-leopard – it seemed like a great 'palaver' of Oomgar-Nuggas, who had had their villages in this valley many years before the Witzaweelwulla.

CHAPTER TWENTY-ONE

The Little Water Midden

When they could no longer see the hilltop for cloud and mist, Thumb lit a second fire on the isle of rock upon the verge of the cataract, where the water could not scatter on it. But no sign came of Ghibba and his five Moona-Men, and Nod began to fret, and could eat no supper for fear that some evil had overtaken them. But he said nothing, because he knew well enough by now that Thumb had much the same stomach for distrust as himself, though he kept a still tongue in his head, and that it only angered him to be pestered with questions no Mulgar-wit could answer. He sat by the watch-fire in his draggled sheep's-jacket, his hands on his knees, and wished he had lent Ghibba his Wonderstone. 'But no,' he thought, 'Mutta-matutta bade me "to no one". Ghibba is cunning and brave; he will come back.'

The Men of the Mountains coiled themselves up by the fire. They fear neither for themselves nor for one another. 'We die because we must,' they say. Yet none the less they raise, as I have said, long ululatory lamentations over their dead, and Noomanossi is their enemy as much as any Mulgar's. Thimble, still a little weak and hazy in his head after his sickness, fell quickly asleep; and soon even Thumb with head wagging from side to side, though he sat bolt upright on his heels in front of the fire, was dozing.

Nod alone could not close his eyes. He watched his brother's great face; lower and lower would drop his chin, wheel round, and start up again with a jerk. 'Good dreams, old Thumb,' he whispered; 'dreams of Seelem that bring him near'!

And all the while that these thoughts were stirring in his head he heard the endless echoing and answering voices of the cataract. Now they seemed the voices of Mulgars quarrelling, shouting, and fighting near and far; and now it seemed as if a thousand thousand birds were singing sweet and shrill beneath the leaves of a great forest. The shadows of the fire danced high. But the night was clear. He could see a great blue star shining right over their thin column of smoke, winding into the air. And now from the ravine into which Ghibba had gone down with his five Moona-Men the milk-pale mists began softly to overflow, as if from a pot filled to the brim. If only Ghibba would come back!

Nod scrambled up, and rather warily shuffled past the sleepers over to the other beacon-fire they had kindled. A few strange little night-beasts scuttled away as he drew near, attracted by the warmth of the fire, or even, perhaps, taking refuge in its shine from the night-hunting birds that wheeled and whirred in the air above them. 'Urrckk, urck!' croaked one, swinging so close that Nod felt the fan of its wings on his cheek. 'Starving Mulgars, urrckk, urck!' it croaked.

He heaped up the fire. But he could not see a hand's breadth into the ravine. Calm and still the mist lay, and softer than wool. Nod wandered restlessly back, passed again the camping Mulgars, and hobbled across till he came to the rocky bank of the torrent near to where it forked. Here a faint reflection of the flamelight fell, and Nod could see the drowsy fish floating coloured and round-eyed in the sliding water. And while he was standing there, he thought, like the sound of an ooboë singing amid thunder, he seemed to hear on the verge of the roar of the cataract a small wailing voice, not of birds, nor of Mulgars, nor like the phantom music of Tishnar. He crept softly down and along the water-side, under a black and enormous dragon-tree. And beneath the giant sedge he leaned forward his little hairy head, and as his flame-haunted eyes grew accustomed to the gloom, he perceived in the dark-green dusk in which she sat a Water Midden sitting low among the rushes, singing, as if she herself were only music, an odd little water-clear song.

> Bubble, Bubble,
>   Swim to see
> Oh, how beautiful
>   I be.
>
> Fishes, Fishes,
>   Finned and fine,
> What's your gold
>   Compared with mine?
>
> Why, then, has
>   Wise Tishnar made
> One so lovely,
>   One so sad?
>
> Lone am I,
>   And can but make
> A little song,
>   For singing's sake.

Her slim hands, her stooping shoulders, were clear and pale as ivory, and Nod could see in the rosy glimmering of the flames her narrow, beautiful face reflected amid the gold of her hair upon the formless waters. Mutta-matutta once had told Nod a story about the Water Middens whom Tishnar had made them beyond all things beautiful, and yet whose beauty had made beyond all things sad. But he could never in the least understand why this was so. When, by the sorcery of his Wonderstone, he had swept all glittering the night before across the jewelled snow, he had never before felt so happy. Why, then, was this Water Midden – by how much more beautiful than he was then! – why was she not happy, too? He peered in his curiosity, with head on one side and blinking eyes, at the Water Midden, and presently, without knowing it, breathed out a long, gruff sigh.

The still Water Midden instantly stayed her singing and looked at him. Not in the least less fair than the clustering flowers of Tishnar's orchard was her pale startled face. Her eyes were dark as starry night's beneath her narrow brows. She drew her fingers very stealthily across the clear dark water.

'Are you, then, one of those wild wandering Mulgars that light great fires by night,' she said, 'and scare all my fishes from sleeping?'

'Yes, Midden; I and my brothers,' said Nod. 'We light fires because we are cold and hungry. We are wanderers; that is true. But "wild" – I know not.'

'"Cold," O Mulgar, and with a jacket of sheep's wool, thick and curled, like that?'

Nod laughed. 'It was a pleasant coat when it was new, Midden, but we are old friends now – it and me. And though it keeps me warm enough marching by day, when night comes, and this never-to-be-forgotten frost sharpens, my bones begin to ache, as did my mother's before me, whose grave not even Kush can see.'

'The Mulgar should live, like me, in the water, then he too would never know of cold. Whither do you and your brothers wander, O Mulgar?'

'We have come,' said Nod, 'from beyond all Munza-Mulgar, that lies on the other side of the river of the saffron-fearing Coccadrilloes – that is, many score leagues south-ward of Arakkaboa – and we go to our Uncle, King Assa-simmon, Prince of the Valleys of Tishnar – that is, if that Mountain-Chief, my friend Ghibba, can find us a way.'

The Water Midden looked at Nod, and drew softly, slowly back her smooth gold locks from the slippery water. 'The Mulla-Mulgar, then, has seen great dangers?' she said. 'He is very young and little to have travelled so far.'

Nod's voice grew the least bit vainglorious. '"Little and young,"' he said. 'Oh yes. And yet, O beautiful Water Midden, my brothers would never have been here without me.'

'Tell me why that is,' she said, leaning out of her heavy hair.

'Because – because,' Nod answered slowly, and not daring to look into her face – 'because Queen Tishnar watches over me.'

The Water Midden leaned her head. 'But Tishnar watches over all,' she said.

'Why, then, O Midden, has, as your song said, Tishnar made you so sad?'

'Songs are but songs, Mulla-Mulgar,' she answered. 'It is sad seeing only my own small loneliness in the water. Would not the Mulgar himself weary with only staring fish for company?'

'Are there, then, no other Water Middens in the river?' said Nod.

'Have you, then, seen any beside me?'

'None,' said Nod.

The Water Midden turned away and stooped over the water. 'Tell me,' she said, 'why does the Queen Tishnar guard so closely *you*?'

'I am a Nizza-neela, Midden – Mulla-Mulgar Umma-nodda Nizza-neela Eengenares – that is what I am called, speaking altogether. Other names, too, I have, of course, mocking me. Who is there wise that was never foolish?'

'A Nizza-neela!' said the Midden, leaning back and glancing shyly out of her dark eyes.

'Oh yes,' said Nod gravely; 'but besides that I carry with me ...'

'Carry with you?' said she.

'Oh, only the Wonderstone,' said Nod.

Then the Water Midden lifted both her hands and scattered back her long pale locks over her narrow shoulders. 'The Wonderstone? What, then, is that?'

Nod told her, though he felt angry with himself, all about the Wonderstone, and what magic it had wrought.

'O most marvellous Mulla-Mulgar,' she said, 'I think, if I could but see but once this Wonderstone – I think I should be never sad again.'

Nod turned away, glancing over his shoulder to where, leaning amid the stars, hung the distant darkness of Mulgar-meerez. He slowly unfastened his ivory-buttoned pocket and groped for the Wonderstone. Holding it tight in his bare brown palm, he scrambled down a little nearer to the water, and unlatched his fingers to show it to the Midden. But now, to his astonishment, instead of glooming pale as a little moon, it burned angry as Antares.

The Water Midden peeped out between her hair, and laughed and clapped her hands. 'Oh, but if I might but hold it in my hand one moment, I think that I should never even sigh again!' said she. Nod's fingers closed on the Wonderstone again.

'I may not,' he said.

'Then,' said the Water Midden sorrowfully, 'I will not ask.'

'My mother told me,' said Nod.

But the Water Midden seemed not now to be listening. She began to smooth and sleek her hair, sprinkling the ice-cold water upon it, so that the drops ran glittering down those slippery paths like dew.

'Midden, Midden,' said Nod quickly, 'I did not mean to say any unkindness. You would give me back my Wonder-stone very quickly?'

'Oh, but, gentle Mulla-Mulgar,' said the Midden, 'my hands are cold; they might put out its fiery flame.'

'I do not think so, most beautiful Midden,' Nod said. 'Show me your fingers, and let me see.'

Both sly tiny hands, colder than ice-water, the beautiful Water Midden outstretched towards him. He gazed, stooping out of his ugliness, into those eyes whose darkness was only shadowy green, yet clearer than the mountain-water. For an instant he waited, then he shut his eyes and put the burning Wonderstone into those two small icy hands. 'Return it to me quickly – quickly, Midden, or Tishnar will be angered against me. How must the Meermut of my mother now be mourning!'

But the Midden had drawn back amid the reeds, holding tight the ruby-red stone in her small hands, and her eyes

looked all darkened and slant, and her small scarlet mouth was curled. 'Can you not trust me but a moment, Prince of the Mulgars?'

And suddenly a loud, hoarse voice broke out: *'Nod ho! Nod ho! Ulla ulla! Nod ho!'* Nod started back.

'Oh, Midden, Midden!' he said, 'it is my brother, Mulla Thumma, calling me. Give me my Wonderstone; I must go at once.'

But the Midden was now rocking and floating on the shadowy water, her bright hair sleeking the stream behind her. Her face was all small mischief. 'Let me make magic but once,' said she, 'and I will return it. Stop, Prince Ummanodda Nizzanares Eengeneela!'

'I cannot wait, not wait. Have pity on me, most beautiful Midden. I did but put it into your hands for friendship's sake. Return it to me now. Tishnar listens.'

'Ummanodda! Ahôh, ahôh, ahôh!' bawled Thumb's harsh voice, coming nearer.

'Oh, harsh and angry voice,' cried the Midden, 'it frightens me – it frightens me. To-morrow, in the night-time, Mulla-Mulgar, come again. I will guard and keep your Wonderstone. Call me, call me. I will come.'

There was a sudden pale and golden swirl of water. A light as of amber floated an instant on the dark, gliding clearness of the torrent. Nod stood up dazed and trembling. The Water Midden was gone. His eyes glanced to and fro. Desolate and strange rose Tishnar's peak. He felt small and afraid in the silence of the mountains. And again broke out hollow and mournful, Thumb's voice calling him. Nod hobbled and hid himself behind a tree. Then from tree to tree he scurried in hiding under great ropes of Cullum and Samarak, until at last, as if he had been wandering in the forest, he came out from behind Thumb.

'What is it, my brother?' he asked softly. 'Why do you call me? Here is Nod.'

Thumb's eyes gladdened, but his face looked black and lowering. 'Why do you play such Munza tricks,' he said – 'hiding from us in the night? How am I to know what small pieces you may not have been dashed into on this slippery Arakkaboa? What beasts may not have chosen Mulla-Skeeto for supper? Come back, foolish baby, and have no more of this creeping and hiding!'

Nod burned with shame and rage at his jeers, but he was too miserable to answer him. He followed slowly after his brother, his small, lean, hungry hand thrust deep into his empty pocket. 'O Midden, Midden!' he kept saying to himself; 'why were you false to me? What evil did I do to you that you should have stolen my Wonderstone?'

A thick grey curtain hung over the night, though daybreak must be near. A few heavy hailstones scattered down through the still branches. And athwart Moot and Mulgarmeerez a distant thunder rolled. 'Follow quick, Walk-by-night,' said Thumb; 'a storm is brewing.'

The Men of the Mountains were all awake, squatting like grasshoppers, and gossiping together close about their watch-fire. Wind swept from the mountain-snows, swirling sparks into the air, and streamed moaning into the ravines.

And soon lightning glimmered blue and wan across the roaring clouds of hail, and lit the enormous hills with glimpses of their everlasting snows. The travellers sheltered themselves as best they could, crouched close to the ground. Nod threw himself down and drew his Sheep-skin over his head. His heart was beating thick and fast. He could think of nothing but his stolen Wonderstone and the dark eyes of the yellow-haired Water Midden. 'Tishnar is angry – Tishnar is angry,' he kept whispering, beneath the roar of the hail. 'She has forsaken me, Noddle of Pork that Nod is.'

CHAPTER TWENTY-TWO

The Ivory Button

When at last day streamed in silver across the peaks, the storm had spent itself. But Nod did not stir, nor draw near the fire to drink of the hot pepper-water the travellers had brewed against the cold. Thumb came at last and stooped over him. 'Get up now, Ummanodda, little brother, and do not mope and sulk any more. I was angry because I was afraid. How should we have gone a day in safety without the Nizza-neela and his Wonderstone? Come nearer to the fire, and dry your sodden sheep's-coat.'

Nod crept forlornly to the fire, and sat there shivering. He could not eat. He crouched low on his heels, nor paid any heed to what was said or done around him. And presently he fell into a cold, uneasy sleep, full of dreadful dreams and voices. When he awoke, he peered sullenly out of his jacket, and saw Ghibba with three of the five Moona-Mulgars that he had taken with him sitting hunched up round the fire. They had come back bruised and bedraggled, and torn with thorns. One of them stumbling in the gloom on the green rocks, had fallen headlong into the cataract, and had not been seen again; and one had been pounced on and carried off by some unknown beast while they were hobbling back in the torchless darkness towards the beacon above the cataract. There was no way beyond the ravine. All was dense low forest, rocks and thorns, and pouring waterways. And the travellers knew not what to be doing.

Nod could not bear to look at them nor listen to their lisping, mournful voices. He covered up his face again, weary of the journey and of the dream of Tishnar's Valleys, weary of his brothers, of the very daylight, but weariest of himself.

After long palaver, Ghibba came shuffling over to him, and sat down beside him.

'Is the Mulla-Mulgar ill, that he sits alone, hiding his eyes?' he said.

Nod shook his head. 'I am in my second sleep, Mountain-Mulgar. A little frost has cankered my bones. It is the Harp Nod hears, not Zevvera's zōōts.

Ghibba sat with a very solemn look on his grey scarred face. 'The Mulla-Mulgars say there can be no turning back, Nizza-neela. And, by the way I have come, it is certain that there is no going onward. Then, say they, being Mulgars-of-a-race, we must float with the mountain-water into the great cavern, and trust our hearts to the fishes. Maybe it will carry us to where every shadow comes at last; maybe these are the waters of the Fountains of Assasim-mon.'

'I see no boat,' yapped Nod scornfully. 'The only boat my brothers ever floated in was an old Gunga's Oomgar-Nugga's Bobberie that now is a nest in Obea-Munza for Coccadrilloes' eggs.'

'Already my people are gathering branches,' said Ghibba,

'to make floating mats or rafts, such as I saw one of the Fishing-Mulgars squatting on while he dangled his tail for fish-bait. Comfort your weary bones, then, Eengenares. Tishnar, who guards you, Tishnar, whose Prince you are, Tishnar, who feasted even Utts like me on fruits of sleeping-time, will not forsake us now.'

Nod turned, cold and trembling, as if to tell this solemn Man of the Mountains that his Wonderstone was gone. But he swallowed his spittle, and was ashamed. So he rose up and listlessly hobbled after him to where the rest of the travellers were toiling to gather branches for their rafts.

The storm had snapped and stripped off many branches from the trees. These the travellers dragged down to the water. Others they hauled down with Cullum-ropes, and some smaller saplings they charred through with fire at the root. When they had heaped together a big pile of boughs and Samarak, Cullum and all kinds of greenery, Ghibba and Thumb bound them clumsily one by one together, letting them float out on to the water, until the raft was large and buoyant enough to bear two or three Mulgars with their bags. For one great raft that would have carried them all in safety would have been too unwieldy to enter the mouth of the cavern, besides being harder for these ignorant sailors to navigate. The torrent flowed swiftly into the cavern. And if but two or three sailed in together, Fortune might drown or lose many in the dark windings of the mountain-water, but one or two at least might escape.

They toiled on till evening, by which time four strong green rafts bobbed side by side at their mooring-ropes on the water. Then, tired out, sore and blistered with their day's labours, the travellers heaped up a great watch-fire once more, and supped merrily together, since it might be for many of them for the last time. Nor did the Mountain-Mulgars raise their drone for their kinsfolk beneath the cataract, wishing to keep a brave heart for the dangers before them.

Only Nod sat gloomy and downcast, waiting impatiently till all should be lying fast asleep. One by one the out-wearied travellers laid themselves down, with the palms of their feet towards the fire. Nod heard the calling of the beasts in the ravine, and ever and again from far up the mountain-side broke out the long hungry howl of the little wolves. Only Nod and the Mountain-Mulgar whose turn it was to keep watch were now awake. He was a queer old Mulgar, blind of one eye, but he could stand wide awake for hours mumbling in his mouth a shaving of their blue cheese-rind. And when he had turned his back for a moment on the fire, Nod wriggled softly away, and, hobbling off into the forest, soon reached the water-side.

He crept forward under the gigantic dragon-tree, and down the steep bank to the little creek where he had first heard the singing of the Water Midden. All was shadowy and still. Only the dark water murmured in its stony channel, and the faint night-wind rustled in the sedge. Nod leaned on his belly over the water, and, gazing into it, called as softly and clearly as his harsh voice could: 'Water Mid-den, Water Midden, here I am, Ummanodda, come as you bade me.'

No-one answered. He stooped lower, and called again. 'It is me, the Mulla-Mulgar, child of Tishnar, who trusted to you his Wonderstone, beautiful Midden. Nod, who be-lieved in you, calls – your friend, the sorrowful Nod!'

'Sing, Mulla-Mulgar!' croaked a scornful sedge-bird. 'The Princess loves sweet music.'

A lean fish of the changing colours of a cherry swam softly to the glimmering surface and stared at Nod.

'Tell me, Jacket-of-Loveliness,' whispered Nod, 'where is thy mistress that she does not answer me?'

The fish stared solemnly on wavering fin.

'Hsst, brother,' said Nod, and let fall a bunch of Soota-berries into the stream. The fish leapt in the water, and caught the little fruit in its thin, curved teeth, and nibbled greedily till all was gone. Whereupon, staring solemnly at Nod once more, he let the leaves and stalk float onward with the stream, then with a flash and flicker of tail dived down, down, and was gone. All again was silent. Only the blazing stars and the shadowy phantoms of the distant fire-light moved on the water.

'O Tishnar,' muttered the little Mulgar to himself, 'help once this wretched Nod!'

Suddenly, as he watched, as if it were the amber or ivory beam of a lantern in the water, he saw a pale brightness ascending. And all in a moment the Water Midden was there rocking on the dark green water beneath the arching sedge. But her hands, when Nod looked to see, were empty, floating like rose-leaves open on the water. But he spoke gently, for he could not look into her beautiful wild face, and her eyes, that were like the forest for darkness and the moonlit mountains of Tishnar for loveliness, and still be angry, or even sad.

'Tell me, O Water Midden, where is my Wonderstone?' he said.

The Water Midden smoothed slowly back her gold locks. 'You told me false, Mulla-Mulgar,' she answered. 'All day long I have been sitting rubbing, rubbing with my small tired thumb, but no magic has answered. It is but a common water-pebble roughened into the beasts' shapes. It means nothing, and I am weary.'

And Nod guessed she had been rubbing the Wonder-stone craft to cudgel, and not as the magic went, Sama-weeza – right to left.

'If it is but a water-pebble, give it back to me, then, Midden, for it was my mother who gave it me.'

But the Midden smiled with her coral lips. 'You did deceive me, then, Mulla-Mulgar, so that you might seem strange and wonderful, and far above the other hoarse-voiced travellers, the beloved of Tishnar? You may deceive me again, perhaps. I think I will not give you back your stone. Perhaps, too,' she said, throwing back her tiny chin, so that her face lay like a flower in leaves of gold – 'perhaps I rubbed not wisely. You shall tell me how.'

'Show me, then, my Wonderstone. I am tired out for want of sleep, and long no more for Tishnar's fountains.'

Then the Midden floated out into the middle of the stream, and with one light hand kept herself in front of Nod, her narrow shoulders slowly twirling the while in the faintly rosied starlight. She took with the other a long thick strand of her hair, and, unwinding it slowly, presently out of it let fall into her palm the angry-flaming Wonderstone. 'See, Mulla-Mulgar, here is your Wonderstone. Now in patience tell me how to make magic.'

And Nod said softly: 'Float but a span nearer to me, Midden – a span and just a half a span.'

And the Water Midden drew in a little, still softly twirl-ing.

'Oh, but just a thumb-nail nearer,' said Nod.

Laughing, she floated in closer yet, till her beautiful eyes were looking up into his bony and wrinkled face. Then with a sudden spring he thrust his hand deep into the silken mesh of her hair and held tight.

She moved not a finger; she still looked laughing up. 'Listen, listen, Midden,' he said: 'I will not harm you – I could not harm you, beautiful one, though you never gave me back my Wonderstone again, and I wandered forsaken till I died of hunger in the forest. What use is the stone to you now? Tishnar is angry. See how wildly it burns and sulks. Give it, then, into my hand, and I promise – not a promise, Midden, fading in one evening – I will give you any one thing else, whatsoever it is you ask.'

And the Water Midden looked up at him unfrightened, and saw the truth and kindness in his eyes. 'Be not angry with me, little brother,' she answered. 'I did not pretend with you, sorrowful Nizza-neela!' And she dropped the Wonderstone into his outstretched hand.

Tears sprang up into Nod's tired, aching eyes. He smoothed softly with his hairy fingers the golden strands floating in the ice-cold water. 'Till I die, O beautiful one,' he said, 'I will not forget you. Tell me your wish!'

Then the Water Midden looked long and gravely at him out of darkling eyes. She put out her hand and touched his. 'This shall be my sorrowful wish, little Mulgar: it is that when you and your brothers come at last to the Kingdom of Assasimmon, and the Valleys of Tishnar, you will not forget me.'

'O Midden,' Nod answered, 'it needed no asking – that. It may be we shall never reach the Valleys. For now we must plunge into the water-cavern on our floating rafts, and all is haste and danger. But I mind no longer now, Midden. That Mulla-Mulgar, my father Seelem, chose to wander, and not to sit fat and idle with Princes. So, too, would I. Tell me a harder wish. Ask anything, Water Midden, and my Wonderstone shall give it you.'

And the Water Midden gazed sorrowfully into his face. 'That is all I ask, Mulla-Mulgar,' she repeated softly – 'that you will not forget me. I fear the Wonderstone. All day it has been crickling and burning in my hair. All that I ask, I ask only of you.' So Nod stooped once more over that gold beauty, and he promised the Water Midden.

And she drew out a slender, fine strand of her hair, and

cut it through with the sharp edge of a little shell, and she wound it seven times round Nod's left wrist. 'There,' she said; 'that will bid you remember me when you come to the end. Have no fear of the waters, Nizza-neela; my people will watch over you.'

And Nod could not think what in his turn to give the Water Midden for a remembrance and a keepsake. So he gave her Battle's silver groat with the hole in it, and hung it upon a slender shred of Cullum round her neck, and he tore off also one of the five out of his nine ivory buttons that still clung to his coat, and gave her that, too.

'And if my brothers stay here one day more, come in the darkness, O Water Midden; I shall not sleep for thinking of you.' And he said good-bye to her, kneeling above the dark water. But long after he had safely wrapped his Wonderstone in the blood-stained leaf from Battle's little book again, and had huddled himself down beside the slumbering travellers, he still seemed to hear the forlorn singing of the Water Midden, and in his eyes her small face haunted, amid the darkness of his dreams.

All the next morning the travellers slaved at their rafts. They made them narrow and buoyant and very strong, for they knew not what might lie beyond the mouth of the cavern. And now the sun shone down so fiercely that the Mulgars, climbing, hacking, dragging at the branches, and moiling to and fro betwixt forest and water, teased by flies and stinging ants, hardly knew what to do for the heat.

245

Thumb and Thimble stripped off the few rags left of their red jackets, and worked in their skins with better comfort. And they laughed at Nod for sweating on in his wool.

'Look, Thumb,' laughed Thimble, peering out from under a tower of greenery, 'the little Prince is so vain of his tattered old sheep's-jacket that he won't walk in his bare an instant, yet he is so hot he can scarcely breathe.'

Nod made no answer, but worked stolidly on, bunched up in his hot jacket, because he feared if he went bare his brothers would see the thin strand of bright hair about his wrist, and mock at the Midden. When the sun was at noon the Mulgars had finished the building of their rafts. They lay merrily bobbing in a long string moored to an Olla-conda on the swift-running water. They tied up bundles of nuts, and old Nanoes, roots, and pepper-pods, and scores of torches, and bound these down securely to the lightest of

246

the rafts. Then, wearied out, with sting-swollen chops and bleeding hands, they raised their shadow-blankets, and having bound up their heads with cool leaves, all lay down beside the embers of their last night's fire for their 'glare'.

There were now seventeen travellers, and they had built nine light rafts – two Mulgars for every raft, except two; one of which two was wide enough to float in comfort three of the lighter Moona-Mulgars, who weigh scarcely more than Meermuts at the best of times; the other and most buoyant was for their bundles and torches and all such stuff as they needed, over and above what each Mulgar carried for himself.

In the full and stillness of afternoon they ate their last meal this side of Arakkaboa, and beat out their fire. A sprinkle of hail fell, hopping on their heads as they stood in the sunshine making ready to put off. It seemed as if there would never come an end to their labour, and many a strange face stared down on them from the brooding galleries of the forest.

CHAPTER TWENTY-THREE

Under the Mountains:
and the Kingdom

At last, after fixing a lighted torch between the logs of each raft, the Mulgars began to get aboard. On the first, Ghibba and Thimble embarked, squatting the one in front and the other astern, to keep their craft steady. With big torches smoking in the sunshine, they pushed off. Tugging on a long strand of Samarak which they had looped around the smooth branch of a Boobab, they warped themselves free. Soon well adrift, with water singing in their green twigs, they slid swiftly into the stream, shoving and pulling at their long poles, beating the green water to foam, as they neared the fork, to keep their dancing catamaran from drifting into the surge that would have toppled them over the cataract.

The rest of the travellers stood stock-still by the waterside, gazing beneath their hands after the green ship and its two sailors, dark and light, brandishing their poles. They followed along the bank as far as they could, standing lean in the evening beams, wheezing shrilly, *'Illaloothi, Illaloothi!'* as Moona and Mulla-Mulgar floated into the mouth of the cavern and vanished from sight.

One after another the rest swept off, their rafts dancing light as corks on the emerald water, each with its flaming torch fast fixed, and its two struggling Mulgars tugging at their water-poles. And as each raft drifted beneath the lowering arch of the cavern, the Mulgars aboard her raised aloft their poles for farewell to Mulgarmeerez. Last of all Thumb loosed his mooring-rope, and with the baggage-raft in tow cast off with Nod into the stream.

Pale sunshine lay on the evening frost and gloom of the forests, and far in the distance wheeled Kippel, capped with snow, as the raft rocked round the curve and floated nearer and nearer to the cavern. Nod squatted low at the stern, his pole now idly drifting, while behind him bobbed the baggage-raft, tethered by its rope of Cullum. He stared into the flowing water, and it seemed out of its deeps, faintly echoing, rang the voice of the sorrowful Water Midden, bidding him farewell. And when Thumb's back was for a moment turned, he tore out of the tousled wool of his jacket another of his ivory buttons, and, lying flat in the leafy twigs, dropped it softly into the stream. 'There, little brother,' he whispered to the button, 'tell the beautiful Midden I remembered her last of all things when the hoarse-voiced Mulgars sailed away!'

Green and dark and utterly still Arakkaboa's southern forests drew backward, with the westering sun beaming hazily behind their nameless peaks. Nod heard a sullen wash of water, the picture narrowed, faded, darkened, and in a moment they were floating in an inky blackness, lit only by the dim and wavering light of the torches.

The cavern widened as the rafts drew inward. But the Mulgars with their poles drove them into the middle of the stream, for here the current ran faster, and they feared their leafy craft might be caught by overhanging rocks near the cavern walls. A host of long-eared bats, startled from sleep by the echoing cries and splashings, and the smoke of the torches, unhooked their leathery hoods, and, mousily glancing, came flitting this way, that way, squeaking shrilly as if scolding the hairy sailors. They reminded Nod of the chattering troops of Skeetoes swinging on their frosty ropes in the gloom of Munza-Mulgar.

When with smoother water the raftsmen's shouts were hushed, a strange silence swept down upon the travellers. Nod glanced up uneasily at the shimmering roof, with its jutting rocky spars. Only the sip and whisper of the water could be heard, and the faint crackle of the dry torchwood.

Thumb flapped the water impatiently with his long pole. 'Ugh, Ummanodda, this hole of darkness chills my bones. Sing, child, sing!'

'What shall I sing, Thumb?'

'Sing that jingling lingo the blood-supping Oomgar-Mulgar taught you. How goes it? – "Pore Benoleben".'

So in the dismal water-caverns of Arakkaboa Nod sang out in his seesaw voice, to please his brother, Battle's old English song, 'Poor Ben, old Ben'.

Widecks awas'
   Widevry sea,
An' flyin' scud
   For companee,
Ole Benporben
   Keepz watcherlone:
Boatz, zails, helmainmust,
   Compaz gone.

Not twone ovall
   'Is shippimuts can
Pipe pup ta prove
   'Im livin' man:
One indescuppers
   Flappziz 'and,
Fiss-like, as you
   May yunnerstand.

An' one bracedup
   Azzif to weat,
'Az aldy deck
   For watery zeat;
Andwidda zteep
   Unwonnerin' eye
Ztares zon tossed sea
   An' emputy zky.
Pore Benoleben,
Pore-Benn-ole-Ben!

When Nod's last quavering drawl had died away, Thumb lifted up his own hoarse, grating voice in the silence that followed, and as if with one consent, the travellers broke into 'Dubbuldideery'.

It seemed as if the wall would shatter and the roof come tumbling down at their prodigious hullabaloo. The bats raced to and fro. Scores of fishes pushed up their snouts round Nod's raft, and gazed with curious faces into the torchlight. The water was all astir with their disquietude. But in the midst of the song there sounded a shrill and hasty cry: 'Down all!'

Only just in time had Ghibba seen their danger, and almost before the shrill echo had died away, and Thimble had cast himself flat, their raft was swirled under a huge rock, blossoming with quartz, that hung down almost to the surface of the water. Thimble's jacket was ripped collar to hem as he slid under, lying as close as he could. And the bobbing raft of baggage behind them was torn away in a twinkling, so that now all the food and torches the Mulgars had was what each carried for himself. They dared not stir nor lift their heads, for still the fretted roof arched close above the water.

And so they drifted on and on, their torches luckily burnt low, until at length the cavern widened, the roof lifted, and they burst one by one into a great chamber of smooth water, its air filled strangely with a faint phosphorescence, so that every spar and jag of rock gleamed softly with coloured light as they paddled their course slowly through. In this great chamber they stayed awhile, for there was scarcely any current of water against its pillared sides. With their rafts clustering and moored together, they shared out equally what nuts, dry fruit, and unutterably mouldy cheese remained, and divided the torches equally between them, except that Ghibba, who led the way, had two for every one of the others.

These thin grey waters swarmed with fish, but all, it seemed, nearly blind, with scarcely visible eyes above their snouts. Some of the bigger fish, with clapping jaws, cast themselves in rage or hunger against the rafts. And the Mulgars, seeing their teeth, took good heed to couch themselves close in the midst of their rafts. The longer they stayed, the thicker grew the concourse of fish drawn together by the noise and smell of the travellers, until the cavern echoed with their restless fins and a kind of supping whisper, as if the fish had speech. So the Mulgars pushed off again, laying about them with their poles to scare the bolder monsters off as they glided softly into the sluggish current, until the channel narrowed again, and their speed freshened.

On and on they drifted. On and on the shimmering walls floated past them, now near, now distant. They lost all time. Some said night must be gone; some said nay, night must have come again; and to some it seemed like an evil dream, this drifting, without beginning or end. When sleep began to hang heavily on Thumb's eyelids, he bade Nod lie down and take his fill of it first, while he himself kept watch. Nod very gladly lay down as easily as he could make himself on the rough and narrow raft, and Thumb for safety tied him close with a strand of Cullum. He dreamed a hundred dreams, rocked softly on the sliding raft, all of burning sunshine, or wild white moonlight, or of icy and dazzling Witzaweelwulla; but yet, it seemed, the Water Midden's beauty haunted all.

He woke into almost pitch-black gloom, and starting up, could count only four torches staining the unrippling water with their flare. And, being very thirsty, he stooped over with hollowed hand, as if to drink.

'No, no,' said Thumb drowsily; 'not drink, Nod. Sleepy water – sleepy water. Moon-Mulgars there, drunk and drunk; thirstier and thirstier, torches out – all dead asleep – all dead asleep.'

'But my tongue's crackling dry, Thumb. Drink I must, Thumb.'

'Nutshells,' said Thumb – 'suck nutshells, suck them.'

Nod took out the last few nuts he had. And in the faint glowing of the distant torches he could see Thumb's great broad-nosed face turned hungrily towards them.

'How many nuts left have you, my brother?' Nod said.

Thumb tapped his stomach. 'Safe, safe all,' he said. 'Nod slept on and on.'

'Why did you not wake me, Thumb? Lie down now. I am not hungry, only a little thirsty. Have these few crackle-shells before you sleep, old Thumb.' He gave Thumb nine out of his thirteen nuts, and partly because he was raven-ously hungry, partly because their oiliness a little assuaged his thirst, Thumb crunched them up hastily, shells and all. Then he lay down on the raft, and Nod tied his great body as securely as he could.

There appeared to be some tribe of creatures dwelling in this darkness. For Thumb had but a little while lain down when the stream bore the rafts along a smoother wall of rock, which rose as if it were to a ledge or shelf; and all along this rocky shelf Nod could see dim, rounded holes, of a breadth to take with ease the body of a Mullabruk or Manquabee. He fancied even he saw here and there dim shadowy shapes peering out. And now and then in the hush he heard a flappity rustle, as of some hairy creature scampering quickly along the ledge on four naked feet. But he called and called in vain. No answer followed, except a feeble hail from Thimble's raft far ahead, with its torches feebly twinkling.

Only three of the nine rafts now showed lights, and the last of these had drifted in, and become entangled in some jutting rock or in the long, leathery weed that hung like lichen-coloured grass along the sides of the cavern. As Nod drew slowly near, he saw that on this raft both its Mulgars lay flat on their faces, lost in their second sleep from drinking of the water. He pushed hard at his long pole, and, leaning over, caught their strand of trailing Samarak, and hauled the raft safely into mid-stream again. He stirred and pommelled the Mulgars with his pole. But they made no sign of feeling, except that their mouths fell a little ajar.

Then he lit the last but one of his own torches by the failing flame of theirs. But it hovered sullen and blue. The air was thick. Each breath he took was heavy as a sigh. He was shrunk very meagre with travel, and his little breathing bosom was nothing but a slender cage of bones above his heart. He crouched down in the whispering solitude. His lips were cracked, his tongue like tinder. He mumbled his shells in vain between his teeth. But from first sleep to the second sleep is but a little journey, and thence to the last the way runs all downhill.

He chafed his eyes, he clenched his teeth, he crooned wheezily all the songs Battle had taught him. And now once more the cavern opened into a wide and still lagoon over whose grey floor phantom lights moved cloudily before the advancing rafts. Its roof wanly blazed with crystals. And there was no doubt now of Mulgar inhabitants. They sat unmoved upon their rocky ledges and parapets, with puffed-out, furry bodies and immense round, lustrous eyes, with which they steadily surveyed the worn and matted Mulgars, some stretched in stupid slumber, some fevered and famished, with burning eyes drifting slowly past their glistening grottoes. But none so much as stirred a finger or paid any heed to the Mulgars' entreaties for food. Only their long ears, which peaked well out of their wool, twitched and  nodded, as if their ducketings were a kind of secret language between them.

Nod's raft swam last across this weed-mantled lagoon amid the moving light-wisps. He called with swollen tongue: *'O ubjar moose soofree! ubjar, ubjar, moose soofree!'* But there came no answer, not the least stir in the creatures; only the owl-eyes stared steadily on. He lifted himself on trembling legs, and called: *'Walla, walla!'*

These Arakkaboans only gloated on him, and slowly turned their round heads, still twitching their ears at one another, as if engaged in some strange talk.

And Nod fell into a Munza rage at sight of them. He danced and gibbered, and at last caught up his long waterpole, as if to strike at them; but it was too heavy for him after his long thirst; he overbalanced, threw out the pole, and fell headlong on to the raft. Thumb muttered in his sleep, wagging his head. And with parched lips, so close to that faint-smelling water, Nod could bear his thirst no longer. He leaned over, cupped his hands, and sucked in one, two, three delicious mouthfuls. Water, cavern, staring Arakkaboans, seemed to float away into the distance, as in a dream. And in a little while, with head lolling at Thumb's feet, he lay faintly snoring beside his brother.

Out of the heaviness of that long sleep Nod opened his eyes to find Thumb's great body stooping over him with anxious face, shaking and pommelling him, and muttering harshly: 'Wake, wake, Nugget of clay! Wake, Mulla-Slugga! The Valleys! The Valleys! The Valleys, little Um-mannodda! Taste, taste! Ummuz, ummuz, UMMUZ!'

Something sweeter than honey, something that at one taste wakened in memory Mutta, and Seelem, and the little Portingal's hut, and Glint's towering Ukka-tree, and all his childhood, was pushed between his teeth. Nod sneezed three times, struggled, and sat up.

For a moment the light blinded him. Then at last he saw all among a long low stretch of rushes, in still, green water between the rafts, a picture of the sky. A thread of moon hung like a shell in the pale crystal quiet of daybreak. He scrambled to his feet, still gnawing his Ummuz-cane. There sat Thimble, mumbling like a hungry dog over his food, and the lean shapes of the Moona-Mulgars shuffling to and fro. On one side rose the forests of the northern slopes of Arak-kaboa. A warm, sweet wind was moving with daybreak, and only on the heights next the pallor of the sky shone Tish-nar's unchanging snows. Flowers bloomed everywhere

256

around him, not vanishing flowers of magic now. And as far
as his round eyes could see, golden with Ummuz and Immamoosa, and silver with dreaming waters, stretched the
long-sought, lovely Valleys of Tishnar. This, then, was the
Mulgars' journey's end!

Nod flung himself down in the long grasses, and cried as
if his heart would break. And still with his oozy stick of
Ummuz clutched between his fingers, he fell asleep.

But soon came Ghibba to waken him. Thumb and
Thimble and all the Moona-Mulgars were squatting together round a little fire they had kindled beneath an enormous tree by the water-side. Bees that might, themselves,
be honeymakers from Assasimmon's hives, were droning
in the tree-blossoms overhead, and Tiny Tominiscoes flitting
among the branches. It was a wonder, indeed, that birds
should even approach such scarecrow travellers. More like
the Noomad of Jack-Alls they sat than honest Mulgars;
some toasting the last paring of their beloved cheese to eat
with their Nanoes, some with stones pounding Ummuz,
some at their scratching and combing, and one or two
wearied out, were bonily sprawling in the comfort of sunbeams streaming upon them now from far across Arakkaboa.

Beneath them lay the shallows of the green lagoon in the
morning. But near at hand rose up a gigantic grove of Olla-

257

condas into the windless sky, so that beyond these the travellers could see nothing of the further country.

When they had eaten and drunk, and were well rested, Thumb and Nod, taking again cudgels in their hands, started off towards the hills that rose above the cavern, of purpose, if need be, to climb into the higher branches of some tree, from which they might descry, perhaps, what lay on the other side of this great grove.

Through the thick dews they stumped along together, their eyes roving this way and that, in wonder and curiosity of their way. And in a while they had climbed up through the thick undergrowth on to a wide green ledge, on which were playing and scampering in the fresh shadows a host of a kind of Weddervols, but smaller and furrier than those of Munza. And now they could see beneath them the huge arch through which their rafts had floated out while they lay snoring.

White flocks of long-legged water-birds were preening their wings in the shallows, in which rock and boughs and farthest snow were glassed. There stood the two Mulgars, ragged and worn, snuffing the sweet air, while a faint surge of singing rose from the forests above their heads.

'It is a big nest Tishnar's water-birds build,' said Nod suddenly.

Thumb's great head turned on his stooping shoulders, and, with mouth ajar, he stared long and closely at what seemed to be a heap of tangled boughs washed up in the water far beneath them.

'No nest, Ummanodda,' he said at last; 'it is some Mulgar's tree-roost fallen into the water. Its leaves are dry, and the feet of that long-legs stand deep in Spider-flower.'

'To my eyes,' said Nod slowly, 'it looks to me, Thumb, just like such another as one of our water-rafts.'

'Wait here a little while, Nizza-neels,' grunted Thumb suddenly; 'I go down to look for eggs.'

258

Nod watched his brother pushing his way down through the sedge and trailing Samarak. 'Eggs,' he whispered – 'eggs!' and broke out into his little yapping laughter, though he knew not why he laughed.

Up, up, on sounding wings flew a bird as white as snow from its lodging as Thumb drew near. And there he was, stooping, paddling, pushing with his cudgel, and peering into the tangle at the water-side.

Nod turned his head, filled with a sudden weariness and loneliness. And in the silence of the beautiful mountains he fell sad, and a little afraid, as do even Oomgar travellers resting awhile in the journey that has no end.

Out of his Mulgar dreams he was startled by a sudden, sharp, short Mulgar bark from far beneath, that might be fear or might be sudden gladness.

And, in a moment, Thumb, having cast down his cudgel, and with something clutched in his great hand, was swinging and scrambling back through the thick flowery undergrowth of the hilside by the way he had come.

Nod watched him, with head thrust forward and sidelong, and at last he drew near, sweating and coughing.

'*Sootli, sootli!*' he muttered. 'Magic, magic!' and held out in the sunlight an old red, rotted gun.

Rusty, choked with earth, its butt smashed, its lock long gone, the two Mulgars stood with the gun between them.

'Oomgar's gun, Thumb? – Oomgar's?' grunted Nod at last.

Thumb opened wide his mouth, still panting and trembling.

'*Noos unga unka, Portingal, Ummanodda. Seelem arggutchkin! Seelem! kara, kara! Seelem mugleer!*'

And even as that last Seelem was uttered, and back to Nod's mind came that morning leagues, leagues away, and himself sitting on his father's shoulder, clutching the long cold barrel of the little Portingal's gun – even at that moment a faint halloo came echoing across the steeps, and, turning, the Mulla-Mulgars saw climbing towards them between the trees Thimble and Ghibba. But not only these. For between them walked on high in a high, hairy hat, with a band of woven scarlet about his loins, and a basket of honeycombs over his shoulder, a Mulgar of a presence and strangeness, who was without doubt of the Kingdom of Assasimmon.

CHAPTER TWENTY-FOUR

Tishnar

Tishnar is a very ancient word in Munza, and means that which cannot be thought about in words, or told, or expressed. So all the wonderful, secret, and quiet world beyond the Mulgars' lives is Tishnar – wind and stars, too, the sea and the endless unknown. But here it is only the Beautiful One of the Mountains that is meant. So beautiful is she that a Mulgar who dreams even of one of her Maidens, and wakes still in the presence of his dream, can no longer be happy in the company of his kind. He hides himself away in some old hole or rocky fastness, lightless, matted, and uncombed, and so thins and pines, or becomes a Wanderer or Môh-Mulgar. But it is rare for this to be for very few Mulgars dream beyond the mere forest, as it were; and fewer still keep the memories of their dream when the livelong vision of Munza returns to their waking eyes. The Valleys of Tishnar lie on either flank of the Mountains of Arakkaboa, though she herself wanders only in the stillness of the mountain snows. She is shown veiled on the rude pots of Assasimmon and in Mulgar scratch-work, with one slim-fingered hand clasping her robe of palest purple, her head bent a little, as if hearkening to her thoughts; and she is shod with sandals of silver. Of these things the wandering Oomgar-Nuggas, or Black Men, tell. From Tishnar, too, comes the Last Sleep – the sleep of all the World. The last sleep just of their own life only is Noomanossi – darkness, change, and the unreturning. And Immanâla is she who preys across these shadows, in this valley. So, too, the Mulgars say, 'Nooma, Nooma', when they mean shadow, as 'In

261

the sun paces a leopard's Nooma at her side'. Meermut, which means in part also shadow, is the shadow, as it were, of lesser light lost in Tishnar's radiance, just as moonlight may cast a shadow of a pine-tree across a smouldering fire. There is, too, a faint wind that breathes in the first twilight and starshine of Munza called the Wind of Tishnar. It was, I think, the faint murmur of this wind that echoed in the ear of Mutta-matutta, as she lay dying, for in dying one hears, it is said, what in life would carry no more tidings to the mind than light brings to the hand. Nod's bells that he heard, and thought were his father's, must have been the Zevveras' bells of Tishnar's Water Middens, all wandering Meermuts. These Water Middens, or Water Maidens, are like the beauty of the moonlight. The countless voices of fountain, torrent, and cataract are theirs. They, with other of Tishnar's Maidens, come riding on their belled Zevveras, and a strange silence falls where their little invisible horses are tethered; while, perhaps, the Maidens sit feasting in a dell, grey with moonbeams and ghostly flowers. Even the sullen Mullabruk learns somehow of their presence, and turns aside on his fours from the silvery mist of their glades and green alleys, just as in the same wise a cold air seems to curdle his skin when some haunting Nooma passes by. All the inward shadows of the creatures of Munza-Mulgar are Noomanossi's; all their phantoms, spirits, or Meermuts are Tishnar's. And so there is a never-ending changeableness and strife in their short lives. The leopard (or Roses, as they call her, for the beauty of her clear black spots) is Meermut to her cubs, Nooma to the dodging Skeetoes she lies in wait for, stretched along a bough. Her beauty is Tishnar's; the savagery of her claws is Noomanossi's. So Munza's children are dark or bright, lovely or estranging, according as Meermut or Nooma prevails in their natures. And thus, too, they choose the habitation of their bodies. Yet because dark is but day gone, and cruelty unkindness,

therefore even the heart-shattering Noomanossi, even Immanâla herself, is only absent Tishnar. But there, as everyone can see, I am only chattering about what I cannot understand.

Envoy

Long – long is Time, though books be brief;
Adventures strange – ay, past belief –
Await the Reader's drowsy eye;
But, wearied out, he'd lay them by.

But, if so be, he'd some day hear
All that befell these brothers dear
In Tishnar's lovely Valleys – well,
Poor pen, thou must that story tell!

But farewell, now, you Mulgars three!
Farewell, your faithful company!
Farewell, the heart that loved unbidden –
Nod's dark-eyed, beauteous Water Midden!

Another Puffin by Walter de la Mare

COLLECTED STORIES
FOR CHILDREN

These seventeen tales offer, you might say, seventeen gateways into the country of Walter de la Mare, which is easy to enter, for it shares a border with fairytale, where witches, ogres, ghosts are regular citizens, and where everyone ready to risk it has a chance of a wish coming true.

Illustrated by Robin Jacques.

POWER OF THREE
Diana Wynne Jones

The Moor was truly full of perils but once inside the mound, the right words spoken to close the doors, they were safe in their own world. Or so, for a long time, the mound-dwellers thought.

Gair would spend a lot of time gazing out onto the Moor and brooding. Ayna could answer questions about the future, Ceri could find things which were lost. Gair alone seemed to have no Gift and knew he was a disappointment to his jovial, heroic father. Perhaps his feeling of not fitting in was what made him so curious about the other sorts of being, Giants and Dorig. Certainly it was because he believed he was ordinary that he did his best to become wise, and to learn as much as he could about the three great Powers of Sun, Moon and Earth. And when the crisis came, Gair found the knowledge he had gained was to help save not only his own life but those of all his people.

HAUNTING TALES
Barbara Ireson

Ghosts? No such things, you may be thinking. But this collection has so many different ghosts, exciting ones, eerie ones, romantic, sad and even funny ones, and they are all so vividly real that they may well make you change your mind and become a ghost-fancier yourself.

Barbara Ireson is well known as an editor and selector of anthologies for children, and she chose these stories to appeal mainly to readers of about ten to thirteen though older readers will find plenty to enjoy as well.

UP THE PIER
Helen Cresswell

It might have been the homelessness that made Carrie's eyes able to see the Pontiflex family when she began visiting the pier, noticing first the oddly dressed boy and the dog who were there one minute and invisible the next, and then the signs that someone might be hiding in one of the sales kiosks on the empty winter pier. After all, George, Ellen and Kitchener Pontiflex were homeless too, though the problem with them was that they had a perfectly good home waiting for them back in 1921 where they came from, but now they were stuck in 1971 and having to camp out on the pier . . .

THE SHADOW-CAGE
Philippa Pearce

Quite ordinary things turn out to be haunted in the world Philippa Pearce creates – a funny little statue, an old biscuit-barrel, a nursery cupboard – and in quite ordinary circumstances, memories of past unhappiness can cling to a place connected with them. A man out for his evening exercise can find his hatred of his brother suddenly taking shape as a running companion. Human passions can even reach beyond the grave if they're powerful enough – a mother's longing for her daughter's return to the home which a cantankerous father had closed to her, an old man desperate at the neglect of his once-cherished garden.

Gently chilling, often poignant, these ten stories are written with all the fine perceptiveness and imagination for which their author is celebrated.

THE TWELVE AND THE GENII
Pauline Clarke

Max found the twelve battered toy soldiers under the attic floorboards in his new home. He liked them anyway, because his parents said they were old and special and ought to be in a museum, but he was wild with joy when he tapped on his grandfather's old drum and they began to *move*! They weren't just toys at all, they were real like people. And because he was so much bigger he was their guardian, or Genii as they called him.

The Brontë children, Branwell, Charlotte, Emily and Anne, first brought the soldiers to life, but Pauline Clark has grafted on to their inventions more adventures all her own, adding her own lines to the portraits of Crashey, Stumps, Tracky, and the rest, so sensitively and gracefully that one can only rejoice at the addition. Winner of the Carnegie Medal for 1962, this is a book for imaginative readers of nine and over.

TWO-THUMB THOMAS
Barbara C. Freeman

It isn't very often you meet a boy who's been brought up by three school cats, but such a one was Two-Thumb Thomas, and for most of the time he was perfectly happy even though he had to rely on Linette, Sue and Blackie for such important things as food and clothes and even though they insisted on him getting an education by attending lessons, listening from behind the door of the Junior Cloakroom.

But the shelf in the Third Form stationery cupboard was getting too narrow for him to sleep on, and he wanted to get up in the mornings and to go to school like the other boys – not be there already – so he moved into the empty old house near the village, but soon found that it might not be easy to stay.

HOBBERDY DICK
K. M. Briggs

Long ago there was plenty of secret folk life in England, particularly hobgoblins who guarded the houses and lands and watched over the families who lived in them.

Hobberdy Dick of Widford Manor in the Cotswolds was a good and careful guardian, but the new family who came in after the Civil War did not win his affection like the Culvers, whom he had known and liked for two hundred years. The Puritan city merchant and his spoilt wife worked their servants hard and forbade all country pleasures. There was no mumming or Maying or Christmas dancing or Easter egg-rolling now, and none of the comfortable chat and fireside games that Dick had loved in the past.

K. M. Briggs is a well-known authority on folklore, and Hobberdy Dick is a memorable and charming character.

THE MOON IN THE CLOUD
Rosemary Harris

Long ago, the Lord God stirred and grumbled, 'They're all bad down there, except the Noahs. I'll have a flood.' But there was one other good and deserving couple in Israel – Reuben and Thamar. Even Noah, devoted as he was to the will of the Lord, worried about them, and couldn't help thinking it a little unfair that Ham, his own wayward and selfish son, should be set above this gentle pair. Ham, of course, thought it only right and proper. And he said he could get both Reuben and Thamar on the Ark, when the time came. But it wasn't his job to book places on the Ark – and he forgot, as Noah never did, that the Lord God was a watchful God.

Heard about the Puffin Club?

... it's a way of finding out more about Puffin books and authors, of winning prizes (in competitions), sharing jokes, a secret code, and perhaps seeing your name in print! When you join you get a copy of our magazine, *Puffin Post*, sent to you four times a year, a badge and a membership book.

For details of subscription and an application form, send a stamped addressed envelope to:

The Puffin Club Dept A
Penguin Books Limited
Bath Road,
Harmondsworth
Middlesex UB7 0DA

and if you live in Australia, please write to

The Australian Puffin Club
Penguin Books Australia Limited
P.O. Box 527
Ringwood
Victoria 3134